# Growlers 2
## Strigoi

John Black

ISBN: **9798676527983**

# DEDICATION

Thank you for buying this book and supporting my work.
I hope you'll enjoy it.

To my wife, who helped and believed in me.

To Tiberiu, who helped me with advice and feedback.

To all my readers and friends, who made this second book
possible.

# CONTENTS

# ACKNOWLEDGMENTS

Editing by Nicola Markus
Qualified Freelance Editor & IPEd Member
nicola@nicolamarkusedits.com

Cover art by Bogdan Bratu
https://www.facebook.com/bogdan.bratu.77

# 1 SMOKE

L ook." Lili pointed. "Look… smoke!"

Andrei followed the line of her hand. And, at last, he saw it. Smoke was coming from a chimney about two miles out, uphill, right in the middle of the poor neighborhood ironically nicknamed Las Vegas.

"What does it… Does it mean that…" stammered Andrei.

"It means," said Dan, "that we are not alone."

Andrei froze. The smoke was rising high, like a thick string, curling away into the clouds. "They can make fire now?" he asked, a tremor in his voice.

"Who?" asked Lili, her expression oozing with disbelief.

"The growlers."

"What are you, an idiot? Those are people."

"Ah. Okay then. So, what should we do? Should we go around?"

"First," said Dan, "we should move away from the bridge, so this growler over here can shut up."

The growler on the bridge, the one they woke every single time they passed through, had been making noises throughout their exchange.

The group started moving. Dan was first, followed by Lili and her son, Mat, and last came Andrei. They constantly checked on the smoke still visible uphill. When they reached the other side of the river, Andrei spoke again.

"What do we do? How do we go around?"

"Why go around? These are people. Maybe they can help us," answered Lili. "Why do you want to go around?"

"Well, you've seen the movies. What if they're hungry? Or in need of medicine? Or even worse."

"You've seen too many movies. I think it would be best to have a bigger group. We can help each other and make our lives easier. What do you think, Dad?"

Dan had been looking into the distance while the two had their exchange. Now he turned back to face them. "I think you both make good points. This used to be a dangerous neighborhood, so we do risk meeting some lowlifes. Not everyone is a bad apple though; there are honest, hard-working people around here too." He paused, his expression reflecting some of the thoughts passing through his mind. "I think it's better to meet these people."

"But what if there are ten people in that house and they all need food, clothing, or, even worse, slaves? How can—"

"What slaves?" Lili interrupted. "Jesus, you're such a wuss. Let's go meet them. Let's not assume everyone is evil."

"We can fight them," said Matei. "We can fight them, Dad. You don't have to be afraid."

"Shut up, Mat! Don't come up with—"

"You shut up, and don't yell at the kid!" snapped Lili.

"Hey! Let's focus," said Dan, commanding attention. "You're both right. We must be careful. I say we close in slowly, check the surroundings, see if we can make out anything, and then decide if and how we make contact. Everyone agreed?"

They all nodded with sulky faces.

* * *

The house was on the right-hand side of the main road leading to Grandma's village, a few hundred yards before the place where they'd found the dead dogs.

Lili, Dan, Mat, and Andrei were downhill, squeezing together, trying to hide behind an average-sized tree on the left-hand side as they looked toward the property a hundred yards out. The fence was tall and made of wood, with no signs of weakness or damage.

The house seemed large, and the tall roof, the only visible part, was made entirely out of wood.

There was no sign of movement anywhere, except for the smoke coming from the chimney.

"We need to check closer," whispered Dan. "A friend of mine used to live in that house. If it's him burning that fire, we're good. I'll go look; you stay here. And keep out of sight."

"You sure?"

"Yes, Lili. And whatever happens, don't come unless I tell you to."

Dan moved out. He crossed the street and started moving uphill, keeping as close as possible to the fences on his right.

As he neared the house, he slowed, taking more cautious steps, as silent as possible. The snow didn't help his attempts to be quiet, so he needed quite a lot of time to advance.

He finally reached the corner of the property and gripped the top of the fence to pull himself up to look inside.

\* \* \*

They watched as Dan snuck forward, trying to stay low. They all remained standing behind the tree. Matei was hugging it, then came Lili, and behind her was Andrei.

"You smell nice," Andrei suddenly whispered in Lili's ear.

"What? Impossible."

"No, really. Did you wash your hair?"

"Yeah, this morning in the river," whispered Lili, rolling her eyes, "and afterwards I had a fifty-minute swim in the freezing water."

"Mm, that was a fine idea," said Andrei, taking his hand off the tree and trying to grab Lili.

"What the hell! Stop it! We're supposed to stay quiet and hidden," whispered Lili, shaking his hand away.

"Well, I think I can hug you while staying hidden," said Andrei, trying a loving voice. "Actually, the closer we get to each other, the better hidden we'll be."

Lili smiled for a moment, then elbowed him in the stomach. "Charming. Now, come on, stop it. This is neither the place nor the time."

Andrei scoffed and put his hand back on the tree trunk.

"What?" whispered Matei, looking up.

"Nothing. Be quiet."

"Yeah, now you want silence," whispered Lili, and both started giggling.

Lili suddenly came to her senses. "What's he doing?"

* * *

Dan could see some people inside the house—one older man and two women. They moved around busily but silently.

Dan's grin widened, and he slowly let himself down. He moved quietly toward the gate. It was a wooden one, unlike most of the other gates around here, which were metal.

When he reached it, Dan knocked. "Hey, Albert, open up!"

Silence everywhere. Dan knocked again, a little louder, but not too much. He didn't want to wake any growlers in the surrounding houses.

"Hey, Albert. It's me, Dan. Open up!"

The gate opened and the older man came out, blocking the entrance. He was large and very tall, with strong, muscular arms. Albert was a woodcutter around the same age as Dan.

"Wow, Dan! Is it really you? You survived?" Albert grabbed Dan and hugged him. Although Dan was a sizeable man, in Albert's arms he looked way smaller. "So good to see you, man! How did you survive? What have you been doing all this time?"

"Ugh, I'm good," said Dan, a little embarrassed. "I'm with my family. It's been hard. Maria is gone, but otherwise we're all here," he said, his eyes moistening. "May we come in? I'd feel more comfortable talking inside."

"Yeah, of course. Where's your family? Come in, come in," said Albert, making a wide, inviting gesture.

"Right over there." Dan pointed toward the tree, then started waving.

Lili, Andrei, and Matei came out from behind the tree, a bit awkwardly, and walked toward them.

Once they'd all entered the yard, Albert locked the gate behind them.

"Welcome to our humble home," he said. "I guess you know it already, Dan."

"Yeah, I do. Thank you for your hospitality," Dan said, as they moved toward the house.

Albert opened the massive main door, also made of wood, and he led everyone inside. "Tell me what you want to drink, Dan. The usual?"

They gathered in the living room. It was large for these parts, about twenty-five by twenty feet. Two enormous couches and one smaller one faced the fireplace, which was set into the middle of one wall. On either side of the fireplace were a comfortable armchair and a big TV, now useless. The room had three doors. The one through which they'd entered, another leading to a corridor, and a third which seemed to lead to a guest bedroom.

Everyone was looking at everyone else, even Matei, who did so from his mother's lap. The fire, the one creating all that smoke, crackled, making the living room a warm, cozy place.

"I guess most of you know my daughter, Lili," said Dan, after sipping some whiskey from the glass Albert had passed to him. "This is Andrei, my son-in-law, and the little one over there is Matei, their son."

"Hello guys," said Albert. "Welcome to our home. I'm Albert, an old friend of Dan's. We were classmates and best buddies; we've known each other for a long time. True, Dan went on to Police Academy, while I stayed back here to do my woodwork," he continued, with a brief laugh, "but I still owe Dan a great debt. How you helped me—"

"Not to worry," interrupted Dan, waving away the pending thanks. "I was just doing my job. Plus, your sister used to defend my ass in the schoolyard when I was little, so I already owed you one," he said, laughing.

"Still," insisted Albert, "no other policemen wanted to help, so thank you."

"Wait, wait," said Andrei, grinning as he looked back and forth between Dan and Albert. "What was that about the sister defending you?"

"He was a tiny one, at least in primary school," said Albert, while

Dan nodded in confirmation. "And my sister had a crush on him, I guess. She walked around the schoolyard, and whoever messed with him met her fists."

"But how come?"

"She was very large, forgot to mention that. And one year older. A female version of me, I guess," said Albert, laughing some more with a deep voice, his entire chest and belly moving. "God took her away almost fifty years ago," he continued, with a nostalgic smile, ending Andrei's puzzled look. "Anyway, these are my sons, Bogdan and Victor, and these are their wives, Flo and Andreea. And this is my mum, Grandma Gina."

Bogdan and Victor were both tall, yet very different. Bogdan had a similar body structure to Albert; he was around six foot seven, buff, and perhaps a bit obese, just like his father. Victor was around six foot eight, but the athletic type.

"Bogdan, my eldest, used to work with me at the lumber factory. He still works there. I mean, I guess it's closed now. And his wife, Flo, is doing something with computers."

"Yeah, I'm doing accounting and audits for a multinational down in the big city."

"Flo? Is that a nickname or short for something?" asked Andrei.

"Ah. My name is actually Fleur, but everyone calls me Flo."

"Fleur? Are you French?"

"Nah, just had crazy parents."

Andrei and Flo smiled.

"Right." Albert took over again. "Victor here is the smart one, he's—"

"Come on, Dad."

"What? You are. Victor finished Engineering School and works in the capital. In an office! He's working with Americans and Germans." Everyone could hear the pride in Albert's voice.

"We're doing automotive software development with a company that has its HQ in the US," explained Victor, "but we're mostly working with the German branch. It pays the bills."

"What! You're a big-shot manager. Tell them."

"Yes, well, I have a team. I'm running the whole project. Many people enjoy our work, and we like that we improve people's lives. It's the little things, and we're doing our part… Or at least we used to be, before all this craziness hit."

"And this is Andreea, his wife. She's a famous writer," said Albert.

"I'm not that famous. I write cook books and DIY stuff."

"And this is my mum, Grandma Gina."

By the fire, in the large armchair stuffed with pillows, covered with a blanket and wearing several scarves and a big warm hat, sat Grandma Gina. She was old, very old, probably in her 90s, and underneath all those layers, she seemed skinny. Her skin was pale and had gray spots here and there. She seemed to have white, curly hair, judging from what little was visible beneath her hand-knit woolen hat. She didn't move much, but her eyes were alive and she scrutinized everyone. Around her neck hung two strings: one held small onions, the other garlic. And between these lay a necklace with a large crucifix. They seemed heavy for her frail body, and it looked like a miracle that she could sit up straight with all that weight around her neck.

"I can't believe you're all sitting here, chit-chatting, when the Devil is roaming around freely."

"Oh, Grandma," said Victor. "Don't start again."

"If I'd still been able to use my legs, I'd be preparing for what's coming. You're young and foolish! All of you!"

"I'm not young. I'm thirty-five. And there is no devil. Just stop," continued Victor, waving his hand.

"The Strigoi and Moroi are all the Devil's work! Everybody knows that! It was written more than a thousand years ago by a priest, Bartolomeu—"

"The Divine Warrior," said Victor and Grandma Gina at the same time.

"Yes, the Divine Warrior!" continued Grandma Gina, throwing quick glances at everyone. "He was a good, holy man. A soldier of Christ. He's the one who first discovered them, fought them, and eventually defeated them with his prayers, his sword, and with the help of God! And now the Devil is back once more. You should repent, or you will pay!"

"What do you mean?" asked Andrei, a tremor in his voice.

"I mean, you should start praying, admit your sins, renounce this *pride* and this gluttony! Everything that happens, happens for a reason. And we will all pay for our sins!"

"Grandma, we've seen these zombies around, sure," continued Victor, "but that doesn't—"

"They are Moroi! Call them what they are!"

"Okay, fine, *Moroi*. We've seen them and we've killed them, so the Devil is not making such a brilliant job of ending the world."

"You're lucky you haven't met a Strigoi yet! Don't take this lightly, Victor! We're all going to die!"

\* \* \*

As the exchange took place, Lili observed people's reactions. She saw Andrei getting dragged into it, his eyes getting larger and larger. *He's scared, the dufus.*

Dan managed to keep a straight face, but little signs showed he was amused.

As she looked around, she realized Flo was doing the same thing. Their eyes met, and they smiled at each other, before quickly looking away.

Lili caressed Matei's head, which rested in her lap. She saw his eyes moving around, but most of his focus was on Grandma Gina. Lili whispered in his ear, "Don't mind what she's saying, honey. She's very old, and sometimes very old people talk nonsense. Nothing she says is true."

"But, Grandma Gina, what have vampires got to do with all this?" asked Andrei. He seemed to choose his words carefully, trying not to trigger Grandma Gina's aggressiveness, but still wanting to get some answers.

"What vampires? What do you mean?"

"I mean, you just mentioned the Strigoi. The vampires. Why do—"

"Vampires? The Strigoi are not vampires. Those stupid TVs fill your mind with nonsense!" Flecks of spit came flying out of her mouth. "No. Strigoi are dead people who come back, destroying everything and bringing damnation. They are the worst thing that can happen to a family, as they bring pain and sorrow. You should all wear garlic around your necks to protect yourselves from them!"

"But the growlers, aren't they the same thing?"

"Growlers?" asked Grandma Gina, looking straight at Andrei.

"The Moroi. Sorry."

"The Moroi are but mindless ghouls, doing a Strigoi's bidding."

"Yeah, they're the retarded cousin," intervened Flo. It looked like she couldn't hold it inside anymore.

Lili laughed, while Dan let out a brief smile.

"Flo!" said Bogdan, looking at her.

"Laugh all you want! But I'm telling you! You need onions and garlic!"

\* \* \*

As silence finally settled, Dan spoke. "We should get going. It was nice seeing you alive and well."

"But why?" asked Albert. "You can all stay here. You could take a room for a while, and then you can take over one of the neighboring houses. I recommend the one to our left. We cleaned it up. It's free of those Morois."

"Not a terrible idea," said Dan a few moments later. "We might do that. We still have some unfinished business to take care of, but after that we'll come back. It's definitely safer to have other people around." He looked at Andrei and Lili, receiving their silent agreement.

"What unfinished business? Sorry to pry, but it sounds odd to have responsibilities other than surviving in this day and age," intervened Victor.

"Well, we have a dog that we need to pick up—Howler. He's all alone in my childhood village, and I fear he has no food or water left. And we have to bury my wife."

"Oh."

As silence crept upon them, Albert intervened. "Yeah, we also lost my Pat. She died a few months back, before all this. God rest her soul. She was an outstanding woman."

"She's better off! Pat's in heaven now, away from all this!" intervened Grandma Gina.

"Mom, don't start again, please," said Albert. "But what did you guys do? What happened to you during all this time?"

So Dan told them. They all listened, gasping here and there, as the story unfolded. Grandma Gina huffed and puffed, transmitting an '*I told you so!*' message with every fiber of her being.

\* \* \*

"And now we're here," said Dan, motioning toward his family. "We've learned a few things about the growlers. If someone doesn't eat onions, he gets sick and eventually dies, becoming a fast, non-rotting growler. If one dies from any other natural or violent causes, he becomes a rotting, slow one. And we've also learned, the hard way, that force-feeding onions to a fast growler makes it appear dead for a couple of days, only to wake again as a slow one. We learned this while trying to cure Maria."

Everyone was nodding, looking at Dan, while Grandma Gina rolled her eyes.

"Also, they fall asleep when the surrounding noise becomes background noise, and wake when a new sound appears or an existing one suddenly stops. Oh, and freezing doesn't kill them. They cannot move, but they are alive inside."

"We've reached the same conclusions," said Victor, with a somewhat superior smile. "Smashing their heads make them behave erratically. Only stabbing their hearts makes them die for good."

"I have an additional theory," intervened Andrei. He swept his gaze around the room, taking in everyone except Victor, who he pointedly ignored. "We know that touching a sleeping growler wakes them. So it probably works just like for sounds. Moreover, I believe that when they stop and fall, they have a complete shutdown. At that moment, and for a little while after, you can do *whatever* to them, without activating them. You can touch them or stop touching them, you can make, or stop making, noise. They will basically lie there until they have some sort of—"

"Reboot?" asked Flo, smiling.

"Yes!" said Andrei. "Not sure if you've also discovered this," he continued, again looking at everyone but Victor.

"We're still debating this point," said Lili quickly. "We've never had the time to test it, and I hope we'll never have to. I think it's important to stay away from those beasts."

As she finished, Albert took over. "That's quite a story, what you've all been through. On our side, it was way simpler. Bogdan and Flo live here with us, while Victor and Andreea came to visit for Christmas. Everything seemed normal until people started dying from that damn flu. And when Victor got sick, we stuffed him with onions and garlic."

"But how did you know to... Ah, I see," said Andrei, as he realized the answer.

"Grandma Gina, well, she—"

"Yes! *I* told them! And it's a good thing they listened to me! You need to eat garlic and onions to keep the Devil away."

"Onions are enough, we've noticed," said Lili. "We just eat raw onions and we're fine."

"No, you're not! You need garlic!"

"Jesus, Grandma, please, no more!" begged Victor again.

"Anyway," continued Dan, "in case you need anything from the hardware store, we have built a good shelter inside an office. There is heat, some food, and tons of water. You can spend the night, grab some things, and then return. Just mind the dogs. We don't know what the situation is in that park since we left."

"Sounds like an excellent idea." Bogdan spoke for the first time, glancing at Flo. "We could use a generator. Life without electricity is no fun."

"You forgot how we raised you," said Albert. "Still, a generator would be nice. Maybe we can take a tour and bring one here to improve our existence. And with everything we know about the sounds, we shouldn't fear attracting any Morois."

"You really call them Morois?" interrupted Lili.

"Yes, that's what they are. Why do you call them growlers?"

"We call them growlers since, you know, they growl."

"Sounds better than Moroi. Moroi sounds so ancient," intervened Flo, quickly attracting a strange glance from Bogdan, followed by a scoff from Grandma Gina's armchair.

"If you go to the hardware store," interrupted Dan, trying to stop another apocalyptic speech from the old woman, "make sure you get some walkie-talkies like ours. It would be nice to be able to contact each other when we're in range. And now, we really have to be going. Time is running out, and we need to save Howler." He rose. "We'll talk in a few days, when we return. If you get the walkies, you'll hear from me in advance, before we reach you," said Dan, squeezing his friend's hand.

"Bye, man. See you soon."

Dan took a few steps, but then remembered something. He turned back to Albert. "Hey, about those dead dogs. Is that your doing?"

"Yeah, we had to kill a few. They gathered on the street, making a lot of noise, waking Morois all around. We wanted to drive them away, since it wasn't safe for us. When we tried to chase them, they attacked. We defended ourselves, killing some of them, and the rest ran away."

"Hmm, odd. There are more than a few dead there. And some had bite marks."

"I don't know. Me and my boys, we fought them, the rest ran away, and we never saw them again."

"Okay then. See you soon."

As Albert waved, Dan and his family moved away. The road climbed slowly, and finally, a left curve later, they reached the place where the dead dogs were.

The dried blood was still there. Blood trails, signs of carnage, and death.

However, the dogs were gone. There was no trace of them, not even bones.

"What the hell happened?" asked Lili, looking around.

"What happened, Mummy?" asked Matei, looking up at her.

"Oh, nothing, sweetheart, nothing. Let's walk faster. And don't look."

"But how can I walk if I don't look?"

"I mean, don't think about it. Just look forward. See? Like I do. I just mind the road."

As Lili and Matei advanced faster, they left Andrei and Dan behind.

"There are some tracks, heading in our direction. See?" said Andrei, pointing at footprints into the snow. "Someone carried the dogs away, uphill."

"You're right," said Dan, looking around. "I hope Albert forgot to mention they eventually moved their bodies. And we probably have a different understanding of what 'a few' means," he said, smiling.

They kept walking until, after a while, Andrei paused.

"This is where the tracks lead," said Andrei, pointing to a yard on the right-hand side of the road. "Should we check it?"

"They carried them for quite some distance," said Dan, stopping. "But we don't have time to investigate whatever Albert and his sons did. We have more important things to do." He started to walk again. Then he pulled out his walkie-talkie.

"Hey, Lili. Can you please slow down? We can barely see you."

"Yeah, Dad. Sorry," said Lili in his earpiece, just as he saw her stop and turn. "We wanted to leave that area behind. We'll wait for you. Hey, Mat, wave to Grandpa!"

* * *

"Ah, now that's a nice car!" exclaimed Andrei, when his old hatchback came into view ahead of them. "Don't you just love it?"

"It's an incredible car, yes. I wonder why we didn't get two of them," answered Lili.

"Yes! We could get a second one, a red one, just for Mom," said Matei, jumping around in the snow. "That way you can have matching cars!"

"That's just what I've always wanted: to spend double the money for something mediocre."

"What's 'mediocre'?" asked Matei, right before Andrei could have his comeback.

"It's something average, in the middle, with nothing interesting about it," answered Lili.

"Just like Mom, basically." Andrei couldn't miss the opportunity.

"Pfft! At least I'm eating healthily and I'll live to be a hundred," answered Lili, laughing.

"And eventually transform into Grandma Gina."

"My God, she was crazy," exclaimed Lili, looking at Andrei. "She was so aggressive and negative. That poor family. How do they put up with that?"

"Well, she saved their lives," intervened Dan.

"Those old folklore things finally helped someone," reinforced Andrei. "Still, she was really pushing the Strigoi angle."

"Yeah, and you got scared like a toddler. I saw you."

"No, I didn't! I was just trying to understand what she meant."

"Yeah, just like now you're *not* breathing like a dog that ran ten miles."

"Well, I'm man enough to admit that I am, indeed, trying to catch my breath. See? But I wasn't falling for what Grandma Gina said."

"Yeah, yeah."

"Still, that Flo wasn't half bad," said Andrei, after a moment of silence. "I wonder how old is she."

"Yeah, I saw the way you smiled at each other. And I guess she's about thirty-five. But, yeah, she seemed different, in a good way. I wonder what she's doing with that fat dude, Bogdan."

"I guess she's into fat people," said Andrei, unable to stop a grin. "So, she might want some of this," he said, pointing at his body with both his hands.

"Maybe. But I would suspect she's more into strong guys. That Bogdan looked like he could split wood for half a day, fat or no fat."

"I can split wood!"

"Sure, you can. By the way, Victor seemed like a great guy. Tall, fit, and probably smart."

"Pfft. He was so full of himself. Did you see him? 'Me, me, me. We're just doing our part'," said Andrei in a mocking voice and doing air quotes.

"Well, he had a team and ran the entire project, so…" said Lili, and they both laughed.

They continued walking until they finally reached the top of the current hill, and there, down below, they saw the woodsmen's cabin on the right-hand side.

# 2 BACK TO TOWN

I n the yard, things looked unchanged. The cabin's roof was covered in snow, and, together with the trees in the background, it made for an idyllic image. Still, the mood changed after Andrei took a look in the shed.

"Yeah, she's okay. We can do it."

"Is Grandma okay?" asked Matei, his mouth hanging open.

"No. I mean, you know, she's not okay, but no change since last time. We can bury her."

Lili and Dan threw Andrei a look, then Lili petted Mat on the head.

"No, honey. Grandma is not okay. But we must do the Christian thing and bury her. She would have wanted that, but we had no time. We'll do it soon."

"But don't we need a priest to do it properly?" continued Andrei, somehow impervious to the looks he was receiving.

"We'll go get Howler first," interrupted Dan. "We're wasting time now. Let's go."

\* \* \*

Midway to the village, Andrei was tired.

"We really need to stop awhile guys. I cannot go on," he said, gasping for air. "Let's take a break."

When the group stopped, he sat down, looking into the distance, trying to catch his breath.

"My God, this is difficult. I can barely wait for spring. It should be way better without all this snow, and we'll be able to use the car."

"Yeah, and all the growlers will be able to walk around. That will be something," said Lili, scoffing.

"Hmm. Yeah, I forgot about that." After a few moments, he continued. "What can we do? We should prepare. I mean, when we move back to town, into the empty house next to Albert's, we should make sure we have the right defenses. You know, in case we get attacked."

"Are the growlers going to attack us, Mommy?"

"No sweetie. They're not," said Lili, throwing meaningful, icy glances at Andrei.

"Well, they could attack us, actually," said Andrei, looking back at her. "He needs to know, to be prepared."

"Again with this? We need to protect him until he's ready to understand."

"He understands."

After a while, Andrei had an epiphany. "Oh, man. I just realized. You focus so much on 'protecting him', but you never thought about leaving him at Alfred's for a few days, until we come back with Howler."

"I considered that, you dufus. Obviously, I did. I just thought it was a terrible idea. I wonder why it crossed your mind this late."

"Pfft. You didn't think of that. And why is it such a terrible idea?"

"You would leave your child alone with people you don't know?"

"No, but I would probably stay behind with him, to protect him. And, yeah, I see what you're trying to say—that I want to stay behind. No. *You* could have stayed behind and let me and Dan bring Howler."

"You're such an idiot! I want to be there for Mom. I want to be with Dad when he does the… right thing. I want us to be together for the burial."

"And you would risk our son's life?"

"We're not risking anything!" yelled Lili. Her voice sliced

through the air, making it seem even colder when the noise faded. "We know how the growlers work. We know this road is safe! And if we move during the day, we shouldn't have to fear wolves or dogs."

Andrei finally saw Lili's wet eyes. He paused a bit, then spoke again.

"I'm sorry, honey, I really am. I don't know what got into me. I'm such an idiot. Could be the lack of oxygen, or maybe the stress." He stopped for a while, trying to find his next words. "Of course we're okay here. We're safe. And, yes, it's better to have Mat with us. And it's normal for you to be here for Maria. I'm sorry," he said, getting up and approaching Lili, who started to cry.

"Go away!" said Lili, covering her eyes.

"Please, don't cry! I'm sorry. I was an idiot. Please forgive me."

She pushed him away a few times, before finally letting him hug her.

* * *

Just before they reached the village, they passed through the place where they'd had to kill the seven dogs to save Dan's life. The bodies lay all around, scattered and frozen.

"Howler! Hey boy!" said Dan as he entered the house.

He heard a weak bark from the room where Howler was locked up, and when he opened the door, the dog came happily to him.

"Oh, good boy, you're okay. You're such a good boy! I'll take good care of you from now on, I promise," said Dan, petting and hugging the dog.

The poor creature was in terrible shape. Skinny, hungry, thirsty. He had run out of food and water, and judging by the state of the walls and furniture, he'd tried to eat anything he could find.

Dan gave him water, then fed him, while the others entered the house and looked around.

"Man, this stinks," said Andrei when he reached Howler's room. "We need to clean this up."

"We'll not be here for long, so don't worry," said Lili.

"We'll be here a while," interrupted Dan. "Howler is in no condition to walk the distance. I think we're looking at a week or even more."

"Ugh, okay," muttered Andrei. "Afterwards, we need to go get more food."

"Classic," said Lili.

"What? If you don't want to eat, just say so."

"You're cute," said Lili, smiling.

"You're not!"

"Ha, ha."

* * *

The days passed by slowly as Dan took care of Howler. He fed him a few times a day, played with him, walked him. Slowly but surely, the dog was getting better, stronger, and the bond between them grew.

* * *

Lili, Andrei, and Matei had been spending a lot of time in the backyard. Andrei and Matei, mostly, as Lili took upon herself the laundry duty.

"Damn, this is hard. I wonder how primitive man could do all this," she said, scoffing.

"They probably washed nothing, honey. Plus, they only dressed in animal skins and such. Just imagine how they smelled."

"No, thank you. Still, I have to boil some water, mix it with some cold, handwash everything, and then let it dry. It takes ages. Next time, you'll help."

"But, honey, I can't do this kind of work. I have other things to worry about."

"Yeah? Like what?"

"Like, you know… providing protection."

"What protection?"

"Against the growlers. My mere presence makes you more relaxed, so happier overall. This brings more benefits than washing a few clothes."

"Well, I feel protected enough with Dad around. You, beloved husband, will help me with the drying part. And you'll carry the hot water buckets. And that's final," she said, going back inside.

"Eh, see now, son," said Andrei with a sigh, "our days of freedom are gone."

"Our days? No, Dad, *your* days. She only told *you* to help."

"Well, yeah. But you'll help me with the drying."

"But Daaad!"

* * *

"Let's get ready," said Dan. "Let's be efficient. We go in, grab the food, and come back. And we should gather as much as we can, to take some back to town with us."

They all nodded, and as they prepared to leave, Dan took Howler back inside.

"You'll stay here, boy. We'll be back in a few hours. We can't take you with us, since you're not ready. I need to train you better, yeah, boy? Who's a good boy? You are!"

As he headed out of the room, Howler started barking and whining aggressively, pushing himself through the doorway.

"Hey, Howler, boy, stop! It's just for a few hours. I'll be back, I promise."

The dog managed to escape. Dan tried to get him back in, but now he didn't want to follow.

"He doesn't want to be alone inside the house," said Lili, who was following the scene.

"Wow, you are exceptionally perceptive," said Andrei, making Lili laugh while blowing raspberries at him. "What can we do, Dan? Should we take Howler with us?"

"I guess the time spent in that room scarred him. No, I think we should just split, like last time. Lili, Matei, and Howler will stay home while we go get food."

He saw Andrei's eyes getting larger, so he immediately added, "we'll take the walkies with us, be in contact with Lili the whole time. And we pacified the church, remember. We go in, take the food, and come straight back. We'll have to take a little less, since it's just the two of us, but that's the way it goes."

* * *

Dan was right. It all went smoothly. Even with just two of them, they managed to bring a lot of food, and that evening they had a varied and fulfilling meal.

"Well, things are not that bad. I mean, all things considered," said Andrei, getting comfortable on the sofa. "The food is good and we are safe here. We even have a dog."

"Yeah. I guess so. It's definitely better than a few weeks back, that's for sure," said Lili, cuddling next to him.

Dan was sipping from a glass of wine. He'd taken a few bottles from the priest's cellar. And there was still quite a lot left, ready to be collected in the future.

"Yeah, it could be worse," said Dan, looking into the glass. "It would have been better if Maria were here with us."

"Oh, Dad... let's not go there. I just hope she's in a better place."

"Yeah, me too... me too."

"This proved to be a suitable set-up," said Andrei, looking around the room, trying to change the subject. "But I think the new place will be better. We'll be even safer with the others next to us. We'll have better chances of finding food, too, as the town is larger."

"Yeah, but that means more growlers," said Dan. "Okay, if we go to one supermarket, clean it out, and then go there for food, we should be fine for a while. But we have no idea what will happen come spring."

"What do you mean?"

"I'm talking about the growlers. They will unfreeze and be able to move everywhere."

"Yes, they'll be able to do anything," said Andrei, nodding. "Who knows how many of them are hidden by the snow. We will probably miss winter more than we think."

"You know what I miss?" said Lili, suddenly. "A bath! I would love to take a bath. A nice, warm bath."

"We can do that," said Andrei. "Just like we did with the laundry. I can heat the water, then carry it to the bathtub. Let's do it!" he said, and jumped off the couch.

"But I want a bath too," begged Matei. "You used to give me baths every day!"

"It wasn't every day," said Lili. "We washed you every day, but a long bath in the tub was about once a week."

"Fine. I want a bath!"

\* \* \*

"Ahh, this is perfect!" exclaimed Lili, splashing about in the bathtub as Andrei poured in the last bucket of hot water.

"Yeah, well, perfect for you. I can barely feel my arms after carrying all this water. And I had to do it twice, for you and your annoying kid."

"Luckily I proposed filling the bathtub only a third for him and two thirds for me, significantly reducing your workload," said Lili, giggling. "Is the little rascal asleep yet?"

"Yes, naturally. He's sleeping like a log."

"What did he tell you when he wanted me out of the room, when you started laughing?"

"Ah, he called me to 'see the swimming shark'," said Andrei, air quoting and chuckling.

"What shark?"

"You don't want to know," he said, and both laughed.

"So, you said your arms hurt?" said Lili a few moments later, in a strangely gentle voice.

"Yeah! And all that snow I had to shovel to fill the buckets. Boy, if I only knew I'd need two hours to prepare this bath for you, I'm not sure I would have volunteered."

"Well, why don't you join me? A warm bath might make you feel better," said Lili, with a smile Andrei hadn't seen in a while.

He couldn't stop a grin. "Finally! Well, in that case, maybe it wasn't such an awful idea I volunteered."

\* \* \*

Howler was much better, and the day to return to town finally came. They had everything prepared: clothes and food all stuffed in their backpacks.

They left the village and reached the cabin around midday.

"Will we spend the night here?" asked Andrei.

"Definitely. We must prepare the grave, and that takes time. It'll probably take us the whole day tomorrow," said Dan. "The ground is frozen, so we'll dig for hours. I recommend you unpack a few things and make up a fire."

"And what are you going to do, Dad?"

"I want to check on Albert. He said he would get some walkies, so I'll try to contact him from the hill nearby."

"But why? Maybe we should start digging the hole right now?" continued Lili.

"We could, but why hurry? And I really want to check on Albert. It shouldn't be a problem, but we need to make sure they are okay."

"Why wouldn't they be okay?" intervened Andrei.

"Ugh, no reason, relax. I'm just saying, we don't want to go there, big heavy backpacks on our backs, only to discover that something bad happened to them, right? It's only a precaution, nothing to worry about. And these days it's good to be cautious, don't you think?"

* * *

Dan reached the hilltop nearby. The same place from where they'd first seen the cabin some weeks ago, when they'd fled the dangerous town. Now, they were trying to get back in.

Howler was next to him. He'd wanted to follow Dan, even if he was tired.

Dan leaned the baseball bat he was holding against his leg; then he grabbed the walkie-talkie.

"Testing, testing. Hey, Albert, do you copy?"

Static was all he got. He looked around at the vast ocean of snow. Behind him, he could see the cabin, smoke coming from the chimney, and in front was the winding road taking him back to town.

"Hey, my friend, are you there? Anyone there?" said Dan, a few minutes later. "It seems we're too far out, boy. Do you want to go check? Do you want to go closer? Or do you want to go back?"

The dog barked with enthusiasm.

"Shush! Ugh, boy, I need to train you better. You need to be smart. No noise! No! Noise!" he said, moving a finger in front of

Howler.

"No!" said Dan, when Howler looked like he wanted to bark again. "Go home. Go back. I want to go closer."

The dog didn't move.

"Okay, I guess getting a little closer will do no harm. I just hope I'm not making a mistake taking you with me."

* * *

"Hey, Albert, buddy, you there?" tried Dan, as he got near Andrei's car. He could see the town limits now, and the distance to Albert's house should be well within reach for the walkies.

"What the hell, boy," he said, petting Howler with his left hand. "They probably didn't go get the walkies. Wanna go closer, maybe? Don't answer," he said, grabbing Howler's snout with the left hand and petting him with the right hand. Only to move his hand away, trembling with pain.

"Ugh, I forgot how bad this hurts," he said, looking at his right thumb, as if trying to see through the leather glove. "Good boy, let's go."

They were slowly entering the town. From time to time Dan would tuck the bat under his armpit, then use his walkie, trying to reach his friend.

Finally, he got an answer.

"Hey, Dan, is that you?" It was a woman's voice.

"Yes, this is Dan. Who is this?"

"Hey! Guys, it's working!" a faint voice came through. Then followed, at full volume: "This is Flo. You've arrived? Are you home?"

"No, I was just coming to check on you guys. The others are at the cabin. But where are you? You're not home, I guess."

"No, we're on our way back from the hardware store. Got these walkie-talkies and a generator, and now we're going home."

"You went this late? Is everything okay?"

"Yeah, why wouldn't it be?"

"Oh, no reason, I was only wondering why you didn't go sooner."

"Eh, we never got around to it. We were just lazy, I guess."

23

"Fine, so I'll go back to my family, back to the cabin. Tell Albert we'll arrive, all of us, in two days, okay?"

"Yeah, will do. He's here with us, doing the important thing. Basically, he's busy carrying the generator," said Flo, and started laughing. "See you soon!"

"See, boy," said Dan, tucking his walkie back in his belt. "We worried about nothing. But being cautious is a smart thing. And you need to learn how to be cautious, you hear me, boy? No more of that barking."

They had started walking back when suddenly Dan heard noise in his earpiece.

"Oh my God, Dan, are you there?" He heard Albert's stressed voice. He was whispering, but fast, in scared tones. "Dan, are you there? Please answer. Answer me! Dan. Dan! Please answer! Are you still in range? Dan? Hey, Dan?"

"Hey, I'm here Albert. I heard you the first time. You need to release the button to hear me, otherwise it's just you talking. What's up? Now, I'll release the button, you press it and answer, then release it again to hear me."

"Something's wrong at the house! The gate is open and there's blood everywhere!"

"What gate? Where are you? Are you inside?"

"No, no, we're outside. Some two hundred yards out. We can see the yard gate is open, and there's blood on the ground. Something bad happened!"

"Who's with you?" said Dan, as he stopped at the outskirts of the town.

"I'm with Flo and Bogdan. We were getting the generator. And we just saw this! You need to come to help us! Please!"

"Oh, what to do, boy?" said Dan, turning to Howler. "They probably need help."

He turned around a few times, looking down the road toward the cabin, where his family was, then toward Albert's house, and back again.

"Okay, stay put, I'm coming," he said into the walkie.

\* \* \*

Mat was building a snow fort, and as the sun set over the hill to the west, he turned to his parents.

"Where's Grandpa?"

"Grandpa is out," said Lili, looking at Andrei.

"Out where? Shouldn't he come back?"

"Yes, honey, he should. He'll be here shortly. Don't worry. Go inside, take off your jacket, and get ready for dinner. We'll follow you soon."

As Matei entered the house, she turned to Andrei. "Something's wrong," she said.

"What?"

"Were you even here? Jesus. Where is Dan?"

"Ah, that. Probably plans to spend the night at Albert's. You know, drink some of that whiskey, share some memories," said Andrei, waving away Lili's concerns.

"I don't think so. Something's wrong. We have to bury Mom tomorrow. He wouldn't come late, or drunk, to dig the grave."

"Maybe he can't do it? It's too much for him?"

"It is a lot for him," admitted Lili, "but he's never let us down. I'm afraid. Let's go inside. It's cold," she said, and started moving.

"What's wrong with Grandpa, Mom?" asked Mat as the adults entered the cabin.

"Nothing, sweetie. I mean, we don't know."

"I don't want Grandpa to die!"

"He won't die. He's okay. Your dad is probably right and Grandpa spent some more time with Albert. But he'll be back, you'll see."

# 3 THE DEVIL

Dan headed cautiously downhill. He reached the place where Albert and his family had killed those dogs.

"We need to be quiet, boy. Come slowly," he said, whispering to Howler.

They took another curve, and he could finally see Albert's gate. It was broken into pieces, like someone had busted their way in. Parts of it were still hanging from the fence. Some blood was visible at the gate, and it was obvious something bad had happened.

"Hey, Albert. I'm near your house, uphill. Where are you?" he whispered, using the walkie-talkie.

"We're downhill. Should we move in?"

"Yeah. Come closer, with caution."

Dan started moving. He could now see Albert, Bogdan, and Flo coming toward the gate from the other side.

As they got closer, Howler became restless.

"Stay, boy. Relax. I'm here. Relax," Dan said in a peaceful voice.

Suddenly, with a growl, Howler sprinted forward, past Dan, and entered the yard through the broken gate.

"Howler!" yelled Dan in a whispered shout. "God damn it!" He picked up the pace and entered the yard at a run.

Albert, Flo, and Bogdan immediately followed, and they all barged into the yard just in time to see Howler bite a squirming growler on the back of its neck.

The growler was trying to get up, yet Howler did an excellent job of holding it down. The struggle was loud, and soon other growls could be heard from within the house.

The growler on the ground was a man, rather skinny and of average height, poorly dressed. And with Howler holding it in place, Dan made quick work of killing it, running his knife through its back, right into the heart.

"Good boy," he said, petting Howler. "And good instincts, going right for the neck. But next time, wait for my command, okay?"

As he said that, the growls coming from inside the house intensified, and they all realized the front door had been smashed open.

Suddenly, a fast one appeared. There was something strange about this one, though, as its face was all smashed in and swollen, like an enormous piece of bloody meat. Still, it came running, targeting the group.

Albert was wielding a very large and heavy axe. With an expert move, one he had probably done a million times, he swung the axe horizontally, from right to left. The growler's head flew off, while the body stumbled, squirming on the ground.

The body kept twisting uncontrollably. The head was off, but still, through the open neck, a horrible sound came out. It was still alive, or some sort of alive, and it only stopped when Albert's heavy axe split the growler's back in two, cleaving the heart.

Behind them, two more growlers stumbled out. Slow ones.

"Oh God!" yelled Flo, and a shiver passed down Dan's spine.

Andreea and someone who resembled Victor were emerging. They had turned, and now they came to kill everyone, closing in slowly.

"No!" yelled Bogdan, his thundering voice drowning out everything.

It froze Albert. His axe was down in the snow and he couldn't move.

Soon, everyone could smell the growing stench, the rot. And as Andreea and Victor slowly approached, they could make out more horrible details.

Victor's right arm was fully eaten. His bones were visible, yellow and cleaned, and those were held together only by cartilage. It was the same with his face. He looked like a skeleton, with one eye missing and the other white and pale.

Andreea was even worse. Her belly was open, her entrails gone. Her entire chest had been eaten too, and her ribs were visible.

"We have to end this," said Dan, adjusting his grip on his bat. "Albert, buddy, we have to end this!"

Albert snapped out of it and grabbed his axe. "Can you do them?" he begged.

"Yes, I can," said Dan. "I'm sorry, buddy."

And he closed in, swinging the bat up.

"No, wait," said Flo. "Let's not. Let's do it cleanly."

Dan stopped. He understood. He saw Albert looking at his child and daughter-in-law. He looked older now, and, massive as he was, he seemed way smaller.

"What do you propose?" said Dan, turning to Flo.

"Not smashing their heads in."

"Yeah, I got that. But how?"

"I push them down and you put the knife in. Okay?"

Flo shifted to the side, as what used to be Andreea and Victor moved within arm's reach. Suddenly, she jumped behind them and pushed Andreea's shoulders forward. Andreea stumbled in the snow and fell face down.

Dan sprung forward and ran the knife through her back. However, Victor was close, and he fell on Dan's back, biting.

The growler initially bit the leather jacket, but as Dan moved, teeth grazed the back of his head, scraping his skin.

With a yell, Dan let go of the knife, fixed in Andreea's back, and shook his body, trying to get Victor off. Howler jumped and grabbed Victor's hand, pulling. Combined, these actions made the growler lose its balance. Flo jumped in, pulling Victor further off Dan, until he was down in the snow, on his back.

Dan touched the back of his head with his right hand. A piece of meat was missing, and when he looked at his fingertips he saw blood. He even found one of Victor's teeth. He pulled the knife from Andreea's back and, turning to his right, stabbed Victor through the chest.

As the growler made a final squirm, something fell from its

mouth—a piece of flesh large enough to fit the space on the back of Dan's head.

"Damn, this hurts," said Dan, getting up and moving his head around.

"You okay?" asked Flo.

"Yeah, I guess. He tore off a piece of me though. I must tend to the wound. I don't want it to get infected."

"Yeah, we'll do that inside. Come on."

"Mom!" said Albert, suddenly. "Where is my mom?"

"Albert, wait," said Dan. "Let us go first."

They were cautious as they entered the house. First Dan, quickly followed by Flo. Behind them, a few steps back, were Bogdan and Albert.

Signs of a struggle were everywhere, and puddles of blood, which looked never-ending. Plus, the smell was horrible: rotting meat mixed with blood.

Dan feared the worst.

They finally reached the living room, where they found Grandma Gina.

She was still breathing. But she was in a poor state.

Her breath was accelerated. She was squeezing the crucifix in her right hand, while in her left she grasped the onion and garlic strings. Her eyes were looking left and right, moving relentlessly. Her legs were usually underneath a blanket. At least, that's how they'd been when Dan had visited. But now, the blanket was on the ground and both her feet were eaten, including some parts of her right leg.

"Oh, Grandma Gina!" said Flo, moving nearer the old woman. "How are you?"

"The Devil was here! The Devil was here! We need to repent! We'll all going to die!"

"Grandma Gina! It's me, Flo. You're safe now. What happened?"

"No one is safe! No one is safe!" yelled the old lady. "Repent, as you will soon die!"

"No use," said Dan to Flo, just as Albert and Bogdan entered the room. "But how come she didn't bleed to death from what happened to her feet?"

Although the meat on her legs was visible, somehow there was very little blood on the floor next to her.

"She has been having really bad circulatory problems for many years now. Both her legs were dead. Probably, if she'd been younger, the doctors would have tried to do something, maybe even cut them off, at least the feet, as they risked poisoning her body. But she was so old that no doctor wanted to touch that."

While they had this exchange, Albert jumped in and started hugging his mother. The whole time, Bogdan stood at the back, holding his axe, while tears rolled down his cheeks.

"Mom! How are you, Mom? Oh my God, it's my fault! I never should have left! I should have stayed here to protect you!"

\* \* \*

A few hours later, Grandma Gina was sleeping in her bed. They gave her a strong sedative, tended to her legs, and soon after she nodded off.

The group was in the living room, and Flo was helping Dan with his wound.

"Ugh, he did quite a number on you. You're missing some meat here. We have to clean it, then put a bandage on."

"Clean it thoroughly. Use a ton of disinfectant. I know the human mouth has a lot of bacteria, even without being a dead growler. And an infection is the last thing I need."

"Yeah, well, if we look at the movies, you're up for something worse," said Flo.

"What? No. Those are movies, come on," said Dan, but a shadow of doubt crossed his mind. "Put some onions on," he added, after a few moments of silence.

"What? It will sting like hell."

"No, actually, put some onions *and* garlic on."

"Jesus, are you sure?"

"Yes! Do it. Clean the wound, then make a garlic and onion mash and put it there."

"Well, okay. I'll do it. I hope you can take it."

"I hope so too."

\* \* \*

30

"Ready!" said Dan, lying chest-down on a sofa after gulping from a whiskey bottle. "Do it."

Flo had already cleaned the wound with water and medicinal alcohol. For this last step, she took a few garlic pieces and half an onion and mashed them in the kitchen.

The paste was ready, and the smell was strong.

"You want me to add some salt to it as well? Or maybe some lemons?" she said.

"Ha, funny," said Dan with half a laugh.

"Okay. Here we go."

She used her fingers and pressed some of the mash into the hole on the back of Dan's neck.

Dan bit a pillow, trying to hold in a yell. A second later, he was bellowing, his face turning red, and sweat and tears poured down his face.

Howler started barking at Flo.

"Down, boy," said Dan, barely catching his breath. "Albert, hold the dog, please."

Albert, who was sitting on another sofa, got up and complied.

"Oh," said Flo. "You okay? Should I stop?"

Dan was taking deep breaths while biting the pillow and groaning. He finally answered. "No, do it. Don't stop. Do it properly."

As she put more of the concoction on Dan's neck, he continued his squirming.

* * *

"I don't know how you pushed through that," said Flo, glancing in admiration at Dan.

Dan, Flo, Bogdan, and Albert were all in the living room, while Grandma Gina slept in her room.

The doors were wide open, so they could hear when the old woman woke.

"It hurt like hell. But it had to be done, I think."

"It sure looked like it. I'm impressed. But you really think that was necessary?"

"I don't know. But you said it yourself, in the movies a bite like this can turn you into a monster. Okay, those are just movies. But what if?"

"Yeah, but what if it wasn't enough?"

"That we'll know soon enough," said Dan, with a sad smile.

Silence enveloped the room again, everyone lost in their thoughts.

Dan glanced around. Bogdan and Albert were looking down, the occasional tear rolling down their faces, while Flo kept changing her position, as if trying to think about other things.

"Let's go secure the gate, shall we?" said Dan, suddenly. "We don't know what happened. Grandma Gina will hopefully tell us soon, but until then, let's put up our defenses."

No one moved.

"Hey, guys. Snap out of it. Albert, Bogdan, come on! We need to do this. And after that, we need to build another front door."

"And we need to do something with Andreea and Victor," added Flo. "We can't let them sit around in the snow like that."

They finally stood up.

\* \* \*

"How did this happen?" asked Albert, looking at the broken gate.

"The vehicle entrance was also forced," said Bogdan.

The two gates were next to each other, and the men were inspecting them from inside the yard.

"We reinforced them properly," said Albert. "No man should have been able to get through. But see here? This beam is almost broken. The vehicle gate is weakened."

"Maybe they were a lot of them."

"Looks like it," said Albert. He gazed around the yard and then approached the opening. He couldn't see anything outside, so he turned back to his son. "We need to fix it, but this time let's make sure no one can break it."

"We could move something heavy here, too, to block both gates."

"Like what? One of the cars?"

"Why not? But let's fix the gates first and then we'll see."

Using some strong, sturdy planks, they patched up the broken gate. They also mended the vehicle entryway, and now everything was in good order.

Although they tried to keep it down, all the hammering proved to be quite noisy. Luckily, they didn't wake any growlers. They'd cleared the surrounding houses in the past, so it was relatively safe.

"Let's move the car," said Albert.

"Which one?" asked Bogdan.

"Mine, since it's an SUV. It's taller and heavier."

"Mine is heavy too."

"It is, but still I think mine would do a better job. And we need the best protection possible."

"Okay, let's use your car. Good idea."

They spent the next few dozen minutes shoveling snow, making room to move the truck and block the gates.

As they were contemplating their achievement, Flo appeared in the doorway.

"She's awake."

Everyone was in the living room when Albert came in, carrying his mother in his arms. She was frail and small, but in Albert's arms, she looked even skinnier. He gently set her down in her chair, covered what remained of her feet with the blankets, and then sat on the sofa, close to her. Just as he did so, she started yelling.

"I need my onions and garlic! What have you done with my strings? Bring them back! Bring them back!"

"Yes, Mom. Sorry. I left them in your room. I'll bring them at once."

"Never do that again, you hear? And you should all wear onion and garlic strings!"

Albert hurried back, placed the strings around his mother's neck, and sat back down on the sofa.

"What's that mutt doing here?" said Grandma Gina, pointing at Howler. "Better not get used to this."

"What happened, Mom?" said Albert, in a calm and nurturing voice.

"What happened? What I told you would happen! The Devil came and killed Victor and Andreea. And he almost killed me!"

"Mom… please."

"Grandma, what do you mean? What happened? What did this devil look like?" asked Bogdan.

"The Devil came to lay waste to this world! Why do I have to keep telling you that?"

"You don't have to keep telling us. We believe you," said Bogdan, pleading with her, "but what do you mean by—"

"I mean the Devil came and—"

"Look, Grandma Gina," interrupted Flo. "I know you're upset that we didn't listen to you. And you're right to be upset. We should have trusted you. Still, we believe that 'the Devil' is probably a concept, at most a supernatural being, and he cannot literally walk around doing things. Can you explain this in a way we can understand?"

"I believe the Devil is real," said Bogdan, looking at his wife. "Don't upset Grandma."

"I don't want to upset her, but 'the devil came' means nothing to me! How did he come? Did he just 'appear' here? Or maybe he dug a hole and crawled up from below? Did he have horns and a tail, or what? What do you mean, Grandma Gina? Can you start at the beginning?"

Grandma Gina paused, looking at Flo while playing with her crucifix. No one said anything for a few minutes, engulfed in awkward silence. Finally, she spoke, looking around the room.

"Fine. I'll tell you what happened. I'll tell you." She slowly turned her head toward Flo. "And afterwards, I want you to look me in the eye and tell me the Devil is not real.

"You three left to bring the generator. This was the Devil's work. He fooled you, he tempted you. You went to get an object of gluttony. What, you cannot live without electricity? You cannot wash in a tub if the water comes from a bucket?"

No one answered, so Grandma Gina continued, satisfied.

"And where is that generator, anyway?"

"We left it downhill, a few hundred yards away," said Bogdan. "But don't worry, we'll bring it—"

"Don't! Haven't you learned anything?" She paused, looking satisfied, while Flo shook her head in disbelief. "You left two days ago, in the morning. You were supposed to come back yesterday.

What happened?"

"Walking there took more time than we'd planned, as we went the long way, to avoid the park. And then we spent some time checking the store, choosing a generator. It's a huge place and it was getting dark, so we spent the night," said Albert. "We lost more time yesterday trying to get gas from a gas station. But that's less important. When did this happen?"

"The day you left, right after sunset. Two days ago. We were all in the living room, talking. We had just finished dinner, when suddenly we heard growling. It was a lot of noise, coming from outside. Victor went to check, only to see the gate being hit from the outside."

"What? This is strange. Are you sure you didn't make any noise?" interrupted Dan.

"No! No noise. We were just here, talking. No, not even talking. It was quiet. We lit some candles, and we sat there, doing nothing."

Dan said nothing more, so after a pause, the old lady continued. Her voice sounded like a caw, and her gaze circled the people in the room.

"Victor came back in, yelling. He said the Morois were at the gate, trying to break it in. He and Andreea picked up their bat and axe and went out. It was a big commotion. I suppose the gate broke, as they were yelling, fighting. Soon after, they came inside the house and locked the door. They'd killed five or six, they said."

"What, five or six? There was only one outside, and it was alive and kicking. Impossible," said Dan, while Bogdan, Flo, and Albert looked back and forth between him and Grandma Gina.

"I'm telling you what they told me. What? How many Morois did you find inside the house?"

"The same as outside. One," said Dan with a distrustful voice. "Oh, and Victor and Andreea."

"Well, there were more than a dozen."

"Impossible!"

"Would you shut up and let me tell you what happened!"

"Please," said Dan, raising his hand in apology.

"They came in and locked the door. The noise outside was terrible, and the Morois were banging on the door."

"And they didn't fall asleep after a while?"

"Who? The Morois?"

"Well, yeah. Who else?"

"What do you think?" she asked Dan, her gaze drilling through his head. "They didn't. The door broke and they burst in. Victor and Andreea put down a few, while being pushed back here to the living room. They killed at least six in the hallway, and six more in this very room, but they were overtaken."

Grandma Gina's voice trembled down to a whisper, while everyone in the room got shivers down their spines.

"They put them down in front of me. That's when he entered."

"Who?" they all asked.

"I guess the Devil," said Flo sarcastically.

"No. Or yes. It was a Strigoi."

Everyone gasped, yet remained quiet, while Grandma Gina's gaze moved around the room. She seemed to be enjoying the impact of her words. "Yes. A Strigoi. He was standing right here, in the middle of this room."

"What… How… How do you know it was a Strigoi?" said Flo.

"He *was* a Strigoi. No doubt about it."

"But how do you know? What makes you say it wasn't a growler?" Dan intervened.

"They are called Moroi! And, no, he wasn't one. He was a Strigoi. The Morois were holding Victor and Andreea down, trying to bite them. When the Strigoi entered, he let out a yell, a shriek, and all of them stopped and looked at him. He was the master. No one could deny that."

"What happened next?" asked Dan, after a moment of silence.

"Next, they killed them. Right in front of me. That Devil shrieked again, and the Morois started eating them. My Victor, my beautiful Victor, they started eating his face. The chewing sounds were unbearable," said the old lady, and she started weeping.

Soon, Albert and Bogdan joined her.

"They ate his arm, ate Andreea's chest and belly. It was horrible. They both screamed and yelled until they could scream no more. May God have mercy on their souls."

"We moved their bodies into the barn," said Albert. "We'll bury them today."

"No! Don't do that! That's not the proper way! You need to do the wake. Bring them inside, wash them, dress them nicely, then put them on tables, as is the custom. We bury them on the third day. Only after the wake can they be buried. Maybe their souls can still be saved."

Everyone looked at each other.

"What happened next, Grandma Gina?" asked Dan.

"After they killed Andreea and Victor, eating them alive? Next, the Strigoi came closer. He came to me, that demon! He came to me and raised his hand. And then he stopped. He saw the garlic and onion strings. He looked right in my eyes and let out a scream! But God protected me! I was holding my crucifix and our savior, Jesus Christ, saved me! I prayed and prayed, and he couldn't touch me!"

Grandma Gina was holding her crucifix, her hand shaking as she squeezed the piece of metal. The tears had dried up and her former determined look returned.

"He then ordered his demons to attack me."

"Demons? What demons?" asked Flo.

"The Morois! Have you listened to nothing I've just said? He ordered those Morois to attack me. He shrieked, and they came closer, growling, trying to get me. But they couldn't. My praying, my garlic, and my onions protected me again. They took my blanket away, but it was difficult for them to come closer."

"But, what... what happened to your feet?"

"They started eating them. What do you think?" said Grandma Gina, her shield beginning to shatter. "They started eating me. The Demon told them to eat me. And they did. They started eating my legs. God gave me strength and I didn't feel a thing. But the sounds, their movements, pushing and pulling me... It was horrible. I reckon God put me through this only to show me I was right. To show you I'm right! You need to pray, you need to believe, you need to repent! Otherwise, everything is lost. Just like what happened to Victor and Andreea." Her voice became a whisper as she said those last words.

"I don't feel so good," she said suddenly. "I need to lie down. Take me to my room."

"Yes, Mother," said Albert, and he picked her up.

\* \* \*

"She's weakened," said Flo, breaking the silence.

"What do you mean?" asked Dan.

"She was way more energetic, way stronger. She looks weaker now."

"She seemed energetic to me," said Dan, with a tone of disbelief.

"You saw her break down a few times. I've never seen her like that. And I've known her since forever. No, she's been rocked. Which is understandable. She was stuck in that chair for two days, next to rotting corpses and a dormant Moroi. It must have felt like an eternity," she said, tearing up. "That was too much. I fear for her."

"Shut up, Flo!" said Bogdan. "Don't you jinx my grandma!"

"I'm not jinxing anything. I'm only saying we need to take care of her. And no matter how much we loved them, I don't feel comfortable bringing Andreea and Victor inside the house with us. They've been dead for a while, their bodies are rotting already, and who knows what diseases they might carry now."

"He's my brother!" said Bogdan, his voice a deep rumble.

"He is, yes. And I'm not saying this to disrespect him or Andreea. All I'm saying is, let's have the wake in the barn. It's safer for everyone, and probably healthier. Okay, it's the custom here to have the wake inside the house. But it can also be done at the chapel. Let's do it in the barn. It's less risky."

"And I need to go back to my family," intervened Dan, stopping Bogdan, who seemed to close-off.

"You sure you want to?" asked Flo. "If half of what she said is correct, the path isn't safe."

"That may be, but I need to go defend my family. And we must get far away from this place."

"We might join you. But wait a bit, let's talk. You still have some time, right?"

"It's getting dark soon, so not that much," he said, just as Albert entered the room. "I think I'll be going, Albert. I need to take care of my family."

"Okay, sure. Thank you for your help, Dan. We need to defend ourselves here."

"Or maybe we should go with him," said Flo. "This place

doesn't seem too safe."

"We have the barrier at the gate now," said Albert. "No one will pass."

"But what if they break the fence?"

"It's stronger than the gates. And if that happens, we'll stand and fight. There's more of us now."

"Yeah, and we'll die in the process," muttered Flo. "I don't want to die here. I'd rather go with Dan. At least then we'd die trying to get to a safer place."

"What?" said Bogdan. "You will do no such thing. We stay together."

"Then come with me."

As an outsider, standing in the midst of a family argument was awkward, and Dan cast his gaze around the room, trying not to meet anyone's eye. As he did so, a sudden thought occurred to him—something that needed clarification. "Guys," he said, trying to get everyone's attention.

"I won't come with you," continued Bogdan. "You'll stay here. We need to stay here."

"Why?" asked Flo.

"Hey, guys," pushed Dan.

"Well, first, Grandma can't walk. We cannot leave her behind."

"Let's carry her. You and Albert are strong. It should be no problem for you."

"Guys!" yelled Dan.

Everyone looked at him.

"What happened to all the dead growlers?" Everyone continued to look at him, not saying a word. "You know, from what Grandma Gina was telling us. A lot dead, more than a dozen inside. We only found four, including... the family. What happened to the rest?"

Everyone sat there, quiet. They all looked around, shivers running down their spines.

"We should ask her. We need to know what's happening," continued Dan.

"We need to let her rest," said Albert. "She's weak. She needs her rest."

"But we also need to know what we're dealing with," pressed Dan.

"Yeah, well, we must wait."

"Okay, fine. I'll be going then," said Dan. "I'll keep the walkie turned on. If you plan to go to the village, use it. You might find us."

As he rose from his chair, aiming to leave, Flo said something about going with him. She and Bogdan started quarreling, making quite a lot of noise, until Albert told everyone to shut up, raising his hand as if trying to hear something.

As silence took over, they could hear Grandma Gina calling them with a faint voice.

"You cannot go."

* * *

Grandma Gina was back in her chair, now covered in even more pillows and blankets.

She sipped tea, while ogling everyone around her. It again looked like she was enjoying this attention, as she didn't seem eager to talk.

"Look, Grandma Gina. I'm sorry to bother you, but I really need to go to my family. We were planning to bury Maria tomorrow, and after that we should probably go far away from this place. Why do you say we cannot go?"

"Because it's dusk. Which means night is coming soon."

"So?"

"So? The Strigoi will be out."

"Nonsense," said Dan, but his voice showed less self-confidence than usual.

"You didn't trust me. You didn't listen to what I had to say, and now you scoff at what I'm telling you once more," she said, looking sideways.

"Grandma Gina, I apologize. What do you mean?"

"What do *you* know about Strigois?" she asked, clearly savoring her words.

"Well, what everyone else does," answered Dan. "What my mother told me when I was a kid. It's an evil person who dies and then returns and kills people all around. And as I grew up, I learned that it's all folklore. Oh, and many people mistake them for vampires, but they're not even close. What else is there to know?"

"Folklore, pfft. But you're right about one thing. These are not vampires. That *Dracula* movie took what Strigoi means and perverted it, inventing vampires. No. The Strigois are something else."

"It's a book, actually," mumbled Flo, interrupting.

"What?" asked Grandma Gina, piercing Flo with her eyes.

"Nothing, sorry. Please continue."

Grandma Gina continued to glance for a few moments, then she started talking again. "As I was saying, the Strigois are something else. My grandma told me lots of stories about them. And more can be read in the writings of Priest Bartolomeu, the Divine Warrior, for those who want to learn the truth. They are dead creatures, having sold their soul to the Devil only to be doomed to walk the earth again."

"But that sounds like vampires," interjected Flo, again. "I guess they need blood to survive?"

"No! They don't need blood. That is nonsense, stupid figments of imagination. No. Get it out of your head. Vampires are invented creatures, made to scare halfwits. A Strigoi is real, and it's not a vampire. They need not eat *anything* to survive. Still, they eat. Flesh. Just like the Morois. They never sleep. They come out at night only to do evil. They are smart, they follow through. They hate the living and will do anything to destroy them. All this comes from the blackness in their hearts. They are not mindless creatures! No. They are pure evil, serving the Devil, and they are the masters of the Morois."

"They still sound much like a vampire," said Flo, getting an angry frown from Bogdan. "What? Why are you looking at me like that? Evil creature, up to no good, smart and all that other stuff. If they start to write poetry and dress like goths, it's clearly a vamp—"

"These creatures cannot speak, read, or write! They lost all humanity when they made their deal with the Devil. Why don't you get it? They are pure evil that cannot be stopped or reasoned with. Are you making fun of me with the 'writing poetry' and such?" she asked, looking angrily at Flo.

Everybody was quiet, listening, while Flo looked elsewhere, dodging Grandma Gina's gaze. Dan moved nervously in his chair.

"You want to go? Fine, go. But I tell you, he's out there, watching. He'll come back soon."

"How do you know that? And what happened to the growlers that died here?" asked Dan.

"The Morois, you mean? He resurrected them."

"What?"

"God," puffed Flo. "What is this guy, some sort of Moroi Jesus?"

"Flo!" yelled Grandma Gina. "I've accepted all your rudeness, but this is the limit. Don't take the Lord's name in vain! Yes, the Strigoi resurrected them. I couldn't see how he did it, but he did. He ate the better half of Victor's arm, then he got close to the dead Morois. He leaned toward their chests, or their heads, and did something, mumbled something, and after a while they stood up."

"This is crazy," said Flo, her voice trembling. "I'm out of here!" She rose.

"No! He's out there!" said Grandma Gina, as Flo retrieved her coat and backpack. "And he's waiting for us!"

"How can you tell?" yelled Flo. "How can you know what this, this, made-up, folklore or whatever type of creature thinks?"

"Before finally leaving and letting me be, he pointed at me! He's watching me, Flo! He's watching! He's out there, and he will not stop until he gets me. And then he pointed outside the window. You, all of you. He saw you. He knows you're here and he's waiting for you. If you go out, he'll get you!"

The old woman slumped back in her chair. Her breaths coming fast. "Listen to me," she said, her voice faint. "I have little time left."

"No, Mom, don't say that," said Albert.

"Shush! Let me speak. I *know* I have little time left. I'll die in a few days. I've seen it. The Lord tested me enough, and now He wants me next to Him. My days are numbered. You? You can go. Run. But do it tomorrow morning, when the sun is up. Don't go out into the night. That Strigoi is waiting, and he has an army at his fingertips. The Devil's army, just for you."

After she fell asleep, Albert took her back to her room. When he returned, everybody was quiet, trying to digest all the peculiar information.

"I… think… I think I'll go," said Dan, trying to stand. "I'll take my—" Suddenly, he fell back into his chair.

"Dan?" called Albert, rushing toward him.

"He's burning up," said Flo, touching his forehead.

# 4 HOLED UP

When he opened his eyes, Dan found himself on a bed, Flo beside him. It was dark outside and a candle flickered on the nightstand.

"Ah, good, you're awake," said Flo, touching his forehead. "You're still burning. Here, have these pills, they should help with the fever."

"What happened?" asked Dan, taking the pills and the glass of water she held out to him. "I'm so thirsty. Can you give me some more water?"

"Sure thing. You wanted to leave, got up, then lost consciousness. Here, drink this. Then we moved you into the guest bedroom, and I'm in charge of taking care of you."

"Oh, Howler, I didn't see you there. How are you boy?"

"Yeah, he's been by your side the whole time."

"He's a good boy. Where are the others?"

"They reinforced the barricade, then moved Victor and Andreea into the barn. It's not the best, but we all believe it's way safer. Now Albert and Bogdan are resting a bit, but not for long."

"What did they do to the barricade?"

"They got scared at the prospect of being attacked by dozens of Morois, so they decided the car might not be enough. The ground is slippery and the car might be pushed, so they added a few extra layers of logs. I helped carry the logs. I'm dead tired."

"How will a few logs help?"

"They hammered some large beams into the ground, to the left and right of the gates, and then we moved most of the logs, the ones we have as firewood, from the back of the house. They stacked them on the ground between those rafters. It took a few hours."

"Stacked them how?"

"Pushed them into the gates, perpendicularly. Like bottles of wine would stack," said Flo, laughing and moving her hands forward and backward, showing the stacking direction.

"Yeah, got it. But couldn't that be tumbled over if the gate was pushed?"

"They put four walls like this, each one seven feet tall. That's why I'm so tired. They even added some extra planks, nailing everything together to hold those walls in place. We worked at night, and after Grandma Gina's story, I always felt something was watching me."

"Four? Jesus."

"Yeah," said Flo, laughing.

"Nothing will go through that," said Dan, nodding.

"We hope so."

"And the other two growlers?"

"You mean Morois?" asked Flo, smiling. "They stashed them somewhere in the yard. They'll take them away tomorrow, probably. Not a priority though. They'll be frozen soon. Ah, I forgot. They also made a plan of defense. Grandma Gina scared everyone and we're expecting the worse."

"Well, yeah, who wouldn't. Ah, that hurts," said Dan, touching the back of his neck. "I guess this is the reason for the high fever."

"I agree. Best you didn't leave."

"Yeah, I guess. I just hope Lili and Andrei stay put and don't get any stupid ideas."

"Like what?"

"Like coming to save me."

"I hope not. Something bad happened here. But you don't know Grandma Gina as I do. She's very old-fashioned, very religious. And she sees the devil in everything. When I cut my hair to a medium bob, she saw it as blasphemy for years," she said, and they both laughed.

"My mom was the same. However, while I'm not happy to say this, I'm afraid there is some truth in what she's preaching."

"What, the devil thing?"

"No, no. But the whole Moroi and Strigoi thing. You know, I grew up hearing those stories. And I can't seem to shake the feeling they are more than stories. It seems the people from old saw some things. It can't be random. Ugh, it hurts. Could you please look at my neck?"

"Sure. Turn over."

As Dan turned, Flo got closer and opened the bandage.

"Ugh. Not good," she said, touching the concoction she'd put there. "Odd. It looks like it's gone rotten. Shouldn't have happened this soon. Anyway, I'll clean it up."

She started cleaning and the wound became visible.

"Well, I'm no doctor, but I've seen nothing like this before."

"What is it?"

"It's… strange. You know how a wound should probably be red? With liquids coming out, where the body fights things?"

"Yeah. How's mine?" asked Dan, chest-down on the bed.

"Well, it's very white, with something black in the middle and some black winding strings, like vines, radiating from the bite. And it spreads to the sides. Now that I think of it, it's consistent with—"

"With what happens in the movies if someone gets bitten by the monster," said Dan, with a sigh. "What do you know, this was it. I'll die like an idiot."

"Why like an idiot?"

"Only an idiot would let himself get bitten by one of these things. And a slow one, nonetheless. I mean, I've seen the movies, I'm familiar with the theories. I should have known better. And I've been bitten before on my shoulder, you know. Twice, actually," he said, raising his right hand. "But still I haven't learned."

"We shouldn't assume everything we see in the movies is true," said Flo, with less confidence than Dan would have liked to hear. "This could be something else."

"Yeah. We'll see."

"What should I do? Do you want some more onion and garlic on it?"

"Yes, why not? Let's do this."

\* \* \*

"There. How do you feel?"

"Horrible," said Dan, barely controlling himself. "It feels even worse than before, if that's even possible."

"I'm sorry. I really hope this helps."

"Me too, Flo, me too. And sorry about the dog."

"What, the barking? It's fine. I think he understands it's for your own good."

"How is he?" asked Albert, entering the room. "How are you, Dan?"

"Ugh, like a burden, that's how I feel. How are the defenses?"

"We're fine. We nailed wooden planks across the windows and built a better front door. Way stronger. And we secured it with some horizontal beams, just like they used to do in castles. We put up a barricade, light yet sturdy, so nothing can enter. If that damn Strigoi wants to try something, we'll be waiting."

"Good, I guess. Where's my bat?"

"It's in the living room. Do you need it?"

"Yeah, you know, just in case. I would feel better if it was by my side."

"Sure thing," said Albert, and went out.

\* \* \*

It was deep into the night, past 3a.m. Grandma Gina was sleeping in her bed, and Dan was in a semi-unconscious state. His fever had spiking, and he was twisting and turning. Flo stayed by his side, pressing wet handkerchiefs to his forehead, talking to him now and then. Albert and Bogdan were tiptoeing around the house, checking the windows, squinting between the nailed planks. They couldn't see anything, yet everyone had the feeling something was out there.

"What was that?" whispered Bogdan, frowning as Howler started to move alertly in the living room, whimpering. "Did you hear that?"

"Hear what?" asked Albert, looking around with unease.

"It sounded like a thud."

"A thud?"

"Yeah, like a hit. A deep sound. Coming from outside."

"You could have imagined it," said Flo, looking around the room. The candles made their shadows dance on the walls, and the lack of sleep was deepening everyone's paranoia.

"Yeah, I could be. But I heard it."

"Should we go check?" asked Albert.

"Don't!" intervened Flo, before Bogdan could say anything. "Why? If Grandma Gina is right, there are at least a dozen Morois out there. And a more powerful dude controlling them. You could walk into a trap."

"I guess so," said Albert. "But I want to get this Strigoi, or whatever he is."

"I understand. But maybe it's better to survive until we learn more about it."

\* \* \*

When they woke the next morning, Lili and Andrei realized Dan had never come back.

"We have to go save him," said Lili. "We need to go save my dad."

"And what about Mat? Do we take Mat? You realize this is not what Dan would have wanted, risking our lives."

"But when I came with Mat and saved you from that church, how was it? Was it a good idea?"

"You're right, that was an excellent move. But now, we don't even know he's in danger. He probably stayed up with Albert until late, and now they're both sleeping."

"I want to believe that, I really do. But I can't. He's not like that. Yes, he sometimes likes his alcohol. He does. But still, we had plans. He always does what he's supposed to do. And now he's supposed to bury Mom. He's not drunk in a ditch somewhere."

"I didn't say he's in a ditch. I said he's drunk with Albert."

"I got you the first time! And I'm telling you he's not. He's late against his will."

"Look. I don't know. Maybe you're right. You're probably right. But that means he's in danger. What could have happened? It might be growlers. Or Albert and his family. You saw that Bogdan dude, the way he looked at us. He said nothing, just stood there and observed everyone. What if they did something to him? Do you want to go back there, right into their laps?"

"They seemed to be decent people! It's not right to assume the worst. If I had assumed the worst, you would both be dead in that damn church!"

"You're right. I tell you what. Let's wait for today. If he's not here tomorrow, we make a plan to save him, okay?"

"We should go now," said Matei. "If Albert or Bogdan did something to him, we can fight back. But we need swords. Oh, and shields!"

"Ugh, Mat, you shouldn't listen to our discussion," said Lili, looking around. "We're adults and we sometimes exaggerate."

"Still," said Andrei, ignoring Lili's annoyed glances, "we cannot keep on pushing him away whenever we need to talk about something. He learns things from our discussions."

"Yeah, he learns you're an idiot!"

"No, he learns how the world has changed. And he should also learn that we cannot always go around fighting. It's dangerous. We need to be smart." He nodded to Mat. "Oh, and you should also learn that your daddy is always right," continued Andrei, trying to get a laugh out of Lili.

"Yeah, and irritating," said Lili angrily, making Andrei laugh instead.

* * *

At Albert's house, the morning found everyone finally sleeping. When Grandma Gina woke, she let out a sigh, then started groaning.

In the living room, Bogdan suddenly started awake, panicked, only to immediately relax when he realized the sound was his grandmother.

"Ugh, Grandma, you scared me," he yelled. "How are you?"

"You get scared too easily," she yelled back in her cawing voice.

"If you would believe in God, truly believe, you wouldn't know fear."

"Yes, Grandma," he said, getting up. "I'll go check outside."

He was quickly joined by Albert, who had been sleeping on the other sofa.

They cautiously opened the front door. Albert and Bogdan removed the barricade, then the beams reinforcing their new front door, and stepped out into the front yard.

They moved around, checking left and right. Flo stood in the doorway, bat in her hands, watching them.

"What?" said Bogdan suddenly, in a tone that made everyone shiver. "How did this get here? Oh, no, *these*!"

Albert rushed over, almost running. Near the bodies of the two dead growlers there were three tree trunks.

"I don't remember putting these here," said Albert. "Did you leave them here?"

"No! Of course not!"

"We probably left them here and forgot all about them," said Albert, without confidence. "Maybe Flo dropped them?"

"No, but guys, look at the snow," said Flo.

"What about the snow?"

"What about the snow?" said Flo, in a mocking voice. "Jesus, Bogdan, sometimes I wonder how you don't forget you need to breathe."

"Not sure that was called for."

"Yeah, sorry. Look at the snow. Over here. It looks like the tree trunks were thrown and their landing splashed some snow, see?"

"Yeah, like on that documentary, when they were talking about meteorites."

"Yeah, something like that."

"This means," said Bogdan, carefully checking the snow, "it was thrown from there?" As he finished his sentence, he pointed at the barricade they'd built by the gate.

They went to check it. From their side, everything looked okay.

"Get the ladder," ordered Albert, and Bogdan complied.

"I'll be damned," said Albert from the top of the barricade. "The Strigoi might truly exist."

"What? The logs are from our barricade?" asked Flo.

"Yeah. I remember checking this. A few logs are definitely missing here. Someone took them and threw them in."

"Jesus! I'm going inside," said Flo, and she ran toward the house. The guys quickly followed, constantly checking left and right.

* * *

"We need to leave," said Flo, once they were all back in the living room.

"I agree," reinforced Bogdan. "Go pack some things and let's go."

"Finally!" said Flo, turning around happily to go handle the request.

"Go where?" asked Albert, making Flo stop in her tracks.

"I don't know," said Flo. "Away from this place. To the village. Dan said it's a suitable place."

"Yeah, we could," said Albert. "But what do we do about Grandma? And Dan."

"We can leave Dan here," said Bogdan. "And we can carry Grandma, taking turns. We can do it."

"Grandma is in no condition to take this trip. And I'm not leaving Dan behind."

"Why not? He's not family. What has he ever done for us?" pushed Bogdan.

"He's my friend. He helped me when I was in need. And you can see what kind of friend he is, when he answered our call and helped us the other day, even though it kept him from returning to his own family."

"Well, he's not our family, is he? Family comes first."

"True, but I'm not leaving my friend. And let's not forget, he got sick while helping us."

"Yeah, I agree with Albert," said Flo in a sad voice. "We can't do that. He helped us, and we need to help him. We need to transport him together with Grandma Gina."

"I don't want to die here because of Dan! I'll go alone if I have to."

"The other time, when I said I would go alone, you were raving about sticking together," said Flo, annoyed. "What changed?"

51

"Bogdan, don't be stupid," interrupted Albert. "We will survive together. Separated, we will share Victor's fate."

A cough could be heard, coming from Grandma Gina's room.

\* \* \*

"How are you, Mom?" asked Albert, going to check on her.

"I guess I got a cold," she said, coughing.

"Do you need anything? Some water, maybe tea? Have you eaten anything?"

"I'm not hungry. The Lord wants me with Him, so I don't get hungry anymore."

"What? You have to eat! Don't do this, Mom! And remember what Dan told us, about what happens if you don't eat onions. You'll get sick and become one of those Morois. And it all starts with the cough."

"I'll never be a Moroi. God will not allow that to happen, not to me. Now get out. I want to pray," she said, grabbing her crucifix. She closed her eyes and started to murmur a prayer.

\* \* \*

"I have to go," said Dan, trying to get up. He was feeling a little better, his fever was down, but as he sat up in the bed, he almost fell back. "Ugh, I have such bad vertigo," he said, touching the side of his head. "I hate this."

"You're in no shape to leave. And what are you going to do about that creature lurking outside?"

"Nothing. I'll take my leave, pick up my family, and go to the village, far away from this place. You guys can join us."

"We probably will. But you need to get better. Stay one more day, get well, and then we'll go."

"No, I need to go to my family. I need to bury my Maria," said Dan, getting up, only to fall back on the bed.

"You're still hot, Dan," said Flo, touching his forehead. "Go back to bed. I'll fix you some food, some onions, and garlic with it, and then you should get some sleep. I'll check the wound afterwards, okay?"

\* \* \*

"Is not looking good," said Flo, checking the back of his neck. Dan had finished his meal, and now he was chest down. "It's spreading. The area looks even whiter, if that's possible, and it's larger. It seems like the black thing in the middle grew. And this concoction is rotten again. It cannot be. Maybe because you're hot it rots quicker?"

"No idea. But I believe the wound makes it go rotten."

"Yeah, probably."

"Plus, the onions you fed me tasted terrible. I know, I know, they were fresh. But I suppose I've got that sickness now, although different. I don't like onions anymore."

"Yeah. And the skin, it feels different here."

"Where?"

"Where I'm touching you. It feels hardened."

"I don't feel anything."

"You don't feel it's hardened?"

"No, I don't even feel you touching me."

"You don't feel that?" asked Flo, pushing harder on the whitest part of the wound.

"No. I mean, I sense my body being pushed, but I don't feel the touch."

"Damn. Okay. Do you want some more of that concoction? Or some moisturizer, maybe?"

"I don't know. Maybe both?"

"Why not?"

\* \* \*

"It's not going into your skin, this moisturizer of mine," said Flo. "I rub it and rub it, but nothing."

"Eh, leave it then. Put on some of that concoction, I guess."

"Okay," said Flo, with a visible lack of confidence.

"I'm not sure it will help," said Dan. "But I don't want to call it quits just yet."

\* \* \*

As evening came, they locked up the house. They put the beams back on the front door and got ready for another night of checking windows.

"I want to talk to you," said Albert, motioning to Bogdan and Flo. "Just the three of us."

They gathered in the living room and started talking in a whisper, making sure Grandma Gina and Dan couldn't overhear them.

"I've been thinking. Things are dreadful. Mom's not eating anymore. Dan is sick. And outside we have Morois, and probably a Strigoi, who seem to have it in for us. On the bright side, we have a lot of food and water in our basement, enough to last us for weeks."

"What do you want us to do?" asked Flo.

"He wants to leave," said Bogdan.

"No. I mean, yes and no. I want to convince Mom to eat and to help Dan get better. And then we need to leave."

"I say we grab Grandma, take her with us, and leave Dan here. He can have all the barricades, all the food and water. He'll be fine," said Bogdan.

"We've already been through this," said Flo. "If he would be fine here all alone, we wouldn't leave this place, would we?"

"Do you want to die here, protecting Dan?" said Bogdan.

A long silence hung over the room. Everyone was looking down, thinking.

"We have two sick people, and I need your help," said Albert, interrupting the silence. "Convince Mom to eat, and you take care of Dan, Flo. Help him get well. And then, together, we can leave," said Albert, and Bogdan got up and left, huffing. "And please take care of this one," continued Albert, looking at Flo and pointing toward the door where Bogdan had exited. "I'm afraid he'll do something stupid."

\* \* \*

Deep into the night, Albert and Bogdan were, once more, patrolling the house and checking the windows. This time they were listening for thuds, like the ones from the night before.

They heard something. Only now, it wasn't a thud.

It was a scream. A loud shriek, coming from behind the barricade.

Everybody froze, terrified, and Flo started shaking.

"Oh my God. What was that? What was that?" she screamed.

"Shush. Be quiet," said Dan, grabbing her by the hand and pulling her closer. "We're safe here, see? Just be quiet. And you, Howler, be quiet as well," he said, as the dog started running around and barking.

"How can I be quiet? Look at you, you're burning! That thing on the back of your neck is spreading. You'll soon die, and we'll follow. And maybe you dying like this is for the best. I'll probably die like Andreea!" said Flo, and she started crying and shaking.

"We'll be okay. Trust me," said Dan. But not even he believed his words.

\* \* \*

Morning found everyone in awful shape.

Grandma Gina had a fever. She was delirious, yelling and screaming about how God would cleanse everything and everyone. She was behaving much like Maria had before dying back at the cabin, only with extra spine-chilling messages.

Dan was also running a fever, and the thing on the back of his neck was even larger. His entire neck was now white, and half of his back as well. It had spread up the back of his head, making his hair fall out. Black vines radiated from the bite, and even if he was burning, the skin on his back was hard and cold.

The concoction didn't seem to help at all, yet it wasn't rotting anymore. Applying it meant nothing to Dan, who didn't feel a thing. Meanwhile, that white, hardened skin was doing an impressive job of fending off all Flo's attempts to moisturize it.

Bogdan was tossing and turning on the sofa. He hadn't been able to sleep at all that night, too many thoughts running around in his head.

Albert was on the other sofa, snoring loudly.

Flo finally fell asleep at dawn, only to wake twenty minutes later, screaming. She was crying and shaking, and nothing Dan said got through to her.

That's when the noise at the front of the house commenced.

# 5 TO THE RESCUE

"Okay, what's the plan?" asked Lili, early the next morning. Dan still wasn't back, and she looked determined to save him.

"Well, we'll go look for him. And if he's in trouble, we'll save him."

"We might be too late. You realize that, don't you, Mister 'I'm always right'?"

"What, honey? It was the safe way to go."

"No! It wasn't! Dad could be dead, and maybe, just maybe, going yesterday would have made a difference."

"Is Grandpa dead? Why is he dead?"

"He's not dead, Mat. Jesus. Why do you keep on—"

"Lili, stop. Don't push the kid. He's only asking. He heard us talk. Mat, look at me. We don't know what's happened to Grandpa. He might be dead, but he's probably alive, stuck somewhere. Remember, like we were back at the church? We just need to go save him."

"Let's go save him, Dad! We'll fight and get him out."

"No, you cannot go, Mat," said Lili, tears in her eyes. "We need to split. I'll go, you stay here with Dad."

"What? No!" said Andrei.

"Yeah, no," said Mat.

"Mat, don't get into this. Look, honey, you cannot go alone.

57

Maybe I should go."

"No. I'm fitter and faster."

"And?"

"And"—Lili rolled her eyes—"I can hide better. I'm more agile. I'll not even take my backpack, so I can move at will. What? You need me to draw you a picture?"

"Honey, relax."

"Don't tell me to relax. We need to act. I'll go. You stay with Mat."

"What's gotten into you all of a sudden? You're usually so slow in deciding anything."

"I've had plenty of time to think. And, yeah, if I were better at taking swift decisions, I would have gone yesterday."

Andrei looked down, thinking. He finally spoke. "Are you sure you want to do this? What if you don't come back? What are we supposed to do? Wait for you? Should we follow if you don't return?"

"No! Don't do that. If I don't come back, you just go. Run. Go back to the village. I don't know. Anything but coming after me."

"Mommy! You can't go alone!" said Matei, crying. "I don't want you to die! We need to go together."

"No, Mat. Look," said Lili, fighting off her tears. "I'll be okay. But I have to do this. I have to save my Dad. You, however, must survive. You must take care of your dad, and Andrei will take care of you. Take care of each other, you hear?"

"Oh, honey," said Andrei, and they all started crying.

"See you soon," Lili said a few minutes later as she prepared to depart. "Keep the walkie open. I'll talk to you regularly, as long as I have a signal, okay, Andrei?"

"Yes, honey, I will. Good luck, and please, please pay attention. And don't be afraid to defend yourself, be it growler or, you know, not a growler."

"Yes. I will. I'll be back soon."

\* \* \*

The air was frosty, but Lili liked the way it filled her lungs. The snow lay deep, as always, so advancing proved difficult. In normal circumstances, this would have been an awesome walk, and excellent exercise.

Lili followed their old footsteps back into town. Now and then she stopped, took out the walkie-talkie and tried to contact her father.

"Hey, Dad, do you hear me?"

Static.

"Dad, are you there?"

"I'm here, honey," came an answer.

"What have I told you a million times, Andrei? Get off the line. I'm waiting for my dad to answer."

"I know, I know. I just wanted to tell you we're fine."

"Fine!"

"How are you?"

"Would you stop this? Let me be."

"Okay, okay. Geez."

"Jesus," said Lili out loud, then pressed the walkie-talkie button again. "Dad? Are you there, Dad?"

She continued to walk until she knew the town was close.

"Hey, Dad. Answer me," she whispered into the walkie. "Dad, please answer."

*This should be in range*, she thought. *I hope you're fine, Dad.*

She recognized the hatchback under the huge pile of snow. *That idiot. I hope he's doing okay.* She stopped for a bit, with teary eyes. *I hope they're all fine.* A tear trickled down her cheek. She shook, wiped away the tear with the back of her glove, and started walking again.

\* \* \*

When she finally entered the town there was no blood, no sign of struggle anywhere. *Probably Dad went straight to Albert's.*

She tried the walkie-talkie a few times, yet she got no answer.

*Oh, Dad, I hope you ran out of batteries*, she thought, as she continued to advance.

To the left she saw some footprints going into a yard. The tracks showed clearly that several people had walked through the snow, in and out. Lili stopped for a bit, checking the tracks. They seemed normal human footprints, yet all of them seemed to come from the center of the town. None came from the outskirts.

*Dad moved forward, into the town.*

She reached the blood field—the one with the dead dogs.

She stopped, looking around. The blood and traces of death were everywhere, yet the bodies had disappeared.

*Hmm. This is interesting. I didn't notice this before. Someone has carried those dogs, not pulled them away,* she thought, looking at the lack of blood and the shape of the trails in the snow. *Who could have carried them, besides humans? Could it be wolves? Or bears? Nah, they would have pulled them. And there should be animal tracks. But why would a human take the dogs? What if Dad came this way?*

Lili turned around, following the tracks. They led back toward the outskirts of town. She remembered that yard with lots of tracks going in and out. She stood there for a while, looking left and right until she finally decided.

The tracks converged into the yard. As she touched the wooden gate, she realized it was broken in the middle. The right side sway, barely held in place by the hinges, while the left side was wired and nailed to the fence. Probably someone had tried to reinforce the gate, but hadn't expected it to break in half. Anyone could now easily enter, as the right side moved both ways.

An odd feeling came over Lili as she quietly stepped into the yard. Something was off; she could feel it with every cell in her body.

The place lay wide and empty. About a dozen yards back stood an orange, average-sized house. As she looked around, she saw a blood trail along the right-hand side.

Lili started moving, slowly. She squeezed her bat, trying to be ready for whatever she might find.

Step by step, she drew closer.

Suddenly, she realized the snow in this yard was hardened, like a footpath during winter. *This yard has seen a lot of action.* A desire to leave came into her mind, and she even stopped, pondering. But soon after she started moving again, following the blood trail.

When she finally reached the corner, she could see the right-hand side of the house.

And there were bones. Dozens and dozens of bones. Clean bones, put together in a large pile.

By the looks of it, they were mostly dog bones, but she also spotted a few larger ones.

She gagged and turned back, waddling. She was ready to leave, but then she realized the house's front door was open.

*No, Lili, go! You have to go*, she thought, even as she entered the house.

She stepped into the hallway. Her eyes slowly adjusted to the shade, and she began to distinguish lots of tracks—dirty tracks leading from the entry to somewhere inside the house.

"Dad?" she whispered. "Dad?" No answer.

She followed the trail and saw it lead to some stairs, going down. A basement, she realized, and advanced, reaching the stairs.

It was pitch black down there. Still, she picked up a smell. A mixture of raw meat, blood, and a little rot. Just a little. And damp, very damp. It smelled like mold.

*Dad cannot be down there. Not of his own will*, she thought. "Dad?" She tried another whisper.

*Let's think this through. I have no actual proof Dad is in there. I'll go check Albert's house. If he's not there, maybe Albert will help me check this place.*

She turned, planning to leave, relieved she had reached this conclusion.

It might have been her calling a few seconds earlier, or the noise her feet made on the squeaky floor—a noise that seemed amplified by the cavernous basement below.

A loud scream, like a shriek, came from the dark. Her heart stopped. It was immediately followed by growls, and she could hear people coming up the stairs.

Lili started running.

She got out of the house, out of the yard, and sprinted toward the center of the town as fast as her legs could carry her.

She could hear growlers behind her, closing in. Lili didn't dare look back. *What if my Dad is one of them?*

As the road turned, she spotted the front gate of Albert's house. There, she saw the wooden barricade. A few dozen yards and she would be safe!

With this thought in mind, she finally looked back, to see about half a dozen growlers approaching behind her. They were moving fast, pushing one other, trying to grab the skinny human in front of them. Luckily, Lili was just as fast and very agile, and she jumped over the piles of snow like a rabbit.

The growlers were relentless. They didn't seem to tire like a normal person would. But these were not normal people. If they could grab the woman in front of them, they would maul her and eat her alive.

She took another quick glimpse back. It seemed to her that their faces looked different. The drumming teeth and white, fixed eyes were as expected, yet their faces seemed more swollen and meaty than those of other growlers she's encountered.

The only good news, making Lili feel more confident, was that none of them matched Dan's body type. They were all average size and shorter than her dad.

"Dad? Albert? Are you there? Dad! Help!" she yelled, trying to jump the fence.

# 6 SECOND RESCUE TEAM

Andrei paced the woodsman's cabin. It had been three days since Dan disappeared and one day since Lili left to find him, and now there was no sign from either of them.

He'd tried the walkie-talkie, relentlessly, but to no avail. All he got was static, and fear squeezed his heart.

Matei sat in a chair, staring at him. "Daddy?"

"What?"

"I'm afraid."

"You don't have to be afraid."

"But I am," said Mat, with a trembling voice.

"Well, don't be!" snapped Andrei. "Let me think."

"When is Mom coming home, Daddy?"

"Jesus Christ, Mat! Would you just shut up and let me think? Oh, great, now you're crying. Why do you cry? What do you think you can achieve if you cry there like a baby? What?" He paused, looking at his little boy curled up in the chair. "Oh... I'm sorry, Mat. Hey, little boy, come here." He hugged him. "I'm sorry. I really am. I guess I'm stressed out, and I snapped."

"It's okay, Dad," said Mat crying.

"You're a wonderful kid, Mat. I'm very proud of you, you know that?"

"I don't think you are."

"What? How can you say that?"

"I keep on making mistakes and upsetting you. And it's my fault Mom and Grandpa are gone."

"What? No way. Why?"

"Well, if it weren't for me, if I could defend myself, you could have gone with her and saved Grandpa."

"Oh, Mat. No. It's got nothing to do with that. It's not your fault at all. You're our son and we love you. No matter what happens, me, Mom, and Grandpa, we'll always do whatever we can to keep you safe. It's our choice, not yours. You hear me? It's our choice, and we want to do it."

"Yes, Daddy."

"Plus, we don't know what happened yet. They might be busy doing something, and we have to be patient until they return."

"Yes, Daddy."

\* \* \*

The day was slowly ending. Nothing had happened. They had shelter, they had food. A lot of food, actually, since they'd hauled quite a few things from Grandma's village. They were in no immediate danger, but they had nothing to do. Matei was visibly bored, pestering Andrei to play games. Still, the minutes and hours dragged, like they were living under a spell.

Andrei used his walkie-talkie extensively, and soon he had to replace the batteries.

"We have to be smart about this," he said, talking to the walls.

"About what, Daddy?"

"Nothing."

"No, what do you mean?"

"If I said it's nothing, then it's nothing."

"Sorry, Daddy."

\* \* \*

"Let's go find them," said Andrei, suddenly, a little after midday.

"Yes, Daddy!" squeaked Matei. "I'll get dressed."

"Yeah, we must find you a jacket that's not pink. Sorry you still have to wear that."

"It's okay, Dad. I like this one. It's warm. But I would prefer a green one."

They set out, walking toward the town.

\* \* \*

Andrei tried his walkie again, but unsuccessfully.

"Maybe we should go back?" he said as they reached his snowed-in car.

"No, Dad. We should go save Mom."

"Yeah, I think... Yeah, we should," said Andrei, looking back and forth along the way. "It would be nice if we could take the car."

"But the snow is too deep, Dad."

"Yes, I know. Don't you think I know that?"

"Sorry, Dad. I know you know."

"I love you, Mat," said Andrei, suddenly. "Thank you for the help."

"I love you too, Dad."

\* \* \*

They drew close to the edge of the town, and the sun was already setting. They probably had one hour of light left at most.

"Honey? Dan? Are you guys there?" Andrei tried his walkie-talkie again. "Please answer me." Andrei looked at the walkie talkie. "Ugh, I hope the batteries are not dying again," he mumbled.

"You can change them, Daddy."

"I just did. And I don't have any more on me, Mat."

Andrei stopped, looking back and forth between the town and the road leading back to the cabin.

"Daddy, they need our help."

"We should go back," said Andrei.

"No, we need to save them."

Andrei looked around nervously. He could hear his breaths growing heavier. "Okay, a few more steps. But if we cannot find them soon, we'll go back."

"But why don't we go to Albert's house?"

"Well..."

"Why not? Mom and Grandpa are there, right?"

Andrei gave no answer.

\* \* \*

Step after step, they reached the outskirts and started walking down the road between the houses.

Then, just as Andrei had been considering taking out his walkie-talkie for another try, he distinguished a person coming out of a yard to the left far ahead of them.

It didn't look like either Dan or Lili, but the distance might be playing tricks on him.

Andrei raised his hand. He was about to yell out a greeting when the person turned, looking toward the yard he'd came out of, and let out a shriek.

"What was—"

Andrei covered Mat's mouth with his hand and dragged them both down. He felt icy shivers along his spine as he realized there was no place they could hide.

"Quick, into the snow," he whispered in Matei's ear. "Be quiet. And don't look!"

As they lay there in the snow, Andrei saw a few people coming out through the gate. They walked differently, as if a little drunk.

"Growlers," he whispered.

"Mhhh, mhhh, mhhh." Mat tried to speak, but Andrei's large palm covered his mouth.

"Shush!" whispered Andrei.

He continued watching, and he counted a few dozen, leaving one by one and following the first figure he'd seen. They all headed toward the town, toward Albert's house.

"We have to go back to the cabin," he whispered to Mat, as soon as the group passed out of sight.

\* \* \*

By the time they reached the buried car, night covered the hills and the forest. The moon was making the snow shimmer, so they could see where they were going.

"What was that noise back there, Daddy?" Matei spoke for the first time since they'd started the trek back from town. "That shriek, what was it?"

"Mat, please be quiet, it's important."

"I am quiet, but what was it?"

"It was… I don't know what it was. Probably a bird. Now, be quiet."

They kept on walking, until Mat spoke again a few minutes later. "Why are we going back, Dad? I'm tired. Let's go slower."

"Move!" barked Andrei, pulling on his hand.

"I'm moving, Dad, but I'm tired. I need to stop."

"We need to move, Matei. This was a mistake. Everything was a mistake."

"Why? Were those bad guys, Daddy?"

"Yes, they were. Now, shut up. We need to be quiet," he said, looking back. He couldn't make out anything behind them, but that noise, that shriek, was burned into his memory.

"You said 'growlers', Daddy. Were they growlers? Why haven't you killed them? You can kill growlers, can't you?"

"Yes, I can kill growlers. But that one… I mean, yeah, they were growlers." He looked back, again. Nothing there, but fear nearly choked him. "We need to move."

"Daddy, I can't walk anymore!"

"If I hear any more of this…" said Andrei, frowning. He didn't finish the sentence. Instead, he quickly added, "We need to move. We're not safe out here. Okay, Mat?"

* * *

Andrei was exhausted and he could barely see anything. Sweat trickled down his face, but he soon realized Matei was dragging his feet, and he had to pull him up by his hand, vigorously, to keep him going.

Finally, they could see the cabin.

Looking down at his kid, Andrei noticed he was barely moving. He needed his father's hand to keep him going. As a ray of moonlight fell on the kid's face, Andrei saw he had been crying. Tears were rolling down his face. But they couldn't stop their forced march. They needed to get to safety. They needed to reach the cabin.

When at last they entered the room, both fell down, back against the door. And they both cried then, holding each other.

# 7 SICKNESS AND DEATH

"What's that? Is he back?" said Flo in an alert tone, as soon as the noise began outside. "I can't do this anymore." Her gaze darted about the room, as if trying to find a way out.

"Hey, Flo, relax," said Dan. "It sounds like a normal person. Actually... Lili!" he shouted, and got out of bed, stumbling toward the door.

Dan still had a fever, and between that and the thing growing on his back, his body didn't obey him as it normally would. He rose, only to fall face down, unconscious, a few steps from the bed.

Luckily, Albert and Bogdan were faster.

They heard the noise, heard Dan's shout, and ran to the rescue. They quickly opened the barricaded front door and barged outside in time to see Lili jump the fence.

On the other side, they could hear that awful sound coming from those creatures as they banged on the wooden fence, growling.

"Lili, how come you're here?" asked Albert. "You came for Dan?"

Lili was panting and could barely catch her breath, but she answered quickly. "Yes, I came looking for him! Is he here? Please tell me he's here!"

"Yes, yes, we have him. He's inside. He's not in the best... I mean... you should go see him."

"What's wrong with him?" Without waiting for an answer, she sprinted into the house, calling for her father.

\* \* \*

"Let's take care of this mess," said Albert to Bogdan, when they found themselves alone, near the gate. They brought two ladders and climbed the fence. Down there, pushing and scratching at the fence, they could see six growlers. Their clothes were in a poor state, like almost every growler they'd met, shirts and blouses ripped open, exposing their chests.

The two men made some noise, and the growlers looked up at them.

"Wow, do you see that?" said Albert.

"Yeah, I do. Their faces."

"What is this? It's just like that Moroi we found in the house! Same swollen face!"

"Yes, and look at their chests. It's the same… meat. See?"

"Yeah, looks like some sort of tumor growth."

"Do you suppose they had some disease and died from it?"

"Doesn't matter," concluded Albert. "Let's do this."

The two men used light axes, and their blades moved swiftly, from years of training. Three hits each, and all six growlers were on the ground, heads cracked open. As expected, they continued to squirm and growl uncontrollably.

Then, both Albert and Bogdan picked up long, heavy pitchforks. This part required a few tries. But after several strikes, all six growlers had their strange chests stabbed and finally stopped squirming.

"I say we get rid of them, and the other two inside our yard. I'm not comfortable having these creatures around for too long," said Bogdan. "Should we?"

"Yeah, let's do that." They grabbed the two bodies from their yard, including the cut-off head, and threw them over the fence.

"Here, pass me the other ladder," said Albert from the top of his.

They used one ladder to climb the fence and the other to go down into the street.

"Let's take them to that yard over there, where we stacked the others," said Albert, pointing at a location three houses down, on the other side of the road.

"Now if I think of it, we might want to move all the bodies farther down the road," said Bogdan. "Come spring, or even worse, summer, that place will reek. And it's too close to us."

"You could be right," said Albert, nodding. "Let's keep that in mind for later. But if we leave for Dan's village, we won't have to worry about it."

They picked up two bodies each and started pulling them by their feet. The slippery snow made the job easier.

The dead growlers were average size and weight, and next to the two massive men, it looked like Albert and Bogdan were pulling puppets.

As they advanced downhill, Bogdan appeared to have an epiphany. "I just realized something. Why are these bodies warm?"

"Warm?"

"I mean, not frozen. See? They were moving fast; they don't seem that cold. They should be frozen somewhere, being half naked and all."

"I don't know. Perhaps they were in a warm place until now? We'll ask Lili where she picked them up."

They finally reached the gate.

"I don't remember leaving this open," said Albert. "Did you?"

"No, Dad. Who knows, maybe we didn't lock it properly?"

"Yeah, or that Strigoi really moves around."

Bogdan dropped the legs of the growlers he was pulling and checked left and right, his fists clenched.

"Relax. It's daylight. Remember what Grandma said. 'The Strigoi only goes out at night'. Or something like that."

"Yeah... okay, let's do this." Bogdan turned around to grab his dead cargo, then stopped. "I really don't understand why they have these faces," he said, looking at his growlers. "And similar chests."

"Why do you care? Let's drop them and finish this."

"Yeah, you're probably right," said Bogdan, and started pulling, going through the gate.

The property held a small, frail old house, and they moved toward its left side.

"What the…" said Albert, suddenly.

"What?" asked Bogdan, who was following right behind him.

"Where are all the bodies?"

Bogdan dropped his cargo again and came closer to Albert. He stood there, stunned, unable to say a word.

"We stacked over fifteen Morois here, Bogdan! Where are they?"

"I don't know, Dad! How could I know?"

"Every Moroi we killed we brought here," continued Albert. "All of them! And now they're all gone?"

"Wait a minute," said Bogdan. He went back and turned over one of the growlers he was pulling. "Isn't this old man Radovici from across the street? And that's his ugly wife, over there."

Albert dropped his growler's legs and started checking the bodies. "Oh my God! You're right! These are all our neighbors! We've already killed these Morois. Was Grandma Gina right? They can resurrect now?"

"Let's go back, Dad!"

"How come they can resurrect? And what happened to their faces?" continued Albert, not hearing Bogdan.

"Dad, let's get the other four, drop them here, and get back home!"

"Why? Do they come back to life after a while? Do they reg—"

"Dad! Stop it! Let's go!"

They moved out, fast, picked up the other four, holding the cut-off head by its hair, and stashed them in the same location.

Then they climbed back over the fence and entered the house, always looking left and right, axes in hand.

\* \* \*

"He's in here," called out Flo. "In the bedroom."

"Dad! Are you okay?" asked Lili, bursting into the bedroom. "What happened?"

Lili saw Dan on the floor. Flo was trying, in vain, to pull him back into the bed. On the other side of the room lay Howler, head up, following everything.

"What happened to him?"

"He heard you at the gate and tried to rush out, but the fever got to him and he fell."

"What's that on the back of his head? Oh my God, poor Dad!" said Lili, covering her mouth with her right hand.

"That gave him the fever. I'll tell you all about it. Can you help me put him back on the bed? It seems like all the men left alive in this world have to be at least twice my weight."

\* \* \*


"So that's what happened to him and what I've done so far," concluded Flo, right about when the growling noise outside, near the fence, was put to rest. She was sitting in a chair, legs crossed, a few feet from the bed.

Lili was perched on the bed, next to her sleeping dad, listening to Flo and petting Howler, who had come to her side while Flo was talking.

They sat there, silent.

"Thank you for all your help," said Lili after a few moments. "You didn't have to do that, but you did."

"I wanted to. Dan helped us. He got into this mess because of us. He deserves our help."

"What can we do? Let's look at this thing."

They turned him over, pulling down the neck of Dan's sweatshirt to see as much of the growth as possible.

Lili touched it. It was white, cold, and hardened. The black vines were everywhere and seemed to get thicker, especially closer to the bite.

"And you say it hurt him when you added onions and garlic? Wait, why garlic?"

"That's another interminable story." Flo smiled. "Let's just say Grandma Gina has a good reason for it."

"Ah, I see."

"I can't believe I'm saying this, but she may actually have been right all along."

"What? Why?"

"Let me tell you what happened here in the last few days."

\* \* \*

As Flo finished her story, her voice shaky, Lili sat frozen on the bed, stunned by what she had heard.

"I might have… I think I found a place. Now I can make the connection. What if that's where the Strigoi lives?"

"What place?" asked Albert, entering the room, Bogdan by his side.

"The place where the growlers started chasing me. It was an old house with an odd smell. Uphill toward the town limits. I think that Strigoi could be living there."

"Let's go get him!" said Albert, turning around. "Lili, come with us."

"Wait!" said Flo. "Don't do that! It's not safe! Let's talk first."

"What is there to talk about? We go in, kill everyone, and come home."

"What if he has an army of Morois?" continued Flo. "How many can you kill? What if we can't kill the Strigoi that easily?"

Everybody fell silent, just in time for Lili to speak.

"First, I want to express my condolences, Albert. And to you, too, Bogdan and Flo. I'm sorry. Secondly, yes, I'll show you the place I found. I even heard that shriek Flo mentioned, coming from that basement, so it's safe to guess that's his lair. But we need to prepare for this."

No one said a word, so Lili continued. "However, I want to help my Dad get well before going anywhere. I will spend all my time and energy getting him through this. And if we let him recover first, I'm sure Dan could really help us."

"I say we go kill that thing first. I don't think there's much you can—"

"What Bogdan means to say," interrupted Albert, throwing a meaningful glance at his son, "is that you're welcome to stay here and help Dan. And we need to take care of Grandma Gina, who's in a similar situation."

"Thank you, Albert," said Lili, turning back to her dad, while Albert, Bogdan, and Flo left the room.

\* \* \*

"How can you be so stupid? What's wrong with you?" Flo asked Bogdan, looking up at him. "How could you say such a thing?"

"Leave me alone. They've been nothing but a burden. We have to keep Dan here, feed him and now Lili too, while we defend the place and take care of everything."

"What has gotten into you? You used to be different. You were kind!"

"Well, I've changed. I need to take care of you, of our family. I don't want to take care of strangers. I'm still kind, but only to the people I care about. Oh, and I have to bury my brother and his wife now."

"We are stronger together! We need them, as they need us. And you need not take care of Dan. Do your part, and I'll do mine. Maybe you should go check on Grandma Gina before putting them in the grave. She needs your support," said Flo, turning her back on Bogdan and leaving.

\* \* \*

Grandma Gina was sick in bed, coughing. She was weak, her breath was accelerated, and she had a fever.

"Grandma, please eat something! Have some garlic, onions, anything," begged Bogdan.

Albert was already there, also trying to convince his mother to eat.

"I don't want anything. I'm not hungry," cawed Grandma Gina, accompanying each word with a quick, noisy breath. "The Lord wants me, and He'll get me."

"Mom! Why are you doing this? We'll force-feed you if we have to!"

"You'll do no such thing! It's the will of the Lord, and there's nothing anyone can do about it. Please respect my will. Now, go away. I need to pray!"

Albert and Bogdan left the room, defeated.

\* \* \*

Lili was investigating her father's neck and the back of his head.

That thing was all over the place. She hesitantly touched the black vines, but they felt no different from the white part of the growth. Maybe just a little embossed.

Suddenly, Dan woke up. "Flo, you still here?"

"It's me, Dad," said Lili, just as Howler let out a joyful bark.

"Lili?" he said, trying to turn onto his side. "My beautiful Lili. Don't cry. I'm afraid I'll die soon. This is spreading, and I'm sleepier and sleepier all the time. No, please don't cry. Just take care of Matei and your husband. You really love and need each other."

"Don't talk like this, Dad," said Lili. "We can still fight this. I don't know exactly how, but we can fight. I'll put on some more onions and garlic for now."

"Flo already tried all that," said Dan, in a weak voice. "It's not working. That skin is too tough. Ah, here she is. Thank you, Flo. Thank you for everything."

"You'll be okay, Dad. You'll see," said Lili.

\* \* \*

"They're frozen," said Bogdan with a grunt, touching Victor's body. "We should have kept them inside."

"Relax, son," said Albert. "Flo was right. It was safer this way. Here, grab this and let's go dig a hole," he said, handing out a pickaxe.

"But Dad," continued Bogdan, absently taking the tool. "Grandma was right! What do we do about the resurrected Morois? What if that guy resurrects Victor and Andreea?"

"I don't understand how that works. But if that Strigoi wanted, or was able, to resurrect them, he probably would have taken them with him. As Mom said, he already took about a dozen of his dead."

"True," said Bogdan, thinking. "We need to talk, all of us, about this resurrection thing. I say we should leave as soon as possible."

"I wouldn't tell anything to anyone, son," said Albert, after a moment's contemplation. "I don't want to upset Mom; she's sick enough already. And you know how easily Flo panics. Let's keep this to ourselves for now. Let's go find a spot for your brother," he said, quitting the barn.

\* \* \*

"Maybe I should check the wound again," said Lili, suddenly. "There must be something we can do! We can't just sit around doing nothing."

Dan had lost consciousness once again.

Flo quietly helped Lili take a look.

"We know that onions, eaten by a growler, push back the disease," said Lili, pondering while moving her hand over Dan's back. "This comes from a growler. So it should, in theory, work."

"As I said, I've tried," said Flo. "I've put that mash on his back a few times now."

"Yes, but you said it rotted fast. The same happened with the onions my Mom ate. It's similar behavior."

"You believe it's a defense mechanism?"

"It sounds like it, yes," confirmed Lili, nodding.

"I see. Maybe I should have used the concoction more often. Maybe replacing it a few times a day?"

"Perhaps every few hours. Or at least whenever we see it's becoming rotten."

"Okay. Let's do this! I'll go prepare the concoction. A lot of it. Until then, you get him ready, okay?"

"Yup, sounds great. But do you have enough onions and garlic for such large quantities?"

"We have quite a lot. Grandma Gina made sure we always had tons of garlic and onion strings in storage, in the cellar, even before all this happened. And with what we've gathered from surrounding houses, we have plenty. It should be enough for about three months, depending on how much we use now, of course."

"Nice. Now we only need to figure out how to get it through this thick skin," said Lili, and she started taking off Dan's clothes, which proved to be a difficult task.

\* \* \*

The men were digging the hole fast. They were on the right-hand side of the house, a few feet behind it. The ground was frozen, but they were making good progress.

"They really loved each other," said Albert, fighting to control his emotions. "I say we put them together. They died together, so they should rest together."

Bogdan said nothing, but he continued to strike the ground strongly with the pickaxe.

\* \* \*

"Damn, you're heavy," puffed Lili. Dan's sweater and T-shirt were pulled up, but she wasn't able to get them over his head.

Dan was still lying on his front, sleeping, and anything she tried had no success.

"Albert, is that you? Do you think you can help me?" called Lili when she heard the deep thuds that only Albert's feet could make on the wooden floor.

"Yes, we just finished digging. What's up?" said Albert, entering the room.

"I need to get Dad undressed. Could you hold him please?"

"Sure thing," said Albert, coming closer. "My God this looks bad," he added, unable to hide his disgust.

"Yeah, it's not pretty. But we have to try to do something."

"Yup, that's clear as rain."

They removed Dan's sweater and T-shirt, just in time for Flo to return with a large casserole dish full of mashed onions and garlic.

She had done a marvelous job, as everything was like a paste.

"Phew, that stinks," said Albert.

Looking at Dan's back, Lili gasped. His neck, the back of his head, his whole back, the upper parts of his arms, and even the sides of his torso were white as snow and crossed by thin black vines the size of a toothpick and a couple of inches apart, all radiating from the neck bite. And the bite place, where a piece of meat was missing, now held a bulging black growth.

"Here we go," said Lili. "Yet, seeing all this…"

"I know," said Flo. "But we still have to try."

Lili nodded. She applied some of the concoction to Dan's back and right on the bulging growth on his neck. He gave a slight twitch, but nothing else happened. Lili rubbed the area for a few minutes, but it seemed pointless. It was as if the concoction wasn't even there, and Dan was still sleeping.

"Just like my moisturizer. As if this newly hardened skin doesn't allow it to be absorbed."

During this time, Albert remained behind them, leaning against the door frame, watching.

"Let me rub on some more," said Lili, continuing to move her hand. "We cannot fail now," she said, blinking away tears.

"Why don't you cut it?" They heard Bogdan's voice from behind Albert.

"Cut what?" asked Flo.

"Cut that hardened skin. Then the paste will go through."

"We can't cut…" said Lili, then stopped. "Do you have a good knife? Preferably a smaller one."

A few minutes later Bogdan returned and handed her a small blade two inches long. It was a kitchen knife with a red, wooden handle.

With a shaky hand, she approached the knife to the bulge on Dan's neck. She almost touched the hardened skin, but she couldn't do it. She drew back her hand, sighing.

"Let me do it," said Flo, and Lil happily handed her the knife.

As Flo moved the knife toward Dan's back, though, Howler jumped up, attacking her.

"Howler, no! Get the dog out!" said Lili, and Bogdan obliged, closing the door behind him.

Flo cut the skin on the bulge, and the black growth was now visible. It had a squishy texture, like a piece of fat.

"Should I cut this?" asked Flo, looking at Lili.

"Let's try," she answered, after a moment's thought.

As Flo pierced it, Dan started yelling.

* * *

"Now, do it!" said Albert.

He and Bogdan were holding Dan down by his shoulders, while Lili gripped his legs.

Flo had removed a sizeable chunk of the black thing growing on the back of his neck. There was no blood, yet a few drops of thick, black gel squeezed out, releasing a moldy smell. All the while Dan

79

seemed to be in a lot of pain.

"Oh my God, this hurts!" he yelled, squirming. "What was that?"

"We had to remove something from your back, Dad," said Lili, trying to keep hold of his legs. "Please stay put. It's for your own good."

"I'm trying," said Dan. "But I can't hold back the squirming. The pain is too much. If you need me still, you must hold me down."

"We can hold you, buddy, don't you worry," said Albert, putting more weight on Dan's right shoulder.

"Now, Dad, Flo will put some concoction on you. It will probably hurt, but it should help."

And Lili was right. She had never heard her dad scream like that.

* * *

When things settled, Bogdan and Albert let go of Dan, who was panting.

"It still hurts, terribly," said Dan, catching his breath. "Man, this is horrible."

"I bet it is, old friend," said Albert.

"Why don't you do it everywhere?" interrupted Bogdan.

"What do you mean?" asked Lili.

"Why don't you cut and apply this on every vine?"

"Yes, why not?" asked Dan. "Do it."

"No, Dad. We don't know if it will even work. And if it does and it destroys the center, maybe all the other vines will die too."

"But maybe not. What if it's large enough not to care anymore? Do it everywhere. I want this thing out of me."

"But what if it doesn't work?"

"Then we did it for nothing and I'm dead anyway. But what if it does?"

Lili looked at Flo, who picked up the knife, understanding the message.

She started cutting the skin on top of the vines, revealing the black lines going from the back of Dan's neck.

* * *

Albert and Bogdan held Dan down as Flo cut the last black vine.

Dan was screaming. Even though she had tried to be careful, Flo's knife entered a bit into the vines themselves, causing a lot of pain.

"Ready for the concoction?"

"Ready as I'll ever be," he said. "Please restrain me. It helps me cope with the pain if I can flex as much as I can."

"Sure thing, buddy," said Albert, and he and Bogdan grabbed him even tighter.

Flo started applying the concoction, and for a few minutes, Dan yelled as if being set on fire.

He lost consciousness right as Flo finished covering the last spot.

\* \* \*

Twenty minutes later, everybody was sweaty and tired.

Dan was sleeping, his back covered in onion and garlic mash. Parts of his back twitched now and then, and he didn't seem to be having a relaxing sleep.

"It stinks," blurted Flo.

"Yeah, tell me about it," said Bogdan.

"No, I mean, it's starting to rot."

"What, already?" asked Lili in a distrustful tone, moving closer.

"Yeah. Look here at the bite."

"Wow! Indeed. It's changed color and," said Lili, taking a deep sniff, "yup, it smells bad. It's started to rot! Incredible."

"Should we change it?"

"Again?" Asked Bogdan, clearly annoyed.

"Let's wait for ten, twenty more minutes," said Lili. "Let's see if it all goes bad or just around the bite."

\* \* \*

"Yup, we have to do it all over again," said Lili, twenty minutes later. "It's all rotten."

"Okay, let's clean this up," said Flo. "Bogdan, could you please bring some napkins from the kitchen?"

Bogdan left, mumbling, and soon returned with the needed supplies.

Lili and Flo cleaned all the stinky concoction from Dan's back.

"Ah, look at this," said Lili. "It looks like the hardened skin is rebuilding right here. Here as well. Damn. It looks like we'll have to cut it again."

"Okay," said Flo. "It's not fun, but I'll do it."

"Thank you for this, really," said Lili, forcing a smile. Flo gave a determined nod in response.

"If you two want to be alone, just let us know," said Bogdan, following this up with a laugh that shook the chair he was in.

"You're so stupid sometimes, and also so unoriginal," said Flo, only making Bogdan laugh harder. "Please don't mind him," she said to Lili. "I've married a retard."

Flo started cutting through the areas that were closing up. "These are smaller than before," she said, after a while.

"You mean the vines?" asked Lili.

"Yes. It might actually work!"

They applied the mash again.

And again, Albert and Bogdan were hard at work, holding down a screaming Dan.

* * *

"We should prepare the burial," said Bogdan, looking around the room. Dan was sleeping, and everyone else seemed exhausted.

"Could we postpone until tomorrow, maybe?" asked Flo. "I know the custom is to do it on the third day, but I'm sure in certain cases there could be exceptions."

"Yeah," said Bogdan, upset, "there could be. But it must be some sort of emergency, not 'I'm not in the mood for it'."

"We have two sick people we need to take care of. How's that for a reason?"

"This shouldn't count. If the family can be there, if the priest can join, we have to do it. That's the way."

"We don't have a priest," said Flo. "It should be okay to postpone for a bit."

"The dead deserve to rest," said Bogdan aggressively.

"Hey, relax," said Flo with an annoyed tone. "Our priorities now are taking care of Grandma Gina and Dan. Plus, keep in mind we're already late with the burial."

"What do you mean, late? We have the entire day to do it," said Bogdan, raising an eyebrow.

"This is the fifth day since they died," said Flo.

"Not true," said Bogdan, louder. "Dan killed them two days ago."

"But they actually died four days ago, killed by Morois or Strigois."

"You're such a stupid—"

"Hey," intervened Albert. "Mind your words, son!"

Bogdan stormed out of the room.

Everyone else remained, awkward silence all around.

* * *

"What's wrong, son?" said Albert, finding Bogdan pacing like a lion in a cage, in front of the house.

"That Dan is ruining everything we're doing here," answered Bogdan, yelling, yet trying to keep the volume down. "Everyone is busy around him, using a ton of our garlic and onions, while Victor and Andreea freeze in that barn."

"Victor and Andreea are dead," said Albert. "Trust me, I know what you're feeling. I've lost my son. No parent should ever lose a son," he added, tears streaming down his wide face. "Still, we have to take care of Grandma Gina and Dan. Yes, even Dan. It's already midday. We can bury Victor and Andreea fast, now, and get it over with. Or—"

"What if that Strigoi comes and resurrects them?"

Albert paused for a moment, thinking. "That... would... not be—"

"See? We have to do it," said Bogdan, waving his hands. "Let's do it and make sure they find peace."

* * *

"I'm sorry about all that," said Flo, sighing. "He's under a lot of stress."

"Say no more," said Lili, smiling. "I have a similar beast back home. Ah, speaking of which, I should contact Andrei. Knowing him, he'll be worried sick."

She grabbed her walkie-talkie. "Hey, Andrei, are you there? Hey, dufus, answer!"

Flo quit the room, quietly, leaving Lili and Dan alone.

As she moved around the living room, she could hear Lili's voice, faint, trying to reach her husband. Yet her ears then picked up another sound. It was an accelerated breath, deep, and similar to a growl, coming from the hallway.

\* \* \*

Albert and Bogdan grabbed Victor and started moving his body toward the freshly dug grave.

"Good thing Flo covered them," said Albert, shaking. "What they did to them, those beasts!"

"Should we make caskets?" asked Bogdan, suddenly.

Albert stopped. "You're right, again. It should be—"

"Albert! Bogdan!" Flo's voice interrupted them. "Come quick! It's Grandma!"

\* \* \*

"Hey, Mom, can you hear me?" asked Albert, holding Grandma Gina's hand. She was burning up, her breath was accelerated, and she was barely conscious.

"I... am... going... to... God," she said, large pauses between her words.

"Mom, don't do this," said Albert, crying. "I can't lose you too!"

"You... don't... lose... me, Albert. I'll... live... forever... in... Heaven."

Albert started crying, while Bogdan and Flo watched, fighting off tears.

Suddenly, Flo rushed toward Grandma Gina and uncovered her feet.

"What are you doing?" whispered Bogdan, aggressively.

"I want to check," said Flo. "Mm… strange."

"What?"

"She doesn't have what Dan has."

"What do you mean?"

"They bit her feet, remember?"

"Yeah, how could I forget?" continued Bogdan, keeping the same aggressive tone.

"Right. Still, unlike Dan, it didn't spread. There's no white skin or black vines. Maybe because her feet were dead? The disease didn't find a place to—"

"Stop this! Cover Grandma and let her be!"

"Okay, okay," said Flo, flushing. "I thought this could be important. Sorry," she added, before leaving the room.

* * *

For the rest of the day, everyone was very busy.

Albert and Bogdan spent most of their time checking on Grandma, who drifted in and out of consciousness. They tried to convince her to eat something, but she opposed it fiercely. She even made everyone swear they would not force-feed her, like Andrei had done to Matei a few months earlier, saving his life.

And as much as they wanted to, no one would break such a promise.

On top of this, now and then they joined Lili and Flo in their efforts to cure Dan; although, Bogdan was reluctant and skipped a few trips. Still, Albert was strong enough to handle the situation on his own.

Flo and Lili repeated the process a few more times. They split the skin covering the black vines and then generously applied lots of bad-smelling paste.

With every new try, the black vines seemed to grow smaller, the concoction taking longer and longer to rot, and the hardened skin becoming a little less white.

Only Dan's terrible pain remained constant.

Lili also tried to reach Andrei on the walkie-talkie, but unsuccessfully. She wanted to go out and get in range, but the others stopped her as the daylight was fading.

* * *

When evening came, it was clear the black vines were thinner.

"It's good, Dad," said Lili, with hope in her voice. "It hurts seeing you in pain, but it looks like this is good for you."

"Thank you, honey. I also feel slightly better. That thing on my back feels like a glued backpack. But I think I'm better."

"That's good, Dad. We must do it constantly, but we seem to be on the right track. And now you have to eat. Flo put together a plate for you. And eat the whole onion."

"Ugh, the onion still stinks."

"Remember when you forced me to eat stinking onions? Now I can have my revenge!" said Lili, grinning.

"It was for your own good. And they weren't rotten."

"Neither is this one."

"Yes, I know, I know. I'm just toying with you," said Dan. "I'll eat it, of course I will. It will probably help. Onions on the inside, onions on the outside. No foreign body will survive," he said, grabbing a bite. "Ugh, it's bad," he continued, overcoming a gag reflex. "Can I get some garlic as well? I want to make sure I overload this thing."

Lili was looking at him, tears rolling down her cheeks. Yet, she was smiling.

* * *

It was already dark outside, and the group was preparing to apply the concoction to Dan's back once more.

"This time," said Albert, "you need to be quiet. Really quiet."

Everyone understood why, and they shivered.

"Okay, Albert. I'll do my best. Can I have a piece of cloth to bite down on? It will probably help."

* * *

The night passed without incident. No Strigoi came around, no shrieks or noises.

Still, the family was up almost the entire night.

Lili and Flo checked Dan's back and, about every two hours, cleaned him up and applied a new concoction.

Dan barely slept. His back hurt all the time, and he wasn't allowed to move or touch it.

All the while, Albert and Bogdan took turns, going between Grandma Gina's room and Dan's room.

Grandma Gina was worse. Her breath was speeding up, and it was becoming noisy. Her long-lasting dream of reaching Heaven seemed closer than ever.

And although the reaching Heaven part would probably have been debated by some people, it became a genuine possibility come morning.

After losing consciousness a few times, Grandma Gina took her last breath, her right hand clenched around her cross, just as the sun rose.

# 8 BURIAL

Albert sobbed, hugging his dead mother.

Flo sat next to him, gently caressing his large shoulders. Silent tears ran down her own cheeks.

Bogdan was in the living room, fighting to hold himself together. He was barely making it.

Lili was in Dan's room. She was petting Howler, looking absently toward her father, who was finally resting.

Dan's back was covered with that onion and garlic mash, black vines barely visible beneath it. The white part now had a hint of gray in it.

The house was silent, and, with a few exceptions, remained that way for the better part of the day.

\* \* \*

"Hey, Dad? Wake up," said Lili in a soothing voice. "We need to refresh the medicine."

"Oh, hey, honey. Again?" asked Dan, yawning. "I'm so sleepy, you would not believe."

"Oh, I believe you," she said, smiling. "I wouldn't mind some sleep myself."

"But why are you whispering?"

"It's Grandma Gina… she passed away."

"Oh, I see. I'm sorry for their loss. But make sure you tell them to take her out soon. She could turn."

"Yeah, well, I will not be telling them that. Bogdan looks like he's waiting for the slightest reason to start a fight."

"Okay, fine. But keep your guard up. If anything happens, we should at least be able to lock ourselves in here."

"Yeah, we should be fine. I'm not worried about her. Without her legs, she wouldn't be too much of a threat. How about that medicine? Should we start?"

"Okay, yeah. Man, if I get through this ordeal I'll never complain about pain ever again. Not even about this stupid thumb."

"Yeah, yeah, making promises when in need. Those are the best ones."

They both chuckled, while Lili cleaned Dan's back.

* * *

"Albert?" said Flo, cautiously. "Albert, we should talk. Can we talk?"

They were still in Grandma Gina's room, and Albert was still hugging his dead mother.

"Albert? Let's have a word, please."

Bogdan came into the room and viewed the scene. "Hey, Dad. Flo is right. We need to talk."

Albert stood. "Yes, let's talk," he said, looking a bit lost, wiping his tears. "Let's talk."

They moved into the living room. The door to Dan's room was open, and Flo signaled for Lili to join them.

"Why is she here?" asked Bogdan. "Isn't this a family gathering?"

"Don't be a jerk!" said Flo. "We have to be one team, all of us. It's the only way to survive."

"I'm sorry. I really don't mean to impose. I can leave you to it," said Lili, looking between the others.

"Nonsense," said Flo, while Bogdan avoided Lili's eyes. "Come, sit here, next to me. So, we need to discuss what to do next."

"Why should we discuss this with you? Let me and Dad—"

"Bogdan, I swear to God!" said Flo, with a mean look. "We need to discuss this together! So please behave."

After a few moments of silence, she spoke again.

"Right. What do we do? We all know the situation. We know what Lili saw. What do we do next?"

"As I already said, we need to leave," said Bogdan. "Not much to discuss. Let's pack up and go."

"Okay, but what do we do about Grandma Gina?" asked Flo. "Do we leave her like this?"

"No," intervened Lili. "She could turn. We need to—"

"What do you want to do, smash her head in?" asked Bogdan, glaring at Lili. "Pierce her heart?"

"I'm not saying that," countered Lili, fire in her eyes. "And I really don't appreciate the tone."

"Yeah, and I don't appreci—"

"Would you learn how to shut up and listen for once! I understand you're angry. I understand you're afraid. We are all—"

"How dare you call me afraid?" Bogdan stood, face turning red. "How dare you, a stupid woman, call—"

"What did you say?" yelled Lili, rising, as Flo gasped, looking at Bogdan. "You think you know it all? You think you can survive *a minute* out there if we don't work together? You think that by being able to smash anything, you can make your way in this world? All alone? Well, you can't! And if you think you can, you're a bigger idiot than you seem!"

Bogdan looked at her, stunned. Lili sat down, straightening her clothes with nervous moves.

"Okay, now," she continued, in a calm voice. "What do we do about Grandma Gina?"

"I say we need to bury her as soon as possible," said Albert. "Yes, in theory, we should wait three days. But that's just a custom. We're already late with Victor and Andreea. Equally important, if I understand correctly, we risk Grandma Gina turning. So, let's do it as soon as possible, and I say we bury her at the same time as Victor and Andreea."

"Sounds reasonable," said Flo. "But we need to dig another grave, and that takes time."

"We can start right now. It should be done in a few hours if we put our backs into it. What do you think, son?"

Bogdan was fidgeting on the sofa, arms crossed over his wide chest. Still, it looked like the previous exchange had made him reflect. It was as if a discussion was going on in his mind.

"What?"

"I said, would you help me dig another grave, to bury your Grandma?"

"Yes, Dad, of course. Let's do it."

\* \* \*

Flo and Lili were left alone in the living room.

"I guess he's on the edge, and his grandma dying was the last straw. Still, what he said was appalling, and I apologize for that," Flo said to Lili.

"It's fine, don't worry. I've had my fair share of such behavior and such words. Probably so have you."

"Yes, and people in the back-country are worse," said Flo, and they looked at each other, with agreeing, sad smiles.

Lili opened her mouth, as if meaning to say something, then she stopped.

"I think I know what you're going to ask," said Flo. "Indeed, we're an odd couple, and the visible parts are true. For example, I love to go out and party, I could do it every night, while he prefers to hang out in front of the TV. I like to travel, while he doesn't. I act on impulse, while he's more rational. Except for this recent outburst, when his emotions got the better of him.

"But this is marriage. I skip some parties, he skips some movies, and we meet in the middle. Well, at least we *used* to. Not sure there are any clubs open nearby right now," said Flo, with an even sadder expression. "I wonder if I'll ever get to listen to music again."

"Yes," agreed Lili, grabbing Flo's hand, "our lives have changed, probably for good. We keep on trying to make sense of what's going on. And that takes its toll on everyone. What happened back there is just an example."

Flo nodded.

"My Andrei is in a similar situation," said Lili, still holding Flo's hand. "These horrible times pushed him to the limit, and he got way more aggressive and nervous. Probably just like Bogdan. Most of the time I saw his good side. We got married late in our lives, at least according to my mother's standards," she said, and they both laughed. "However, we've had our fair share of wonderful times. I hope we can get back to that one day."

"Yeah," said Flo, and both paused for a while, in silence.

"But what's your story? How did you two get together?" asked Lili, choosing her words carefully.

"We were high school sweethearts, me and Bogdan," answered Flo, her face lighting up. "We got married young. Those were great times! We were young, healthy, happy. I'm glad we got married. I'd do it all over again. Still, yeah, I know what you mean. If we had met later, say five years ago… I mean, now if I think about it, we probably never would have met," she said, laughing. "I mean, he would have been doing his woodwork, then heading straight home to sit in front of the TV, while I would have been doing 'something with computers'," she said, air-quoting Albert, "and would then have gone out clubbing."

They both laughed.

"Again, I'm sorry for what happened," said Flo, returning from her trip down memory lane and pulling her hand back.

"Not to worry. My conclusion is, I don't know what's wrong with these men. They go really crazy when faced with danger."

"Well, Albert seems to have his feet on the ground. And your dad also."

"Yeah. My dad is something else. They don't make them like they used to, that's for sure," she said.

"I'll go prepare some more medicine for your dad," said Flo, getting up.

And she did, returning one hour later with a large, full jar.

\* \* \*

"It's done," said Bogdan, stepping into the living room. "Go help with the preparations please, Flo. Dad is outside. He needs you."

"Yup, right away," she said, throwing a quick glance between Bogdan and Lili. "Lili, do you want to help?"

"Yes, of course. I was just about to change Dad's mash, but then

I'll come right over."

"Okay," said Flo, going out.

Lili rose from the sofa and moved into Dan's bedroom, closing the door behind her.

At the same time, Bogdan sat on the opposite sofa, acting a little awkward. For an instant it looked like he wanted to say something, but the moment passed quickly.

\* \* \*

"It's cure-o'clock, Dad," said Lili, holding the jar of fresh medicine. "You guys ready?"

"Yeah, I am. I think Howler is too, aren't you, boy? By the way, Lili, what was that all about?"

"Eh, Bogdan. He was a jerk," Lili answered, using a napkin to clean Dan's back.

"Yeah, I heard. But I liked the way you stood your ground. Good for you."

"Thanks, Dad," said Lili, her eyes getting teary. "I don't know what's gotten into me. I was aggressive myself."

"It was fine. He deserved it. And I think the others agreed. Now, can you please clean the rotting onions off my back? If I smell this too much, I'll start hating onions and garlic. And we both know how that would make my life even more miserable."

"Yes, Dad… there. All done. Well, I must say, this looks way better! Many of the vines are gone, especially on the far end side. I can only tell where they used to be from the cracks in your skin. And here in the middle, and at the neck, they've shrunk to half their initial size. Hmm. I wonder why this skin is not getting soft again," she said, pressing her finger where a black vine used to be and trying to squeeze a nail under the hardened skin.

"Yeah, it feels odd now. A few days ago I lost all feeling in that area. Now, I feel as if someone has glued a massive piece of plastic to my lower back. Not sure I can properly express what I—"

"I think I can peel it!" interrupted Lili. She had the tip of her finger underneath a piece of hardened skin, near Dan's waist. That skin was now coming loose, much like a snakeskin. "Do you feel anything?"

"Yeah, I feel relief! Like an itch I had is now gone. Ah, that feels nice! Try to remove all of it?"

"Yuk, this is icky!" said Lili as she peeled back a strip of white, hardened skin bordered by two cuts where there used to be black vines. Underneath, she saw Dan's normal skin.

"This looks like new skin. It seems softer than usual."

"Ah, this feels awesome!" said Dan, happy. "Take it all off!"

"Oh, I can't. Up here, where the black vines are still visible, it seems really glued, still a part of you… I'll tell you what, I'll cut the part I was able to detach, and I'll give it another shot tomorrow, okay?"

She proceeded and removed quite a lot of the white skin. Now Dan's back looked better. The white area was smaller, though it still engulfed the back of his neck and half of his back and head. The other half of the head was now normal. His arms were now too, and so was the lower part of his back.

"Okay, now brace yourself. I'll apply this smelly thing on the vines," said Lili.

She was meticulously applying the mix when she heard a different yell between Dan's screams.

* * *

Bogdan remained alone in the living room. He did raise his hand toward Lili, even opened his mouth, trying to say something, right when she closed the bedroom door behind her.

Bogdan moved around, nervous. He could hear voices from the guest bedroom, as Lili and Dan talked. He finally settled and sat down, again, on the sofa, waiting for Lili to return. He'd get up the courage to talk to her then.

As he sat there, he started to hear a menacing growl somewhere in the back of his mind. The growling intensified. No, it wasn't in the back of his mind. It was coming from the hallway.

"Grandma?" he called.

The growling was different, more alert and restless than usual.

"Grandma?" he yelled. "Who's there?" he called again, just as Lili burst into the room, quickly followed by Howler.

94

\* \* \*

She could hear Bogdan screaming.

"It's Grandma Gina. I bet she turned. We must silence her," she said, and sprinted toward the door. Howler quickly followed.

"Take care!" yelled Dan behind her.

She met Bogdan in the living room.

"I… I think… I think Grandma is… awake," he said, looking awkwardly around the room.

His massive frame next to Lili's small body only augmented the difference between the two.

"Something is odd. It's a distinct growl. Let's go," said Lili, with confidence in her voice.

Bogdan and Howler followed. They approached Grandma's room. And, yes, she was there.

She was sitting up in her bed, squirming. Her white eyes were wide open, the eyeballs not moving at all, yet she waved her hands a lot and seemed scared.

"Oh, it could be the onions," said Lili, just as Howler started barking.

Grandma Gina still had the onion and garlic ropes around her neck, and her hands were moving around as if trying to push away an invisible enemy.

"What do you suppose we should do?" asked Lili, raising her voice, as Bogdan stared at the scene, looking lost.

"I… I think we need… to stop her," Bogdan stammered. "Let's call Dad. Dad!"

"No! Don't call him," urged Lili, reaching toward Bogdan. "Let's deal with it ourselves. I don't think he needs to see this."

"Oh, you're right," said Bogdan. "What should we do?"

"Take Howler out. I feel my head will explode from all this barking."

Bogdan happily obliged, then closed the door.

"Okay, now, here's my knife," said Lili, handing it over.

"Ah… can you… do you think you can do it?"

"Okay," said Lili, in an understanding tone. "But you need to hold her down."

Bogdan grabbed his grandma's shoulders and pushed her down

on the bed. She continued to growl and squirm, but, probably due to the intoxicating smell of the onions, she never even had the reflex to bite.

Bogdan looked the other way while Lili unbuttoned Grandma's clothes, reaching for her chest. She then pressed her knife into the skinny body with a swift move.

A final, long growl was heard. Then Grandma Gina died for the second time. This time, for good.

\* \* \*

Bogdan and Lili were in the living room, sitting quietly on opposite ends of the same sofa.

"I want to say," started Bogdan, but then he stopped. It looked like he was searching for the right words.

"I know. It's okay," helped Lili.

Bogdan looked relieved. "And thank you for what you did earlier. And how you put her clothes back together, so my dad won't see the stab wound."

"Yeah, I think it's best if he doesn't know, at least for now. Don't tell him yet. And don't worry about it. Glad I could help. Now, I must go take care of Dad's back."

\* \* \*

Later that day, everyone was outside, behind the house. Even Dan, who'd had his back cleaned, put on some clothes and joined the others.

Albert had knocked together three rude coffins, and with help from Lili, Flo, and Bogdan, they slowly lowered them into the freshly dug graves using ropes.

Victor went first, followed by Andreea, in the large one they'd dug the day before, and Grandma Gina went into the other they'd just completed.

As they did this, the sun was setting behind the hill.

The women were quiet, praying silently, as Dan, Albert, and Bogdan covered the coffins.

At the end, Bogdan added two crosses made of small planks, and they all stood there in quiet contemplation.

# 9 KNOCK, KNOCK

Night came, and everyone except for Dan, was in the living room. They sat there, silent, absorbed in their own thoughts.

Dan was back on his bed, chest down, gently patting Howler. Lili had finished covering his thinned vines with the concoction a few minutes earlier.

Suddenly, they heard a noise, like a thud, coming from outside the house. Howler became alert.

"Oh, not this again," said Flo, looking around, scared. "What do we do?"

"We should get ready to leave," said Bogdan. "As soon as Dan can go, of course."

"I fully agree," reinforced Flo.

"I think I can already go," answered Dan from the other room.

"We should wait until you are fully up for it, Dad," said Lili. "But in the meantime, we can prepare."

"By the way," asked Flo, "why aren't they attacking? I mean, they attacked when Victor and Andreea were alone. Why not now?" she said, as Howler relaxed again and lay down on a rug.

"I don't know, but I hope they never will," said Bogdan, getting up from his chair. "Come on, Dad, let's start our rounds."

They moved around the house, looking through the nailed planks, trying to get a glimpse of what was happening outside.

\* \* \*

Deep into the night, Howler became restless. At one point, he spent most of his time near the back of the house. He kept moving left to right, as if trying to find an invisible exit through the wall. And now, they could all hear muffled noises, especially from behind the house.

"What's up, Howlie?" asked Lili, getting nearer to him. "What do you hear?"

Howler barked.

"Shush, Howlie. We need to be quiet."

Howler let out a tiny yelp, then started pacing again.

"Something's by the window!" said Bogdan, suddenly, and everyone moved to the right-hand side of the house.

They could make out a skinny silhouette drifting toward the front of the house. They kept moving window to window, trying to understand what was going on. Unfortunately, there were a lot of blind spots, and they couldn't see all around the house. Still, it looked like someone was out there.

*Knock!* The sound coming from the main door reverberated through the house. Lili yelped, as everyone else froze. The men looked around, as if hoping to see that maybe one of them was making the noise.

*Knock!* At the second one, Lili and Flo shifted closer together, looking around the living room.

*Knock!*

Bogdan took a few steps toward the front door.

"Don't open it!" whispered Flo, running and grabbing his hand. Bogdan stopped, squeezing his axe.

A few moments after the third knock, they heard a shriek. The women looked at each other, holding their breath.

"Yeah, we need to leave first thing in the morning," said Lili, and Flo nodded.

Then the growling started. Initially faint, it soon became loud enough for everyone to hear. And it was coming from the front of the house, behind the main gate. Soon, it was ear-splitting.

"They're at the fence!" yelled Bogdan, looking out a window.

"Let's go out!"

"Are you sure?" said Flo. "Maybe it's better to stay inside. Remember that knock."

"Yeah, what if it's just taunting us, trying to lure us out?" said Lili, supporting Flo's idea.

"That's the only way we can hold the fence. And anyway, I can't wait to meet that Strigoi. Let's go!"

Albert and Bogdan grabbed their heavy axes.

"I'll join you," said Dan. "Is there a spare axe around here?"

"Yeah, get Tiny," said Albert. "It should be by the front door."

They got to the door and started removing the barricade, and Dan found a heavy axe in a nook to the left.

"So, you call this huge thing 'Tiny'," he said, grabbing it in his left hand.

Albert removed the last beam, and the men headed out.

"Lock it behind us," said Dan to the girls. "Open it only when we tell you to. Oh, and keep Howler with you."

* * *

The women were inside, in the living room. They both had weapons: Flo a small axe, Lili her trusty bat. And both of them had knives.

Howler paced between them, alert, moving left to right. They tried to get him to settle, but the dog was restless.

Lili and Flo could hear the sound of fighting and yelling outside. Thuds, grunts, hits. It seemed like it took forever, it was loud and terrifying, but eventually it all ended.

They rose slowly and approached the front door.

They stood there, waiting, but nothing happened. They tried to see something through the plank-covered windows and even called for Dan, Albert, and Bogdan, but all they got was deafening silence.

The hours passed, and soon the sun came up.

* * *

The three men rushed to the front of the house.

"To the fence," said Dan, squeezing Tiny in his left hand. "Let's go!"

Bogdan and Albert grabbed the ladders and put them against the fence, left and right of the barricade holding the gates. Once up there, they saw over two dozen growlers pushing against the wall.

Farther back, uphill, stood another. They could only distinguish a silhouette, but they could tell the growler was immobile, looking toward them. It was just standing there, watching.

The fence was shifting violently. Albert and Bogdan kept swinging their axes, hitting growlers with every pass.

Trying to help, Dan pushed against the side of the wall, trying to stop it from falling.

It seemed they were going to make it, when, suddenly, the silhouette in the distance let out another shriek. Dan felt the pushing intensifying. He fought back with all his strength, screaming. Bogdan and Albert joined the cry, moving their axes left and right, cutting growlers into pieces.

Still, it wasn't enough. With a loud groan, the wall gave in on both sides, tumbling all over Dan.

Albert and Bogdan fell back, but they jumped off their ladders just in time and landed on their feet, a few yards back. Bogdan dropped his axe mid-fall and it fell to the ground a few steps in front of him.

And a few steps farther, stumbling on the fallen fence, about ten growlers were trying to get up, and a few more appeared from behind the reinforced gates, which were still standing.

\* \* \*

"My axe!" yelled Bogdan, and sprinted to take it. Albert found his equilibrium after the jump and hit a growler that was just getting up, splitting its head and neck in half.

"Take it!" yelled Albert, running toward Bogdan. "I'll hold them!"

Bogdan picked up the axe, and then, together with his father, started moving back, slowly, fending off incoming growlers. They hit a few, cutting limbs and shoulders.

Still, the fight was tough, and the growlers were fast. They couldn't just swing, hoping for a hit, since for every one they got, another five moved forward ready to jump and bite. No, the growlers kept coming at them, and the two men needed to push them back, waiting for one to wander from the group.

"Look, Dad, the same faces. And the chests!"

"Yeah, I noticed that. Just kill them!"

The fight was raging on, and they slowly got pushed back, step by step, toward the left-hand side of the house, and farther behind it.

And then, taking another step back, Albert let out a loud yell as he fell into a freshly dug grave.

An empty grave.

\* \* \*

Dan was trapped. He found himself face up, the fence on top of him, with growlers squirming on top of the fence. They soon started standing up, charging Albert and Bogdan. Luckily, some of the logs from the barricade had detached during the fall and got trapped beneath the fence as well, preventing Dan from being crushed.

Dan tried to push the fence up and squeeze out. It was heavy by itself and having growlers on top made it an impossible task.

He realized he could try to crawl out. He started turning and caught his right hand beneath him. A sharp pain made him pause. Still, he pushed through, just like he had when they were applying the cure to his back.

Finally, he was on his belly, and he could see Albert and Bogdan being swarmed by running growlers.

He started pulling himself forward, crawling out from under the fence, finally freeing his head and shoulders.

Then, he felt a heavy foot on his back.

\* \* \*

"What the…?" yelled Albert. He was in one of the graves they'd dug only a few hours ago.

He could see Bogdan fighting off the incoming growlers to his left.

Behind his son, a tiny shadow appeared. And it was getting

closer, hands forward, ready to attack.

"Bogdan, watch out!" yelled Albert, trying to get up, just as the shadow grabbed Bogdan.

Bogdan, taken by surprise by the unexpected touch, turned. He looked at the growler and froze, axe in hand.

A few seconds later, the other growlers grabbed Bogdan from behind. They started biting his neck, head, and shoulders, pulling the huge man to the ground.

The silhouette turned, attracted by Albert's thundering scream.

It jumped into the grave, growling.

"Mom?" said Albert.

And then he saw her open chest, with that meaty tumor growing inside, and he froze.

\* \* \*

The growler jumped on Dan, biting the air.

*Not again*, he thought, trying to get it off.

As the growler neared his neck, it stopped and sniffed at the black bite Dan already had.

For a few seconds, the growler stood there, on top of Dan, smelling the back of his neck. Then it got up and went for Bogdan, just as the last five growlers were putting down the large man.

Dan heard Albert's scream. He got up, took Tiny, and ran toward Bogdan. He started hitting growlers in the back of their heads, one by one. His left hand was strong, and most of his hits were well placed. However, his injured right hand required him to spend more time positioning Tiny before every swing.

Soon, all the growlers eating Bogdan were on the ground, squirming uncontrollably. Dan turned and he saw one more growler fighting with Albert in the grave.

Albert was on his back, pushing at what used to be his Mom, while she tried to bite him.

Dan acted quickly and struck her head with the axe, splitting it open, and brains and liquid fell on Albert in the freshly dug-up grave.

Albert started screaming and crying, yelling indistinguishable words.

Dan couldn't understand what he was saying, but he left him and ran to Bogdan. His neck and chest were raw, and he was lying in a pool of blood.

"Hey, Bogdan, do you hear me?"

But Bogdan couldn't answer. He wasn't breathing.

\* \* \*

Suddenly, Albert remembered something. He stopped screaming and pushed the body to the side. He got out of the grave, picked up his axe, and ran toward the broken fence.

Out there, uphill, the shade was gone.

"Let's go back inside," said Dan, who was right behind him.

"I want to kill that son of a bitch," said Albert, grinding his teeth.

"I know, and if you want to, I'll come with you right now. But maybe, just maybe, it's smarter to go back inside and take care of the girls."

"No, let's go get him now and finish this!" said Albert, and they both started moving.

\* \* \*

The women were holding each other. Howler had settled down, and was now lying on the wooden floor, a few feet away from them.

"I'll go out," said Lili, suddenly. "We can't stay here inside forever."

Flo said nothing. It looked like she was holding back tears.

"Yes, let's do this," she said, with glazed eyes.

They removed the barricade and slowly opened the door.

Outside, there was a scene of real carnage. Almost a dozen growlers lay in the snow in front of them. As they took a few steps and made some noise, most started squirming. But luckily, all of them had their heads smashed in. They couldn't hurt anyone.

"There." Lili pointed toward the left-hand side of the house. "The trail of growlers leads there."

Holding their weapons tight, they took cautious steps until they saw the open grave.

And Bogdan was next to it, face up, near a pile of five dead growlers.

"No! Bogdan!" yelled Flo, running.

As she hugged her dead husband, Flo heard a hissing noise behind her and turned.

She soon discovered Grandma Gina. The old lady was on her back, inside the open grave, head cracked open, twitching.

"What the hell?" she said, and jumped into the grave, plunging the knife into Grandma Gina's chest for the second time.

* * *

"It's us." They heard Dan's tired voice about ten minutes later. "We couldn't find him," he added, dropping Tiny and sitting on a bench.

"Oh, Dad, you're back," said Lili, joining him and hugging him tight, while Flo continued to hold Bogdan, crying, not hearing anything going on around her.

Albert was next to them, leaning on his axe. Both he and Dan looked exhausted, and Albert looked especially troubled.

"That son of a bitch! I'll get him if it's the last thing I do!" he said, spitting on the ground. "Look at what they did to my boy! Both my boys! He's killed all my family!" yelled Albert, waking all the living growlers around the house.

"I will kill you all!" he yelled and started smashing chests all around, silencing every moving growler.

"Let him be!" said Dan to Lili, as she stood up from the bench. "He needs this. Until then, let's get ready to bury Bogdan."

* * *

Dan was shoveling, covering Bogdan up. They put him in the same grave they'd dug for Grandma Gina, laying him next to her. And this time, without a casket. There was no time, and everyone wanted to leave this place as fast as possible.

Flo and Albert were a few dozen feet away, holding each other and crying, while Lili was with Dan, assisting him.

"I can help," she said. "Just give me a lighter shovel."

"No, don't you worry," said Dan. "This is a job for me. Plus, I need the exercise. I've been lying in bed for days."

"But you barely slept last night."

"I'm fine. What worries me now is, maybe..." Dan lowered his voice, throwing glances toward Albert. "Maybe we should have stabbed Bogdan's and Grandma Gina's hearts. Just to make sure they don't come back. Yesterday when you had to 'silence' Grandma Gina, I thought you meant putting a knife through her chest."

"I did," said Lili. "I stabbed her heart before the burial. She turned anyway. Albert doesn't know."

"Really?" said Dan, interrupting his shoveling.

"Yeah. She turned. You heard her growling in her bed. It was lucky Albert was busy making the casket. Anyway, we stabbed her. And look at her now."

"But how did she get out?" asked Dan. "Maybe she dug her way up, somehow breaking through the casket, impossible as it might sound. Maybe you missed her heart? This is crazy."

They both looked down at the corpse with worried looks.

"What's that on her chest?" Lili suddenly asked. "See? Like all the other growlers around here. The only difference is her face is normal."

"Yes, I know. This is strange. All the growlers here," said Dan, "have the same tumor-like thing on their face and chest. And Albert told me today about the place where they used to dump growlers corpses. They went there only to find it empty. And they were carrying growlers with them that should have already been there— some turned neighbors they'd killed before. I bet some of these, if not all, have already been put down by Albert and his family. That means they can—"

"They can resurrect!" said Lili, her jaw dropping.

"I didn't want to believe it, but all evidence points to that direction. That, or they never actually died for good."

"No, I think they die. Just think of Mom," she said, with a shade of sadness on her face. "But do you remember Grandma Gina's story, about how the Strigoi did something and returned to life the growlers Victor and Andreea had killed? What if he can resurrect dead growlers? What if it's him mending their heads and chests, bringing them back?"

"If that's true, we're in deeper shit than before. And we were in very deep shit to begin with."

"Language, Dad," said Lili, but her smile quickly switched back to a focused look.

"Hey, honey. Don't you worry," said Dan, touching her arm. "Mat and Andrei are okay. We'll go pick them up, then we'll get away from this godforsaken place, away from this Strigoi and his doings. Together."

"Yeah, I hope so. Finish the grave, Dad. I'll start packing."

* * *

They put together the backpacks. Clothes, food, onions, and some garlic. Flo and Albert insisted on the garlic, and Dan took their side.

Lili received an old backpack, and now she could carry a lot of food, medicine, and other useful supplies.

They also prepared some fresh concoction to go. Lili quickly examined Dan's back and noticed that only a small portion around the initial bite was still stuck to Dan, so she applied some of the mash to the back of his neck and covered it with a plaster. She was able to peel off all the remaining hardened skin.

"One more day and you'll be fine," said Lili, smiling at her dad.

"Well, this thing actually saved my life, if you can believe it."

"What? How?"

And he told her about the sniffing growler.

"It just left you alone after sniffing your neck?" asked Lili, gasping.

"Yeah. Just like in that movie, *Alien* or *Aliens*, I think."

"Yup, *Alien 3*. I was about to mention the same thing. Why? You think the growler sensed you'll become one of them soon?"

"Probably. Who knows?"

"Anyway, I'm so happy you're okay, Dad," said Lili, hugging him.

* * *

It was past midday, and they were all ready to go. Lili, Flo, Dan, and Albert stepped out of the yard, walked over the flattened fence, and set off toward the village. Howler went with them, walking beside Dan.

"We'll stop by the cabin to pick up Mat and Andrei," said Lili. "They must be worried sick. I wasn't able to contact them all this time."

"Maybe tell them to pack and be ready to go when we get there," suggested Dan.

"Excellent idea, Dad," said Lili. She then quickly grabbed her walkie. "Hey, Andrei, do you copy? Come on, pick up!" She waited a bit, then shut it down. "We're still not in range, I guess. We'll try again once we pass the town limits."

\* \* \*

"How are you, Flo?" asked Lili a short while later, when they found themselves a few steps behind the two men.

"Peachy."

"Yeah, I guess."

"I've lost Bogdan. I can't believe he's gone. He's been a part of my life for so long! And Victor, Andreea… even Grandma Gina. I didn't mention this before, but my parents died many years ago. This has been my family. And now they're all gone. I have no one."

Lili paused for a moment. "I know it doesn't feel like much now, but you have me. And Dan, whose life you saved. And Albert. Let's not forget about him. You've been a part of his life for so many years. You made Bogdan happy. I'm sure he sees you as part of his family."

"Thank you," whispered Flo, and she started sobbing.

"Here's the house with the strange basement," said Lili, suddenly, pointing to a house on their right. "That's where they—"

"Yeah, we saw that," interrupted Albert. "We came here last night. The smell was odd, like you said: a mixture of blood, rot, meat, and mold. But there was nothing odd inside, except for a few body parts. It's just a dark basement. And not as damp as you suggested."

"Wow! That's strange," said Lili, thinking. She then continued. "I guess he changed places?"

"What do you mean? Did he pack and move? We're not even sure that Strigoi ever lived there."

"But a bunch of growlers chased me! They came from that basement, and I heard that shriek! It must have been him."

"What if a bunch of growlers went dormant down there?" asked Dan. "I mean, they wouldn't freeze in a deep cellar."

"And what about the dampness?"

"No idea, Lili," continued Dan. "But anyway, we went there, looked around, and went down the stairs. We found nothing."

"You found a few bodies you said."

"No, not bodies, just parts."

"Hmm. What if that's his food?"

Everyone looked each other, and then they continued walking, in silence.

* * *

"That's our car," said Lili to Flo. "Andrei really loves it. We'll probably come pick it up once the snow melts. He will not shut up about it."

"It's cute. Bogdan had a large one. It was huge! It sometimes felt too big."

"We're still talking about cars, right?"

"Yeah. I mean, not only about that," said Flo, and both giggled. "He always said the bigger the car, the smoother the ride. Oh, and it had to be a German brand. Those are real cars. The others, he said, are just vehicles."

"I see. I guess he had an older model, right?"

"Yeah," admitted Flo, and both giggled again. "Ugh, I miss him," she said, switching to tears.

"Can you please check on Howler?" said Lili, trying to change the subject. "He's a little behind. I'll try to reach Andrei."

"Sure thing," said Flo. "Hey, Howler. Come on. Dog! Come here."

Lili pulled out the walkie-talkie. "Hey, Andrei? You there?"
Static.

"Hey, Dad?" called Lili. The men, who were a few dozen feet ahead, turned. "I still can't get a hold of them."

"Don't worry, honey," said Dan, looking into the distance. "It's still far out. There's also this hill between us and them. Keep on trying. You'll get them soon. Oh, damn, it's starting to snow."

A few large snowflakes were slowly falling. And as the sun set, a chilly wind blew, chasing away any slight warmth.

\* \* \*

As they advanced, the snow and wind intensified. It would have made an idyllic scenery if watched from the window, with a glass of mulled wine, but the four people and one dog were walking in the snow. And everyone was either worried or very sad.

They were almost at the top of the hill, from whence they would have a proper view of the cabin.

"Hey, idiot! Pick up that walkie-talkie! What the hell are you doing?" tried Lili for the millionth time. "Dad," she said, with a tremble in her voice. "They still don't answer!"

Dan made no comment, but he picked up the pace slightly.

They finally reached the hilltop, and everyone gazed toward the cabin.

"Damn, this snowfall. I can barely see what's down there," said Dan, squinting. "Let's get closer."

They advanced, Lili lagging behind, talking on her walkie. As they approached the cabin, unwittingly, she lowered her voice almost to a whisper.

"Hey, Andrei! Answer. Do you copy? Please don't play games, just answer. I'll kick your ass if this is one of your retarded jokes! Andrei?"

Dan suddenly stopped, pointing at the cabin. They could see the cabin door standing open, swinging in the wind. The shed door was the same.

"Oh God," said Lili, and she started moving faster. The others followed.

They reached the house and Dan entered first, making a lot of noise. He looked around, but all was clear.

"They're not here," he said, looking back at the group.

"I bet the idiot didn't close the door properly," said Lili, with hope in her voice. "Best thing they left. Smart move, getting away from here."

"It's such a mess," said Flo, looking around and getting used to the darkness.

"Yeah, it was probably the wind," said Albert.

"What about that table?" asked Flo with a distrustful voice.

Lili and Dan froze. They looked around, now really noticing the environment. The entire room was a mess, and some furniture had been overturned.

"That's my backpack," said Lili, pointing at it. "Look, Dad, that one's yours. And cans, cans everywhere."

Dan looked around, silent, frowning at the sight.

"I need to take my clothes," she continued, as she started grabbing some things. "We'll have to come back for our backpacks; we're too loaded now. Was this done by other people? But why would anyone leave supplies behind?"

Lili turned to the group, just as Flo spoke. "Do you think it was the Strigoi? Raising the dead and trashing the place?"

Dan ran out to the shed, followed by the others.

"She's not here!" he yelled.

"Who?" asked Flo.

"Maria. She's not here anymore."

# 10 NEW BEGINNINGS

Mat twitched and Andrei woke up. It was past midnight, and they were in each other's arms, on the floor by the cabin door.

"We need to move," said Andrei, looking around frantically. The cabin was cold, and they'd fallen asleep in their winter jackets.

Matei was still sleeping, so Andrei carefully placed his son on the floor, tucking the hood of his jacket under his cute little head. He took his backpack and started stuffing in his things. He took about a quarter of the food, focusing on onions and perishables, like salami and a few vegetables, leaving behind most of the cans.

"Why did you have to go?" he asked, mumbling. "Why, honey? We should have gone back to the village together. Why did you go into that trap? Here, I'll leave the cans. Right here on this table. See? If you come back, there's food waiting for you."

He finished his backpack and started looking for Mat's, continuing to mumble.

"Where is that thing? Ah. Good. I'll put his clothes in. Ugh, these need washing. I must do the washing now, I guess. Your plan finally worked. You got me started with heating the water, then carrying it. Then hanging them out to dry. I see. Now you did all this so I'd have to do the actual washing. Smart move."

Backpacks done, he looked out a window that was facing the front yard.

112

"Coast seems clear. Yup. We have to go. We'll wait for you back in the village."

He stopped, and big tears started rolling down his face.

"No! I have to be strong," he said, or thought. He couldn't even remember if all this was in his head, or if he was speaking aloud.

"Daddy? Are you crying?" He heard a tiny voice.

*Be strong!*

"No," said Andrei, sniffing. "It's the cold. It makes me tear up. It's like an allergy. So! Ready to go?" he continued, still watching out the window.

"To save Mom?"

"No, no, to go back to the village."

"But it's the middle of the night."

"It's the best moment to walk, little boy. The best air, the nice, you know, moonlight."

"But why don't we go save Mom?"

"Because Mom doesn't need saving."

"Really? Why?"

"I talked to her, on the walkie-talkie, while you were sleeping," said Andrei, finally turning around to look at his son, as he finished wiping his tears.

"Really?" asked Mat again, his big eyes getting even larger. "What did she say? Why didn't she talk to me? Call her back!"

"You were sleeping, so I said not to wake you up. She said she has to stay behind, to take care of Grandpa. Remember his finger? It hurts him badly and she's stayed behind with him, back at Albert's."

"But call her back! I want to talk to her."

"Ah, we can't. She had to come closer, to be in range. Then, she had to go back to put some more medicine on the thumb. She'll be back in a few days or weeks, depending on Dan's recovery, don't you worry."

"But why isn't Grandpa Dan coming back with his finger like this? He walked before with the hurting finger."

"He could, but you know how Grandpa Dan is very old. Yes, and very old people sometimes need to rest for a few days. Or even more."

Matei threw a suspicious look at his dad.

"Come on, let's move. We'll go to the village and wait for Mom and Dan there, okay, little man?"

"But why isn't Grandpa putting his own cream on the finger?"

"Remember one year ago, when you hit your foot on the bedpost?"

"Yeah."

"Remember how you couldn't touch it, and barely let me and Mom take a look, so we could check if it was broken or not?"

"Yeah."

"Well, it's the same with Dan. He can't touch his finger, it hurts so much, so he needs someone else to do it for him."

"I see. But why isn't Albert doing this for Grandpa?"

"What's up with all these questions? Come on, get up, and let's go. We can talk on the way there."

"Okay, Dad."

They got out, and Andrei carefully closed the door behind him. He turned around, looked left to right, and let out a relieved sigh.

They started walking toward the village, under the moonlight.

* * *

They had been walking for an hour now. The air was frosty, but it was beautiful outside. The moon and the stars were sending rays of light into the snow crystals, making the surrounding hills shine.

Andrei was silent, and he constantly looked around, especially behind them.

"Why isn't Albert putting the cream on Grandpa's finger?"

"What? Ah, that. Well, Albert's hands are too large. Did you see his huge hands?"

"Yeah."

"They need a smaller hand, to make sure it gets to all the right places, to help Dan heal faster."

Matei said nothing for the next few minutes, and they continued to walk.

"Are they coming soon?" Matei suddenly asked.

"Who?" asked Andrei, pivoting to look behind.

"Mom and Grandpa."

"Ah. I don't know. They'll fix Grandpa up, and then they'll

114

come. But don't worry about that. We'll be just fine, the two of us. We'll live like fat rats!"

"But I want my mommy."

"Me too," whispered Andrei.

"What?"

"I said 'I know'. But don't worry; she'll be back. Until then, we'll have a blast, you and me. We can finally play those games together. See? Your plan worked. Now you got me to play with you."

"Wow! Can we play now?"

"No, not now. We need to walk. And I need to catch my breath. Plus, be quiet."

"Why? Can growlers attack us here?"

"No. They cannot walk when frozen. And it's freezing out here."

"But the ones from the town, why could they walk?"

"You saw that? I told you not to look."

"I didn't. But I saw them."

"Yeah, *that* makes sense," said Andrei, sarcastically.

"It's true! I saw them, and then I didn't look anymore."

"Fine, okay. Yeah, they were probably coming from a warm house. They weren't frozen. But out here there are no houses, so no growler can move around."

"Where were those growlers going, Daddy?"

"I don't know. Probably just crossing the street. Maybe they heard a noise. Don't worry about it."

"Were they going to Albert's house? Are Mom and Grandpa in danger?"

"No, no, clearly not. Don't worry. Grandpa and Mom are safe. Albert has a sturdy fence; you've seen it. Nothing can go in," said Andrei, with a tremor in his voice.

"And what was that shriek? Was it a Strigoi?"

"I don't know, honey, Jesus. It probably was. But it's far away now, and we're safe here. Now be quiet. Remember what I've been telling you about the importance of conserving your energy."

They continued walking, quietly, with Andrei looking around from time to time.

"What about wolves?" came back Matei, a few minutes later.

"What about them?"

"Can they move? Could they attack us?"

Andrei paused for a moment. "That, actually, could happen. That's why I'm saying we should move fast, and be quiet."

"Daddy, I'm scared!"

"There's nothing to be scared of. Remember! The best way to be safe is to move fast! And to be quiet. And you conserve your energy if you keep quiet while walking. So let's be quiet. Okay, Mat?"

"Yes, Daddy."

\* \* \*

They saw the village, as the sun sent its first rays over the horizon.

"Ah, finally," said Andrei, checking behind him again. "I'm so tired."

"Me too! I want to sleep."

They slowly approached their former shelter, the house right at the beginning of the village. Everything was in order. They opened the gate, and a few moments later they were inside the house.

"Ugh, I'm dead tired," said Andrei, dropping his backpack. "I'll go start a fire. Can you bring some snow in a bucket? We need water."

"Yes, Daddy," said Matei, grabbing his toy shovel.

"And let me know when you're finished, so I can lock the door!"

"Yes, Daddy."

"Ah, damn!"

"What, Daddy?"

"Nothing. You go get that snow. I realized I have something to do."

\* \* \*

Andrei set out, looking for some planks. He remembered seeing some in the house over the street, the one under construction, so he had decided to head there.

"Wait here, Matei. I'll be back soon."

He came back with a few planks and, using a handsaw, a hammer, and some nails he'd found in the shed, he nailed shut the back entrance to the house. The one with the tarp attached on the inside.

* * *

"Daddy?"

"What?"

"I'm hungry."

They were both in bed, in their improvised pajamas, tucked beneath a warm blanket. The sun was up, but they were both yawning and sleepy.

"What? No way, you fatso."

"But I'm really hungry! And I'm not fat, you're fat."

"Am I fat?" asked Andrei, starting to tickle Matei. "Am I?"

"N… o… o… o…, Daddy," said Mat, laughing. "You… are… not… fat."

"Okay. Now go to sleep."

"But I'm starving. I wish Mom was here. She would give me some food."

"Actually, I don't think she would. She would tell you it's too late for food and that eating before bed is unhealthy. But okay, fine, I'll fix you something. What would you like?"

"What do you have?"

Andrei got out of bed and opened one of the food bags. "I can give you some beans."

"No."

"Meat? I have canned pork."

"No."

"That's all I have."

"No, there's more. Mom always had more."

"Choose one."

"No!"

"Fine, then don't eat."

"But I'm hungry!"

"If you're hungry, you will eat either pork or beans. Look, we can mix them up and we'll eat together. How about that?"

"No! I want eggs."

"We don't have any eggs."

"Mom would have made me some eggs."

"Then go eat with Mom!" yelled Andrei. "Sorry. Look. I'm exhausted. Choose something and let's eat, so we can finally go to sleep."

Mat said nothing, so Andrei continued. "I forgot about the onions. You'll get onions with that. What do you think?"

"Fine," said Mat with a sigh.

\* \* \*

"Daddy?"

"Hmm?"

"Why did we leave Mom's and Grandpa's backpacks in the cabin?"

"Why do you think?"

"Um… because you're not strong enough to carry everything?"

"Are you trying to get yourself beaten to death with a pillow?" said Andrei in a playful voice.

"Ha, ha, no, Daddy."

"Yeah, you're right. They were too heavy. We might go back for them later. We'll see."

"But Mom and Grandpa, when they get back, might also need them."

"Yeah, right. That too," said Andrei, turning his face away from Matei. "Now, be quiet. We have to sleep. Goodnight."

"Daddy?"

"What?" asked Andrei with a sigh.

"Do I lose energy if I talk?"

"What do you mean?"

"You said, while we were walking, that I lose energy if I talk. Is it true?"

"Yes! Please be quiet."

"How do I lose energy talking?"

"I don't know, you just do. It's better if you're quiet."

"But I like to talk."

Andrei said nothing and moved under the blanket, trying to find a better spot.

"Do you want to play catch? Or hide and seek?"

"What? No."

"Why not?"

"Matei! Please! Can you please be quiet? Close your eyes and focus on sleeping. Look at us. We've been walking all night and now you want to play catch?"

"It would be fun. Mom always plays catch with me."

"Even when you're supposed to go to bed?"

"No. But in the yard—"

"Please shut up and go to sleep!"

\* \* \*

Andrei woke in the middle of the night.

*Wow, we slept through the entire day*, he thought, turning to look at his son. Still, it had been a good, well-deserved sleep.

Matei was still sleeping, his little face toward him. They were in a large bed, yet Matei had found a way to sleep cuddled up against Andrei the entire time.

The fire had been out for a while now, but the room was still warm. *I should probably start another one*, he thought, looking around without enthusiasm.

As he was yawned, he looked out the window and saw that it was snowing. Also, judging by the creaks made by the house, the wind was blowing hard.

He got out of bed, reaching for a mug to get some water.

*Knock!* he suddenly heard at the front door. Andrei froze.

*Knock!* Again.

*Knock!* A third time.

# 11 ONE TEAM

"**H**ey, open up!" yelled Lili from behind the door. "It's freezing out here. Open up!"

"Why would you knock like that?" Dan's voice could also be heard, muffled. "Do you want to give him a heart attack?"

"It seemed like a good idea at the time," said Lili. "Hey, open up!" she yelled again, knocking.

The door cracked open, and Andrei peeked out, dressed in pajamas and holding a bat.

"Oh my God, Lili! Is it really you?"

"No, it's sexy Santa Claus."

"You're alive?"

"What's wrong with you? Of course we are! Now, move aside, let us enter."

She had barely taken two steps into the house before Andrei jumped forward and hugged her, stopping her in her tracks.

"I thought I'd lost you," said Andrei faintly in her ear, tears in his eyes.

"Same here," said Lili, tearing up too. "We noticed your backpacks were missing from the cabin, so we had some hope. I was so happy to see this door was locked." She then continued in a more confident voice. "Now, step aside, you dufus, and let us in."

The group entered, one by one, dropping their heavy backpacks by the entrance.

"Oh, hi Flo," said Andrei, trying to rest his left arm on a cabinet. "How are you?"

"Peachy."

"Great!" he said, trying to smile. "Come in, all. What took you so long? Oh, hi Dan! What happened? Where's everybody else?"

"Would you shut up and let us catch our breath?" interrupted Lili. "We've been walking for hours. We're cold and we're hungry. And tired. Could you start a fire; I see it's out."

"Yes, yes. I was just about to do that. Come right in. Oh, hey Albert, good to see you."

"Hi, Andrei," mumbled Albert as Andrei left the living room.

"Where are you going? Didn't you forget something?" asked Lili. "What?"

"The fire!"

"Ah, yes. I'll go put some clothes on, you know, to be more presentable. I'll come right back."

"That's a first. Okay, go."

"So good to have you back! I can't wait to hear everything!"

"Yeah." Lili sighed as Andrei left the room.

\* \* \*

The fire was burning, and everyone sat around the table, quiet. They were all eating.

Even Howler had his own food in a bowl on the floor.

Matei was still sleeping in the bedroom, and Lili and Andrei let him be.

Andrei was looking around, checking people's faces. "How you've all been? Dan, what happened? Why didn't you come back?"

Dan didn't answer, and Andrei pressed on. "You guys are kind of down. Where are Bogdan, Victor, and Andreea? And Grand—" Suddenly, Andrei looked like he'd had a Eureka moment. "Hmm. Do you want some more beans, Lili?" he continued with less enthusiasm.

"A lot of good people died, Andrei," Dan finally answered. "It was a terrible time for everyone, especially for Albert and his family. Same for Lili and myself. We almost died on several occasions."

"How about you, honey?" asked Lili. "When did you get here?"

"Yesterday," answered Andrei. "First, we tried to come rescue you. I was an idiot. It was an impulse decision, and we reached the town at dusk. I think we saw the Strigoi, followed by a few dozen growlers. That's when we rushed back here. I thought you were all dead," he said, glancing at Lili. "After seeing that big group, we ran back to the cabin. We slept a bit, then we came straight here."

"Yes, you probably saw the very group that attacked us. It was terrible," said Lili.

"When was that? Last night?" asked Dan.

"Yeah."

"Was Maria still there?"

"Still where?" asked Andrei.

"In the shed. Was she still there?"

"I don't know. I didn't check. Why?" asked Andrei, his eyes getting larger.

"She wasn't there when we got to the cabin, a few hours back," said Dan with a sigh.

"What? How come?" asked Andrei, this time looking terrified.

And they all started talking, going through what had happened over the last few days, pulling together all the threads.

"The only great thing, if we can call it that," concluded Flo, "is that we are finally safe. Ever since we left for that generator it's been one awful thing after another."

"Also, you forgot your old backpack back at the cabin," said Andrei to Lili, while Lili rolled her eyes.

Everybody sat there, quietly, with sadness in their eyes, listening to the fire crackle.

"That disease sounds strange," said Andrei, suddenly. "You said it was spreading all over the body? Do you think if would have covered you completely?"

"I think so," said Dan, nodding. "I don't know if I would have died before the end of it, but it was certainly growing fast. It felt like I didn't have much time left, that's for sure."

"Good thing you discovered the cure. If this ever happens again, to any of us, we'll know how to fix it. Maybe sucking out the bite, right when it happens, could also help, on top of adding onions and garlic. I wonder what the garlic's role in all of this is."

"No idea," said Lili, "and I'm not that keen to find out."

"Come to think of it," said Andrei, grinning at Dan. "White with black stripes. You started to look like a zebra, didn't you?"

"No, more like a tiger," said Dan, making Lili laugh and the others smile. "And they were vines, not stripes."

Everyone went quiet again, the joy quickly replaced by the old sadness.

"Well, I'm off," said Dan, shaking everybody from their thoughts. "I'll go to bed. It'll be morning soon."

The others all followed.

\* \* \*

"Mommy," said Mat, in his sleep, as Lili got into bed and hugged him.

"Mommy?" he yelled, opening his eyes. "Mommy, you're back!"

"Yes, baby, I'm back. I've missed you so much! How are you?"

"I'm fine. How's Grandpa's finger?"

"Oh, it's better now," interrupted Andrei. Matei was between them, and Andrei could throw a quick glance at Lili. "He could finally walk, so he and Mom came back."

"Oh, I'm so happy, Mommy!"

"Yes, it's so good to be together again. Now, go to sleep, honey. We'll talk in the morning. Okay, sweetheart?"

"Yes, Mommy," said Matei, and he fell fast asleep, a broad smile on his face.

\* \* \*

Around midday, everybody was up.

"Let's get organized," said Lili as they finished a late breakfast. They were all enjoying a nice cup of coffee that Flo had brew over the fire in the living room.

"Mat? Honey? Do you want to go out and play with Howler? See, it's not snowing anymore. Just stay near the house."

"Yeah!" said Mat, suddenly cheering up. "But I want you to come with me."

"I can't. I have some chores. Unless you want to help with the dishes?"

She barely finished that sentence. Mat was already at the door, getting dressed.

"Good. Now, gather around." People joined in, and Lili continued. "I can think of a few points we need to discuss, but everybody, please chip in."

"Wonderful idea," continued Andrei. "Let's all list our priorities, sort them according to the impact on our wellbeing, assign a person in charge, an owner, if you will, and then we'll get right to it."

"Would you like to create an Excel file as well, while we're at it?" asked Lili.

"Yeah, it would help keep track of everything."

Lili rolled her eyes.

"Okay, so speak up. Anyone?" continued Andrei. "Okay, I'll go first. We need to find enough food."

"Ha, ha. I could have sworn you would say that."

"Yeah, well, honey, it's for all of us. We're a team here. One team, to be precise."

"Right. No, nothing, go on," she said, moving her hand just as Andrei wanted to say something else.

"Okay. Moving on to 'food gathering'," said Andrei, air quoting. "We need to have a way to get food in an organized manner, so we never starve. Yeah, yeah, stop snickering, Lili. We should probably also look at maybe planting something ourselves come spring, and why not have some chickens, ducks, and such? Maybe even some cows for milk. Hopefully some of them survived the winter."

"That's a big hope," said Dan.

"Yeah," agreed on Andrei. "If not, maybe we can find somewhere else, who knows. Still, that's for the future. To conclude, in the short term, we should organize a way to never be out of food. Especially onions."

Everybody nodded.

"Okay, next?" said Andrei, looking around the table.

"We should look at the way we share the house," said Flo. "You know, for privacy."

"I agree," said Lili. "As you probably noticed, one room and the living room are well insulated. There are those two extra rooms. Maybe we can get them ready, one by one."

"How?" asked Andrei, with a specific tone he usually used when trying to nudge Lili into some lighthearted banter.

"By insulating them."

"With what?" asked Andrei, with the same attitude.

"With insulation materials."

"Stop, guys," said Dan.

"Sorry," said Lili, and both she and Andrei smiled. "I don't know how. We just have to do it."

"Yes," took over Andrei, "we insulate them with whatever we can find around. Wood, hay, clay even."

"After that, we can all have decent accommodation," said Lili. "Until then, I guess us girls can take the good bedroom that me, Andrei and Mat used until today. And the men can take the living room."

"Four people in one room and two in another?" asked Andrei raising his eyebrows.

"No, we'll take Mat with us. Three and three."

"But I want to sleep with you," said Andrei. "I mean, you, Lili," he immediately added, turning a bit red.

"Yeah, we got the nuance. Then make sure you insulate a room as soon as possible."

"But I have no idea how to do that. True, I studied the subject in the past, but I've never done it myself."

"I know how," interrupted Albert. "Been doing woodwork and building houses for over forty years. In fact, even longer. I started helping my dad when I was ten."

"Great!" said Andrei, pointing at Albert. "We have our 'man in charge'."

"No, I cannot be in charge of this," said Albert. "I'm not sure what that even means. Just tell me what to do and I'll do it."

"I can be responsible for that," said Flo. "We'll work together, Albert."

"Perfect! But who's the owner for food gathering?" asked Lili, looking at Andrei and smiling.

"Let's wait until we have all the subjects on the table, then we'll decide the split," replied Andrei hastily.

"Another thing," continued Flo, "is to make sure this house is safe. Remember what happened last time. We need reinforced fences so no one can force their way in."

"There's a whole subject related to security," intervened Dan. "The fence is one of many. But we need to make sure we have the weapons and the proper tools to survive. We all need basic training to be ready to fight. We need to prepare for the worst. And, yeah, that includes being ready to meet another Strigoi in the future."

"So that's it," said Andrei, nodding. "I'd hoped there was still a chance we were wrong, but we have to assume Strigois are real."

"Yes, we do," said Lili in a sad tone. "Everything we talked about last night points to that."

"Well, no one saw one up close. Might very well be just another growler," said Andrei, sulking.

"And as a first step," continued Dan, interrupting them, "I will take it upon myself to train Howler."

"To fight?" asked Andrei.

"He could sense the Strigoi before we could see or hear him," answered Dan. "Back there at Albert's house. He has good instincts when attacking growlers and he's not afraid to bite. He's an excellent companion. He just needs to learn how to control the barking, and not to attack until instructed."

"Fine, okay. What else?"

"And Flo was right," continued Dan. "We need reinforced fences and reinforced windows, should they ever get near the house. We need better weapons, ones that can efficiently stop an advancing growler. I think I can work on that with Albert."

"Great!" said Andrei. "There's one more thing left, I think."

"Which one?" asked Lili.

"Washing, cleaning, cooking. I guess those are right up your alley, Lili and Flo?"

"What a superb idea," said Flo, while Lili glared at him. "I've always wanted to be a housekeeper. And a maid. And a cook."

"No, I didn't mean it like that, it's—"

"We'll do it like this. You clean up after your fat ass and I'll clean up after mine," interrupted Lili. "We'll do the laundry the way we did to so far. As for cooking, it's true we'll need to ration food, and it makes sense to cook for everyone at once. Still, we'll take turns, and at some point you might have to cook for everyone."

"Sorry, honey, I didn't mean it that way. I was just, you know, saying that I need to do more strategic things."

"Ah, you do?"

"Yeah," said Andrei, grinning. "I love you. You're so cute when you get annoyed."

"Yeah, well, I am annoyed. But at myself, for indulging you for too long. Now," she said, turning to the others, "do we have anything else to worry about?"

Everybody was silent until Flo finally spoke. "Yeah, water. What do we do about it?"

"There's a well at the house across the street. Plenty of water there."

"Here's a thought," said Andrei. "Why don't we split? Some go live in that house, some stay here? That way, we can continue to sleep together."

"I personally don't think it's a good idea to split. Why do you think that is?" asked Lili sarcastically.

"Mm… no idea. Because you don't want to sweep two houses?" answered Andrei in a similar tone, trying to push Lili's buttons.

"For security reasons," intervened Dan. "Splitting means we would have to reinforce two fences, instead of one. We would separate our best fighters, having me and Albert in different locations. We wouldn't be able to synchronize and adapt during the night, should there be an attack. There are a lot of reasons. That's something for the future, if we find more living people."

"Right. Okay, that makes total sense."

"So? Who handles food gathering?" asked Lili.

Silence all around.

"Fine, I'll do it," said Lili.

"I would totally do it, honey, but I have to be ready to intervene when needed. You know, together with Dan and Albert," said Andrei, visibly relaxed.

"Yeah, sure you do."

Everyone laughed.

"So, that settles it," concluded Lili. "Dan handles security, Flo handles the house improvements, and I'll handle food gathering."

"And I will help everyone. Just ask me," said Albert. "I'm best at anything woodworking."

"Yeah, same," said Andrei quickly. "I mean, I'm not qualified about the woodwork." He coughed a bit, then continued. "See? This is awesome! We are one team."

# 12 ONE DESIRE

The next day, Dan was getting ready to go. Howler was next to him, waiting. As he tied his boots, Dan knocked his injured thumb and twitched.

"You should fix that," said Flo, approaching.

"Yeah. It's been on my list for a while."

"In your Excel spreadsheet?" asked Flo, and they both giggled.

"Yeah. But there was always something bigger or more important to take care of. Now is a suitable moment to handle it. Unfortunately, I have little knowledge about taking care of such an injury. True, as police officers we get some first aid training, but it's mostly related to emergency trauma. I don't really know how to handle a fracture that's a few weeks old."

"How's the neck injury?" said Flo, stepping behind him and touching his neck. "Ah, it's healing nicely. No more black vines, and Lili peeled off all that white skin."

"Right. I don't need that concoction anymore. I still have an ugly scar, but other than that I'm good. I'm not sure I've thanked you enough for taking care of me. Now I only have to fix my thumb."

"Well, let's fix it! What should you do in case of a fracture?"

"Do you have medical training?"

"No, no," said Flo, laughing. "But let's try something. What if we build an improvised cast using splints? It should help. I mean, it can't be worse than it already is, right?"

"You're right. I've gotten so used to going to the doctor every time I have a health issue, I forgot about trying to fix it myself. I think we need some properly sized splints and a way to bind them together." Dan felt his thumb with his left hand. It was painful, still swollen, and he couldn't move it. "Yeah, every time I try to move it, it hurts."

"Then don't move it," said Flo, smiling. "I'll go look for some splints. Maybe you could try to get some bandages on your supply runs. We have a few, but not nearly enough. You must keep the splints on for a few weeks at least, so you'll need to change the bandages now and then."

"Okay, great. I'm going out now, and I'll keep an eye out."

"Where are you going?"

"Around. I want to check some houses, see what I can find. We need food and building materials, especially if we want to reinforce the fence. And I want to train Howler."

"Nice. I still want to move some stuff in the house and talk to Albert about what we can do regarding the insulation. Otherwise, I would have loved to come with you."

"Maybe next time," said Dan, and they both smiled.

* * *

"Damn this thing," mumbled Andrei as he carried two buckets of water from the well across the street. "I should be doing something more important."

"What was that, honey?" said Lili, who was scrubbing some clothes.

"I said I should do something more important."

"Oh, is that right? Well, if you want clean underwear, keep on doing what you're doing. We need to rinse these, and we need that water."

"Yeah. Come spring, I'll go get a generator. And a pump. I won't have to carry water ever again. I'm an engineer. You'll be amazed at what I can build."

"That would be nice," said Lili. "But how are you going to do that? Are you okay to go to the hardware store?"

"Why n— Ah, you mean the Strigoi?"

"Yes."

"Yeah, I know. I'm still trying to remember what I did when we left that cabin. Did I close the door or not?"

"I think you did. Even if you didn't, the wind couldn't have knocked down all that furniture. It's clear someone else was there."

Andrei put down the buckets, thinking.

"Other people, maybe?" he said, but he immediately shook his head. "No, I don't think so. They wouldn't have trashed the place."

"Indeed. And the important things, like our backpacks and the food, were still there," said Lili, taking a break from rinsing.

"In that case, we should stay the hell out of that town, that's for sure."

"Yeah, but what if that thing followed us?" asked Lili, looking deep into Andrei's eyes.

"Oh, don't even say that! I've seen all those movies. In every one of them, someone says something like that, and then it happens."

"This isn't a movie. Relax. But no matter what, we need to be ready. Why do you think we're building all these defenses? Now, come on, hang these up to dry."

* * *

"Hey, Dan, are you going out?" asked Albert as he saw Dan and Howler leaving the house.

"Yeah, why?"

"I need some wooden beams to reinforce the wall. And some planks for doubling the walls on the other two rooms. And some filler. I was thinking maybe I should come with you?"

"It's best if you stay here and guard the location," said Dan, after a moment of thought. "We don't know yet what we're up against. I'll keep an eye out and let you know where you can get those supplies. Okay, buddy?"

"Oh, I hope that beast shows up. He's mine!" Albert paused for a while, looking over the fence and into the distance, while Dan sighed. "Okay then," continued Albert, "I'll take a look and decide what we can use from these two yards."

"Great. Thank you," said Dan, nodding.

"How's training Howler going?"

"I've taught him to bark on command. I know, I know," he quickly added with a smile, "the whole point is to teach him the 'quiet' command. As silly as it sounds, the first step to achieve that is to teach him to bark when instructed."

"It looks like you know what you're doing, I guess," said Albert with half a smile, still looking into the distance.

\* \* \*

Dan was finally away, walking down the middle of the street. Next to him was Howler.

The snow was even deeper than last time, thanks to the snowfall from two days ago.

"Good boy. Now, we'll go slowly and silently, and we'll look for the stuff we need. You, however, need to learn to keep quiet. Okay, boy?"

The dog started yelping happily.

"See, that's not good," said Dan, squatting while grabbing the dog and reaching for his snout. "Be quiet and you'll get a treat," he continued, when Howler finally stopped making noise. "Good boy! You were quiet. Here, have this. Good boy!" he said, petting and feeding the dog. "No, don't yelp. Be quiet! Good, good."

Dan stood up and looked around. "Don't worry, we got this."

\* \* \*

They stood before the access gate of a yard. They hadn't reached the church yet, and even if all the local houses were poor, this one looked slightly better. Plus, it was one of the few that had two stories, the top part being a mansard roof. It was an old house, yet freshly painted green.

"We'll try here, okay, boy? And if we find some good stuff inside, we'll take it with us."

They approached quietly, and Dan checked the front gate. It was locked, but he was able to pass his left hand over the fence and reach for a latch. He could open the gate, but unfortunately, the lower part was stuck in the snow.

"Okay, boy, I have to push this," he said as he started pushing and puffing.

Finally, the opening was large enough for him to squeeze through, while Howler followed, without hesitation.

"Let's see if there's anybody home," he whispered, and Howler let out a faint whimper. "Now, see? *That* you need to control."

They climbed the porch and Dan used his bat to knock on the front door. Faint growls soon followed, getting louder as the growlers inside approached the door.

Howler started barking.

Dan ignored the barking, then gently put his hand on Howler's head and looked into his eyes. When the dog stopped barking, Dan waited a few more seconds, then rewarded him with a treat.

"It's clear we must get you accustomed dealing with stimulus, especially from growlers."

They heard growls all around them, in the neighboring houses. Dan squatted and grabbed Howler's snout.

When the growls stopped, Dan said. "We'll do it again."

He hit the door. The growls inside the green-painted house resumed, and so did Howler's barking.

"Well, I guess we'll be here awhile," said Dan, giving him a treat as soon as he became quiet.

* * *

Albert entered the yard of the house across the street. He saw the well and an angry Andrei pulling up a long rope. At its end was a bucket three quarters filled with water.

"Ugh, I hate this," said Andrei with some resentment in his voice. "And my back is killing me. How are you, Albert?"

"I'm fine. I'm looking for building materials."

"Ah, these are poor people. I don't expect you'll find much," he said, pouring the well bucket into another one.

"Yeah, I fear so too. Nevertheless, I can probably round up some scraps."

"That's a good idea. I have to get these two buckets to Lili. See you," he said, picking up the buckets and leaving.

Once Andrei was gone, Albert started checking the surroundings. Moving around, he soon reached the backyard, where

Lili had seen the old lady in the armchair, a few weeks ago. He, too, saw the woman. She was still frozen, but the noise he made brought her back to life.

"Ah, you stupid things!" said Albert with hate in his voice. "You killed my family, you stupid, ugly monsters!"

Then he heard another growl coming from the backyard. He couldn't see the growler yet, but he squeezed his heavy axe, grinning.

\* \* \*

"Oh, Andrei, please use your extensive computer game experience and your massive knowledge about war strategies to assess our strengths and come up with some high-level strategic moves."

Andrei was talking to himself, mockingly, while he crossed the street with his two heavy buckets.

"Andrei, please help us draw up a defensive plan of the premises. Can we treat this like a tower defense game?"

He looked around the street, stopping right before the gate. "See? A tower should go there, another there. And we need some obstacles."

He put down a bucket and opened the gate.

"Oh, Andrei, you're an engineer, someone who actually knows how to modify the electrical installation to be able to work with a generator as is, instead of pulling power cords everywhere. Why don't you start with that? But no, I have to carry these stupid buckets," he continued to mumble.

"They're not stupid," said Lili, right as he entered the yard. "You want to have clean clothes?"

"Yes, yes. I also want to go with Albert."

"Where?" asked Lili, as she poured a bucket of water into a huge basin full of dirty laundry.

"He came by the house with the well, looking for materials."

"What? When?" Lili jumped up.

"Just now. Why? What's wrong?"

"Shit," she said, drying her hands on her coat. "There are two growlers out the back."

"Really? How come?"

"I put them there. Let's go!" she said, grabbing her bat and running.

Andrei took a few seconds to look around before he finally followed her.

* * *

Albert grabbed the old armchair and started pulling.

"I would kill you right here," he said, talking to the growling old lady while studying the wooden roof above their heads, "but I can't swing my axe properly here."

As he pulled, the chair broke into pieces. It was too old and frozen to withstand his assault, and the growler fell onto the ground.

He grabbed her by her frozen clothes and continued to pull. She maintained her sitting position, fully frozen like a statue.

"No," he could hear Lili yelling. "Albert, pay attention! There are growlers there."

"Yeah, I know. I'll finish this one, and I heard another here in the snow. Ah, it's up and at it now."

A muffled growl was coming from beneath the snow. The last snowfall had covered the growler, so he could only roughly estimate its location.

Before Lili could say another word, Albert swung his axe and split the old lady's chest. But he didn't stop there. He continued to hack away at the body.

"Let's go," said Andrei, pulling Lili back, and she quickly followed.

"Ah, you have no legs? Well, how about no hands as well?" they heard Albert ask as they moved away.

* * *

"We'll do it again, boy, but please be quiet." Last time, Howler hadn't barked that loud, but he had let out some whimpers, which was still too much.

Dan hit the door and the growls started again. There was banging coming from the inside as well now. Howler let out only a tiny yelp, instantly becoming alert.

"Good boy!" said Dan, with pride in his voice. "That's a good boy," he continued, petting Howler and giving him yet another treat. "That's the way to do it. Now, let's see how you handle a growler face to face."

He waited for the noise to end. He then heard the three expected thuds, as the three bodies on the other side of the door fell to the ground, dormant.

Right after the growlers fell, he put his hand on the doorknob and turned it. Luckily, it was unlocked.

The door made a loud squeak, and it even touched one of the growlers. However, they didn't move.

"Son of a bitch," said Dan. "Andrei was right. They do get some full shut down."

Howler started growling at the fallen growlers, ready to attack.

"No! Down boy. Don't! Be quiet."

Dan grabbed a growler and pulled it outside. At the same moment, all three became active.

He quickly closed the door. The growler outside was already up and it attacked Dan. Just in time, Howler latched onto its ass, pulling it away.

* * *

"Boy, Albert is in a bad place," said Andrei to Lili as they returned to the house.

"You can say that again."

"Boy, Alb—"

"Stop it! You know I hate that joke."

"You're so cute when you're mad," said Andrei, grabbing her waist.

"Yeah, and you're not."

"I just realized one thing."

"What?"

"We need to repopulate."

"What? The earth?"

"Yes! See? We think alike," said Andrei with a grin.

"Are you out of your mind? We're almost forty, and being

pregnant is the last thing I need right now. Unhand me," said Lili as they entered their yard.

"No. I meant to talk about the process of making babies. Not to have one," continued Andrei, while still holding Lili.

"Well, little chance for that, after your stupid joke. If you love kids so much, why don't you go play with Mat? I think he's inside, bored, now that Howler is with Dad," she said, pushing him away.

Flo was just coming out of the house, carrying a large garbage bin.

"Hey Flo," said Andrei. "What are you up to?"

"Oh, hey guys. I'm cleaning up a bit. Where's Albert?"

"He's back there, slaughtering some growlers," answered Andrei, pointing behind him. "Why? Do you need anything? I can surely help," he added, offering a charming smile.

"I need someone to raise a bed, so I can sweep under it."

"Oh, I can do that," said Andrei proudly.

"Perfect, follow me," said Flo, heading back into the house.

"Mind your back, you dufus. And wipe that grin off your face," whispered Lili to him.

"Well, now that I think of it," he whispered back in a playful tone, "we have to repopulate with children as well. I wonder if Flo wants some of this," he said, pointing at himself and continuing to grin.

"She just lost her husband, you idiot."

"Oh," said Andrei, with less enthusiasm. "Right. Okay, so not now, but later. Still, I should make a good impression. Damn, I should have been wearing fresh clothes today."

"You grin like an idiot. I know you're just pulling my leg, but I'll bite. You think fresh clothes would make a difference?"

"Yes. What if she tries to kiss me while I raise the bed?"

"Don't worry honey, you're safe," said Lili, rolling her eyes and trying to hold back her laughter.

"You only say that because you want to keep me all to yourself."

"Yeah, good luck with the bed. At least stop grinning when you get in there. You look like a retard," she said, and puffed, continuing to smile, while he went inside, laughing.

\* \* \*

The growler used to be a young man in his twenties. It was short, yet well built, dressed in raggedy pajamas. It was trying to get to Dan, but Howler was biting its ass, pulling it away from its target.

Strange enough, the meat wasn't frozen. It looked very cold, but not quite frozen.

Dan grabbed his bat and, making a move he'd learned and practiced many times while on the force, put down the growler with one expert blow.

"Good boy," he said, when Howler let go. "Now, I'll hold it down, and, according to Andrei, it should soon fall asleep. Hear boy? It will fall asleep," he said, holding down the growler. "No, don't bark. Remember what we learned! Good boy. Now, let's both be quiet."

They struggled for a while until the growler finally fell asleep.

Dan gave Howler a treat. He then stood up, and Howler attacked the growler, this time at the neck, waking it up again, along with the two growlers left inside.

"No! Ugh, Howler. You really have to pay attention, boy. Let it be. Let. It. Be. Come here, and be quiet."

As the sun set behind them, Dan and Howler woke the growler a few dozen times. And with every repetition, Howler got better and better at understanding when to attack, when to let go, when to be quiet, and when to bark.

Still, there was a long way to go.

"Let's get back now," said Dan, when the growler fell dormant again. "Come now, let's go," he said, and started moving.

The growler lay there, fully dormant, as man and dog got out of the yard and headed back toward their home.

* * *

"What happened to him?" asked Dan, pointing at Andrei.

Andrei was coming to sit at the table, but he looked stiff, and he was groaning and moaning at every step.

"He helped Flo lift a bed," said Lili, shaking her head in disapproval.

Dan laughed. "Could you pass some onions, please?"

They were all eating and had been quiet for a while now.

"We still have enough food to last us for over a week," said Lili, "but we must do some supply runs soon. I suppose we can go to the church again. There's plenty of food there."

"Yeah, we can do that," said Dan. "Albert, I think I have some ideas about how to source wooden planks, if we cannot find any elsewhere, and some beams as well."

"Tell me."

"From fences. There are quite a few good fences around here, and no one would mind us taking some planks and beams."

"Yeah, sounds about right. Today I grabbed most of the firewood from the house with the well. You know, the one with the old couple."

"What old couple?" asked Dan.

"There was that old couple outback. You didn't know?"

"No, not really. Anyway, great job with the firewood. Now I realize we'll need a lot of beams to support the fence from the inside, in case of a firm push."

"Why do we need to do that, Grandpa? Is someone going to push our fence?"

"No," intervened Lili, petting Mat, "but we need to be prepared."

"Yeah, in case a growler comes knocking," said Andrei almost at the same time, moaning as he changed his position a bit. Lili looked at him, and he nodded. "It's fine. He's not a baby."

"By the way, I found some bandages, Dan," said Flo. "I've been cleaning the house and found a medicine shelf. We can take care of your hand after dinner."

"Wow, great. We didn't have time to look for bandages. Actually, we didn't get any supplies today, did we boy?"

Howler looked up and yawned, quickly putting his head down again, resting it on his front paws.

"He's sleepy, Grandpa. Let him sleep!"

* * *

"How's this?" asked Flo, trying to adjust a few splints around Dan's thumb.

"It looks good. Make sure you block this direction. Yeah, that. Ugh, it hurts a bit."

"I don't think it's supposed not to hurt at all when we set it on. But it shouldn't hurt like hell, and if left untouched, it probably won't hurt anymore."

"Yeah, it's not that painful. It's bearable. Put the bandage on now."

Flo started winding the bandages, while Dan held the splints in place.

Soon after, Dan was the proud owner of an improvised cast.

"This looks good on you," said Flo, smiling.

"Yeah, like socks on Howler's paws."

Flo laughed.

"Thank you, Flo. You keep on saving me. I hope I'll get better with this."

"Don't mention it. Now, remember not to use the hand too much. Let it heal. You need a few weeks."

\* \* \*

Two weeks flew by, and it snowed a few times.

Dan was getting out every day, no matter the weather, to train Howler. They went farther and farther, and soon enough they were walking up to the church and back, sometimes covering the whole distance two times or more per day. They sometimes went farther, but only for a bit. Dan didn't suspect any real danger, but he wanted to make sure the village was safe before venturing beyond.

Equally important, he liked to stay within range of the walkie-talkies, which were good enough up to the church.

The three growlers in the green-painted house were excellent training material, and they always stopped there before returning home from the last tour each day.

As the days passed, Howler advanced in his training. Now, he could stay put, follow, attack, retreat, be quiet, or bark at Dan's command. He was even reading some of Dan's hand gestures and could understanding when and how he should act.

There were still some details to iron out, but Howler had proved to be a talented student, and the bond between him and Dan grew even stronger.

During the first week, Lili, Albert, and Flo did a quick run to the church's cellar and grabbed enough food for at least three weeks, while Dan, Howler, and Andrei stayed home, protecting Matei. Protecting Matei and Andrei, actually, as Andrei was bedridden, barely able to move due to his painful back.

Still, the cellar reserves would not last forever, so they had to look for other options.

Andrei's back was better, ten days later, and now he was finally able to walk around, instructing people about what they should and shouldn't do.

Flo and Albert spent a lot of time improving the interior of the house. One extra bedroom became available—the smaller-sized one—so Andrei, Lili, and Mat could finally take their old room back, while Flo slept in the newly available room. Albert and Dan were still in the living room for now.

Flo and Albert then started working on the last room, the medium-sized one. When that was finished, they would have to decide who moved where. But the plan was to free up the living room.

Finally, and probably most importantly, Dan and Albert had spent quite some time reinforcing the fences. It was an enormous yard, and they needed a lot of wooden beams.

In addition, taking their cue from the vast majority of nearby properties, they built another perimeter fence right behind the house, splitting the enormous backyard in two. The fastest solution was to carefully detach the back fence and bring it a few dozen yards closer. They left the remaining left- and right-hand sides of the fence in place, just in case they ever wanted to put things back to their original state and have a large, reinforced back garden.

With this move, they lost part of the backyard, but they gained better security. Having a shorter property fence allowed them to reinforce it better. And now they had a fully reinforced yard. Every dozen feet there was a long wooden beam, propped up against the fence, at an angle. On the ground, each such beam was pushing against another, shorter beam hammered vertically into the ground, for extra resistance. Along the fence, where needed, they nailed additional planks to make it thicker.

And the main gate got upgraded with two horizontal large beams to hold it shut, in case someone tried to force it. Finally, by the gate there were two more beams, ready to be propped up against the gate, again at an angle, to help further support it.

Throughout all this work, Albert had been like a restless bear. He carried planks and beams from all around, working all day and long into the night.

Things were looking up, and they all felt more relaxed and secure.

\* \* \*

"I plan to go to Grandma's house," said Dan, suddenly, during lunch.

"Right," said Andrei. "We came to this village with that objective in mind." He switched to a grave tone. "But we failed."

"Yeah. We have a good thing going here, so why move? But I know I could find a few cans, some medicine."

"That's why you're going?" asked Lili.

"I'm not going for that really," he confessed. "I want to see my childhood house. Plus, it should be safe now. I guess it's time to go farther away from the church. Anyway, I'll take Tiny with me, just in case."

"I can come with you," said Flo. "Remember, we talked about going out together at some point, to see Howler train? Now I finally have some free time on my hands."

"Okay, perfect. We'll go when we're ready. Grab an empty backpack. We should get hold of some supplies while we're there."

"Can I go too?" asked Andrei.

"No, you can't," said Lili, killing his momentum. "You have laundry duty."

"Oh, damn it!"

"Language!"

"If you want 'language', don't make me do laundry!"

"That's how you're teaching your child to handle chores and responsibility? Behave!"

\* \* \*

"Now, stay!" said Dan, as he and Flo continued to walk. Howler stood there in the snow, quiet but alert, following Dan with his eyes.

Dan hit his left thigh, and Howler came running and jumping happily.

"Oh, wow, he's fantastic," said Flo with admiration in her voice.

"Yeah. I love this dog. He's awesome, aren't you, boy?" he said, petting Howler and slinging him a small treat.

"How's your hand?"

"Looks like it's healing. I'm not sure how well, but it's definitely less swollen. I think I must do some exercises when I get rid of the cast, to regain control and strength, but it's an improvement. With a bit of luck, in a week or two it will be safe to remove this."

"That's great," said Flo, smiling.

"Thank you, again."

"Don't mention it."

"This is odd," said Dan when they reached the church.

"What is?"

"There are so many tracks here at the church. What did you guys do when you picked up the food? Walk all over?" asked Dan, looking around the church's yard.

"Yeah, but they seem covered by snow, don't they?"

"Yes, they're old; that is clear. I was just wondering why there are so many."

"No idea," said Flo, concern furrowing her brow. "I was inside the cellar with Lili most of the time. Andrei didn't want to go near it."

"Oh, yeah. I get a similar feeling when I see that house over there," he said, with a tremor in his voice. "Anyway, let's go."

"Ah, a mini store!" said Flo a few minutes later, clapping her hands and looking toward the left-hand side of the road.

It was a rectangular building, probably forty by thirty feet, built at the edge of a fence. It had a large neon sign above its door, though it was turned off.

"Perfect!" said Dan, happily. "We'll check when we come back. It probably has a lot of food."

"And alcohol," said Flo, smiling. "Let's get some."

"What, now?"

"Yes, why not? Don't you want some tonic for the road?"

"Well, if you put it that way," he said, and they both laughed.

They smashed open the front door's glass and waited. No noise came from inside the store, yet a few growls started in the house behind it. As the noise settled, Dan squeezed his hand through the gap and unlocked the door. When they entered the frozen mini store, they felt as if they'd hit the jackpot. There was a ton of cheap alcohol and plenty of canned food. They also found bread, oil, sugar, flour, packed cold cuts and cheeses, plus lots of sweets. With the store now acting like a large freezer, everything was frozen except the wine and the strong alcohol, which luckily only froze at lower temperatures.

"Now that's a bounty," said Dan, happily. "This should keep us alive and well for months. We'll grab as much as we can later, before we head back."

"Let's get bread and some cans for later today," said Flo. "And pick a bottle or two."

"Yes, ma'am," said Dan.

\* \* \*

"Ah, here it is!" said Dan, opening the gate. "My childhood house."

"It's nice," said Flo, looking around. She was holding an open bottle of cheap wine, almost finished now. "Want some more?" she asked, passing it to Dan.

He grabbed it and took a sip. "Eh, you're just being polite. It's old and falling apart. But I love it."

They started moving around, checking the surroundings.

"These are some old plum trees. There were more of them, and my dad used to make rakija brandy out of the fruit. And back there you'll find some apple trees. Man, those were good apples. Ah, and over there, see the big one, that's a walnut tree."

"I guess you had a great childhood," said Flo.

"Indeed. We weren't rich, not by a long shot, but Mom and Dad took good care of us."

"You had siblings?"

"Yeah, three brothers and two sisters. We were quite a family."

"What happened to them? I mean, you know… before all this."

"Yeah, well… we eventually lost touch. One of my brothers died when I was very young, taken by diphtheria. It was a big deal back then. My sisters married, and they both moved away, across the mountains, following their husbands. Another brother moved down south to the capital, for some fancy job. He died a few years ago. That's the last time I saw my sisters, at his funeral. As for the last brother, I don't even know."

"Oh, sorry," said Flo, placing a comforting hand on his back.

"Don't worry. He left the country thirty years ago. Germany first, then Spain. After that, he moved again, but where, I don't know. We believe he crossed the ocean, went to the US or Canada. He used to contact us now and then, but after a while, we only heard from him at Christmas and Easter. And after he'd crossed the ocean, not even then."

"I'm sorry to hear that," said Flo.

"Ah, don't be. We've been separated for so long, I barely remember his face," said Dan, trying a laugh. "But how about you? Lili told me you lost your parents a while back," he said, slowly turning around and walking toward the house's front door.

The snow was nearly three feet deep and untouched, so they had to raise their legs high for each step they took. They advanced slowly, talking all the while.

"Yes, that's right," answered Flo, fighting with the deep snow. "I was a teenager when they died. Some stupid car accident. Luckily, or not, I have no siblings. I was already with Bogdan; we were in love. He and his family took me in and treated me like their own. They loved me and I grew to love them."

"That's sad, losing your parents like that," said Dan. "I'm sorry."

"Don't be. I got over it. I'm okay now. And as I said, people took good care of me."

"Glad to hear it. I'm sure Bogdan loved you a lot, although he seemed a bit on edge during those last days."

"Yeah, he did. We loved each other. We *used* to love each other is closer to the truth. As you might suspect, we weren't that compatible," she said, taking a break and looking at Dan. "The last few years were mostly routine. And I'm not a big fan of routine." She laughed. "But, yeah, I don't know what would have happened if it weren't for this situation."

"Yeah, I understand. I was lucky. Me and Maria, we were the perfect match. She helped and supported me, and I did the same for her. We loved each other a lot."

They both stood there, quiet and still, for several moments.

"But that's all in the past," said Dan, trying a smile. "Want me to show you inside?"

They did the tour of the house. Dan showed Flo the living room, the small bedrooms and the kitchen, and for each room he had an interesting story or two.

When they reached the pantry, they discovered some old cans. Some were way past their expiry date, but they were cans and might still be okay.

They grabbed everything, and time flew by. They realized that in a few hours the sun would set.

"Ah, we need to go back," said Dan, standing on the porch and checking the sky. "Not too much time left."

"We could spend the night here," said Flo, looking at the sky as well and playing with a pork liver pâté can. "I'm tired. It's been a long day and it's an even longer walk back home. I mean, we should be safe here. Plus, we'll need at least an hour to pack the food from that store, and walking at night might prove problematic."

"Looks like tonight the moon will shine bright. And we can use the flashlights."

"Maybe, but it's better to do it during the day. There are no Strigoi around, thank God, but I feel safer travelling during the day."

"But what about the others? They'll be worried. Let me try the walkie, although I have little hope."

He tried but, as expected, all he got was static. "Damn," he said, looking around, thinking.

"Don't worry. We didn't leave until after lunch, so I already told Lili we might not come back until tomorrow."

"Oh, really? Okay then," said Dan, glancing at Flo. "I should start a fire."

"And I'll open some of these old cans from your mother's pantry. I used to really like this brand, with the blue pig on the label. I'll also try to make some toast out of this frozen bread. We're in luck as it's already sliced."

* * *

"That was some good pâté," said Dan, finishing up his food. "I forgot how much I loved it. I don't think they make this brand anymore."

"Yup, it was yummy," said Flo, taking her last bite. "That's why I wanted to eat it. Mm, I just remembered, some of those sweets from the store would have been nice now."

"You mean some of these?" asked Dan, producing two candy bars from his left pocket.

"Oh my God, you took some? Awesome!" said Flo, grabbing one. "You're full of surprises, thank you."

"You're welcome."

"Should we open the other wine bottle?"

"You mean unscrew the bottle cap?" asked Dan, and they both laughed.

* * *

They were sitting there on the couch, by the fire, quiet. Each held a glass of wine, and the second bottle was still three quarters full.

"This is some shit wine," said Flo.

"Yeah, it is."

Flo snuggled closer, resting her head on Dan's left shoulder. "You know," she said with a strange tone, "I didn't really tell Lili anything."

"I thought as much," said Dan, looking toward her. "I'm old enough to be your father, you know," he added after a few moments.

"But you're not." She turned her face toward him. "Age is just a number. It doesn't bother me. Does it bother you?"

Dan paused for a few moments. "It doesn't. However, I can't. Oh, trust me, I would. But I'm still mourning Maria's death. I'd feel like I'm somehow cheating on her, and I never did that."

"I know what you mean," said Flo, turning back toward the fire. "Me and Bogdan, we'd lost that. Deep down, we were already separated."

"I understand. And don't get me wrong. I think I'm not in my right mind for saying no. It just doesn't feel right, at least not right now. I need more time, if you'd give that to me."

She spent a few seconds composing herself. "We should finish the bottle, don't you think?" she said, taking another sip from her glass.

"I'll drink to that!"

\* \* \*

"Where the hell are those guys?" said Lili, pacing the living room.

"Relax, honey," said Andrei, although he wasn't that relaxed. "They'll come. They might have so much stuff to pick up that they needed more time to put things together. Plus, they left midday and it's a long walk. I'm sure there's a reasonable explanation."

"There's always a suitable explanation, Andrei. But so far, every time someone has gone missing, it was because something bad happened."

"Hey, guys, what's this?" asked Albert, coming into the house.

"What?" asked Andrei.

"This."

"Ah, that's Lili's backpack. Put it there, by the door."

"Okay."

"What? What backpack?" intervened Lili.

"That one. Isn't it yours?"

"Yes, it is," she said in a concerned voice.

"And? What's the big deal?" continued Andrei, looking alternately at Lili and the backpack.

"Where did you find it?" asked Lili, ignoring Andrei's question.

"It was outside, hanging by the front gate. Why?"

"Yeah, why?" asked Andrei, but his face suddenly paled.

"I left this back at the cabin," Lili said faintly.

# 13 SIEGE

L ili was outside, late into the night, perched on a double staircase that Albert had pillaged from one of the surrounding houses. The moonlight allowed her to see far along the main street, both left and right.

To the left stretched the path leading to the cabin, lost in a sea of snow. She could see well into the distance, and the road looked deserted. To the right of their yard were two other lots, without any buildings. Because of this, and also thanks to the shape of the landscape, she was able to see a few hundred yards into the village. No one could approach unseen from either side.

Upfront, however, across the street, the layout restricted her view. Each property had some trees, then there were the houses themselves, plus other annex buildings like barns, kennels, or henhouses. Still, an approach from this direction would be difficult, as any respectable growler would be slowed down by the various fences and other obstacles.

Andrei stood guard behind the house. He was up on a regular ladder, propped against the house itself. He could see the new, reinforced fence that Albert had built a few yards back from the house, and behind it the left and right extensions of the old fence. Just like Lili upfront, he had a clear view beyond the fences, seeing a similar sea of snow.

"Anything?" Lili asked through her walkie-talkie.

"Nope. All is quiet," said Andrei, looking around. "I don't think anything will come this way."

"I hope so. But we don't know. Just keep looking."

"Yes, my liege," said Andrei, sarcastically.

"Shut up," said Lili, smiling.

* * *

As the hours passed, nothing moved or broke the silence.

Albert, who had been sitting on the bench, a heavy axe in hand, had passed out and was now snoring loudly. Luckily, he was in a nook, so it was unlikely the noise could be heard beyond their yard.

"My feet are killing me, and I'm freezing my ass off," said Lili, pressing the push-to-talk button. "The sun cannot come up soon enough."

"That's a pity," said Andrei.

"What is?"

"That such a sexy ass is freezing."

If anyone had been watching him, they would have seen an enormous grin.

"Pfft! I thought you liked Flo's better."

"It is larger, so yeah. But yours is also acceptable." Even if it seemed impossible, a third-party observer would have noticed his grin getting even larger.

"You can kiss goodbye to ever getting near it again."

"I can kiss anything."

"So delicate. A genuine gentleman," said Lili, sarcastically. "Now, shut up, maybe Dad is now in range. We don't want to make him nauseated."

The sun finally came up on the horizon, and they could go back inside to sleep.

Albert woke up just long enough to crawl to the sofa, where he continued sleeping for another few hours.

* * *

It was midday, and the group gathered around the table. Andrei and Albert were thinking, while Mat was yapping about some video game he used to play. Lili was using the walkie-talkie, trying to contact Dan and Flo, but with no success.

"You know, if I win enough rounds, I get a better card. And then I can use that card in other rounds. I can be invincible, don't you think, Daddy?"

"Yeah, I do." Andrei's tone suggested he was beyond bored.

"And then, if I'm invincible, I will get all the other cards. I can be the best player there is."

"Great."

"Look, Mat," said Lili, suddenly, putting down the walkie-talkie. "We need to talk about something. Adult stuff. Can you go outside?"

"But I have nothing to do. Howler's not here. He's with Grandpa. Where is Grandpa? When is he coming back?"

"We don't know," said Andrei.

"Is he having trouble with his finger again? Is Flo putting cream on his finger?"

"What?" asked Albert, looking at the adults.

"Ah," said Andrei, blushing, throwing urgent glances at Albert. "Yeah, you know, it's Dan's finger that needs tending. It might be. We don't know. Now," he said, turning to Matei, "go out and let us be."

"But I'll get bored outside. Daddy, do you want to come out with me?"

"No, let me be."

"You go play by yourself," said Lili, still trying the walkie-talkie.

"But I don't want to play alone!"

"Then stay outside!" yelled Lili, losing patience with the walkie-talkie and startling Mat. "Why do we have to keep on repeating things?"

"He's just a boy," said Andrei in a peaceful tone, grabbing and hugging Matei. "Don't yell at him. Can you go out, little man, to give us some space to talk?"

"Yes, Daddy," said Mat.

"I'm sorry for yelling at you, Mat. I shouldn't have lost my temper. Thank you for going out."

"Okay. Where do we start?" asked Lili, when Matei finally went outside, closing the main door behind him.

"I wonder what's up with the backpack," said Andrei.

"Ah, that's simple. He's toying with us."

"Yeah, but why?"

"Come on," said Lili, rolling her eyes. "He wants to scare us. To wear us down. He will give us signs that he is there, night after night, until he finds the perfect moment to attack."

"Lili is right," said Albert. "That's what this evil creature did back at my place."

Andrei paled, and his eyes grew larger. "We need to do something. What do we know?"

"We checked for footprints out front, but we left so many ourselves. There's nothing we can make out from that," said Albert. "He could have come from any direction. But we know we have a Strigoi that wants to meet my axe, and at some point, he will attack. We have better defenses than before, but there's only three of us, with Flo and Dan still out."

"What weapons do we have?"

"We have axes, bats and knives," said Albert. "I sharpened wooden spikes out of some stakes. We can stab growlers with them at a distance. I've placed them all around the yard. I think that's it. Oh, and let's not forget the shield that Dan made me build."

"You mean that thing over there?" asked Andrei, pointing at a sizeable object made of planks nailed together and sporting some sharp spikes.

"Yeah. It's just like a police shield, but with spikes. You grab it, keep it close to you, and just charge through the Morois… ahh, growlers. You'll definitely put down a few," said Albert proudly.

"Let's hope we don't need to get that close," said Andrei. "We also need light."

"At night?" asked Lili. "We have the moon and the stars. I can see pretty well after my eyes adjust."

"Yeah, me too. But remember what Grandma Gina used to say, how the Strigoi only goes out at night. I guess that's because he cannot stand the light. 'I hope' would be a better term, perhaps. We need some big fires to cast bright light all over the yard. Hopefully, that will keep it away."

"Excellent idea, Andrei," said Lili, nodding. "Albert, can you make that?"

"Where do you want them?" asked Albert.

"Near the corners of the inner fence," said Lili. "Oh, and I need a better way to be up."

"Up?"

"I need a higher and more comfortable observation point, for checking the surroundings. Sitting on that stupid ladder for hours is not fun."

"I'll see what I can do," said Albert, rising from his chair. "Come help, Andrei."

* * *

The sun was setting, and Albert showed Lili what he and Andrei had built.

In all four corners of the yard, they had put together huge campfires. They'd taken some bricks from the under-construction house across the street and stacked them to build three-foot-tall rectangles. On top, they'd placed metal grills they'd sourced from all around the village. Everything was ready to go, with flammable materials resting on top of the grills.

"See? In case of need, we just start these campfires," said Andrei, enthusiastically, "and then we'll have a lot of light, all over the yard. Even outside, as the light will glow over, and the flames will surely be higher than the fence."

"Nice," said Lili. "I'm impressed."

"This was short notice," added Albert, "but tomorrow we can build one double the size in the middle of the yard. I must check the brick supplies. We need to ensure it doesn't tumble. But I think we can do it."

"That's great. Thank you, Albert," said Lili. "If what Grandma Gina said, and what Andrei is suggesting, is true, with these fires the Strigoi should be unable to come inside our perimeter."

"We should start the fire only when needed, however," said Andrei. "We don't have enough firewood to keep them going all night every night. So we need to set these ablaze only when we think the Strigoi wants to mess with us."

"Do you have any news on Flo and Dan?" asked Albert, suddenly.

"No. I tried the walkie all day. I fear the worst."

"We should go after them!" said Albert, with rage in his eyes. "If anything's happened to Flo, I swear I'll take my axe and go kill every growler, Moroi, Strigoi, demon and devil on this planet!"

"We'll go tomorrow morning," said Lili, with a concerned look. "But I don't know how to make the split, since we need to take care of Mat, and we cannot take him on a rescue mission."

"Yeah, like this didn't happen at least twice before. By the way, where is Mat?" asked Andrei, looking around the yard.

"He's sleeping."

"No way! This early?"

"Yeah. All that playing outside in the snow got to him. I made him some hot tea, he drank it, ate something, and bam! He fell asleep."

"The fat rat!" said Andrei, with a sneer.

"Anyway," continued Lili, "we'll talk tomorrow about a rescue mission. Maybe you'll have to go alone, Albert, with me or Andrei as backup. We'll see. But what is this? Is it the new observation tower?" asked Lili, smiling.

"That's right," said Albert. "You can climb through here. You can stand up there or sit on a chair. It can hold my weight, so you should be okay."

At the front corner of the house, the one closest to the village, Albert had put together a three-by-three-foot platform. It stood on four wooden beams, and Albert had nailed it tightly to the house itself. Albert had also added a ladder, so anyone could reach the top of the eight-foot-tall structure.

"It's nice! I can take a small chair up there with me, and even wear a blanket. You built one on the other side as well, for Andrei?"

"No. There wasn't enough time," said Albert, in an apologetic tone. "But I'll do it tomorrow!"

"Ah, no sweat. You are amazing," said Lili, touching his huge shoulder. "We'll be way better off than last night. Now, let's just hope we have another quiet night."

\* \* \*

They heard a shriek in the distance, just as the sun went down behind the hills. It was coming from the center of the village.

"He's here!" said Andrei, looking around, scared.

"Let's go!" said Albert, grabbing his axe.

They got out of the house, closing the door behind them.

"What do we do about Matei?" asked Andrei.

"He's sleeping. Let him be," answered Lili. "Go to your ladder and check for growlers!"

Lili climbed to the top of her new observation post. She had an eagle's eye view over the front side of the house. It was still quiet, no sign of anything moving.

Suddenly, she made out a shadow. It was on the main road, far away into the village. The moon shone behind it, so it was impossible to distinguish anything but its shape.

"Dad?" she said into the walkie. "Dad, is that you?"

No answer, just as she'd feared. That shade looked skinnier and shorter than her dad. But the distance might have been playing tricks on her, so she had to try.

"What do you mean? Do you see Dan? Over," came Andrei's response in her earpiece.

"I see something. It's approaching."

"What do you see? Over."

"A person. Far away, walking on the street. Check your side. It might be a trick to distract us." Lili continued louder, for Albert to hear. "Hey, Albert. Incoming."

Albert rose from his seat on the porch, axe in hand. "Let them come," he said, determined.

"Well, so far it's only one. We'll see."

"It's him," said Albert, voice filled with hate.

The shadow was approaching. When it was about a hundred yards from their house, it stopped. It looked like it was waiting for something. Suddenly, it raised its hand and pointed toward Lili. As it moved, it became clear that, until then, the shadow had been holding its hands behind its back.

It just stood there, pointing, for a few seconds which seemed like forever.

Lili felt an icy shiver move down her spine. And it got even more intense when the creature let out another shriek.

As this happened, Lili could make out a movement on the road, behind the shadow. It wasn't clear, yet, what it was. But as the seconds passed, she was able to see better and better.

"Oh my God, it's an army!" said Lili into the walkie-talkie.

"What do you mean?" said Andrei, his voice trembling.

Albert climbed the double stairs Lili had used the previous night. "I don't see it," he said, squinting into the distance. "I only see the Strigoi."

"Maybe I have better eyes. But something is far out there in the village, right behind that Strigoi, and it's coming. Yeah, I guess we can assume that is the Strigoi."

Suddenly, everyone heard the noise. It started as a background rumble. But now that noise transformed into growls. Dozens and dozens of growls, overlapping each other.

A few seconds later, Lili could see even better. The army of growlers was fast approaching. They were running, plowing through the snow.

"I can see them!" yelled Albert, suddenly. "They are coming! And they are many!"

As the growlers passed the Strigoi, the noise became overwhelming.

"Anything out back?" yelled Lili into the walkie.

"Nothing!" came Andrei's terrified voice. "What's going on? I can hear growling!"

"Come up front! It's a horde!" yelled Lili, while racing down the ladder.

"I guess that makes us the Alliance?"

"What?"

"Nothing, nothing. It's from a video game. I'm coming!"

Albert was already placing a wooden ladder against the reinforced fence up front.

The growlers reached the front wall just as Albert, Lili, and Andrei made it to the top of their wooden ladders, swinging their axes. Or bat, in Lili's case.

The shade let out another shriek, and the growlers attacked the fence.

Just like at his old house, Albert was swinging his large axe, hitting at least one growler with each move. He was cutting limbs, opening heads. Andrei was doing the same thing, although with less success.

The pile of dead or disabled growlers was growing, but the horde seemed to be overwhelming.

They started pushing the fence. It held, Albert's beams doing an amazing job, but some beams started popping out of place, and Lili saw that.

"We need to secure the beams!" she yelled, as parts of the walls started to shake.

Albert stopped for a moment, looking around. "I'll go push them back!"

"No," said Lili. "You do the killing. You're good at it. Andrei, can you do it?"

"Do what?" asked Andrei, busy swinging his axe.

"Push back the beams, you fool!"

"Oh, yes, I can!"

He got down and started mending the fence. His efforts paid off and the part of the fence which had been in danger of falling was soon reinforced. Still, Andrei had a lot of work to do, as the beams were popping out in various locations.

"Use a spike!" said Albert, seeing Lili's bat swings. "You're not killing anything with that!"

Lili dropped her bat, climbed down, picked up a long spike, and got back up. She started using it at once and landed a few hits, piercing one growler's head and another's belly.

"Yes, it's better!" she yelled, spiking another opponent in the shoulder.

"Mommy, what's going on?" Lili heard a small voice from behind her.

She turned around, only to see Mat standing in the doorway, rubbing his eyes.

"Go back inside!" yelled Lili. "God damn it, Matei! Go back inside!"

"Mommy, I'm scared!" yelled Mat, crying. He froze, large tears running down his cheeks. He was too shaken up; he didn't seem able to move.

"Shit!" said Lili, getting down the ladder. "Go back inside. It's dangerous out here!" she yelled. "Andrei, take Matei back!"

"You take him. I have this beam to hold in place!" yelled Andrei as he shoved a beam that kept popping out at the area of the fence that was the most hard-pressed.

There came another shriek and, just like at Albert's house, the growlers intensified their attack.

"The Strigoi!" yelled Albert. "The Strigoi is coming!"

"Start the fires!" yelled Lili, turning away from Mat. She ran to the one in the corner closest to the village and, with shaking hands, set it ablaze.

"Andrei, get the fires at the back!" yelled Lili, as she dashed toward the campfire at the other corner of the front yard.

Andrei threw down the troublesome beam and darted toward the backyard. He saw Mat in the doorway, crying. "Go back inside, little boy! Go back! Stay inside!"

Matei didn't hear him. He curled down, crying and covering his ears.

\* \* \*

Andrei headed around the house to light the two fires at the other corners.

"What the hell?" he yelled. "Lili! They're attacking from behind as well!"

The fence was moving violently, and a lot of the beams had already toppled.

"Lili! I need help!" he shouted, picking up a beam and trying to put it back in place in the middle of the shakiest part of the fence.

He did a decent job, as the wall's movement decreased.

Still, there were at least three other areas in danger of being torn down, and the fence was creaking all over.

\* \* \*

The shadow was slowly approaching. However, the two fires up front caught fast, and the firelight glowed bright. The pyres shed their light over the whole yard, and now Lili could better grasp what they were up against.

The growlers looked the same. Chalk-white faces, blank yet aggressive stares, always drumming their rotten teeth. They didn't have the strange faces or chests, like the ones from Albert's house. As they tried to get in, they were scratching and biting the fence, sometimes looking up. Their white and dirty hands were getting scraped, cut, and ripped, and teeth were breaking and falling out. A few of them got their upper lips torn off when their teeth got caught between two planks that worked as a lever, yet they didn't seem to care. They were as aggressive as ever, and they weren't tiring.

Lili glimpsed the Strigoi, as the flames cast a light over the street. And he was different.

Lili froze, looking at his face. It was white, like the growlers, but it seemed even paler. However, his eyes were pitch black. The blaze made the Strigoi cover his eyes, shrieking, but she retained the impression of two pieces of coal. And his face was streaked with black lines.

"What the hell! I saw him! I saw the Strigoi!" she yelled, coming back to her senses as soon as the Strigoi covered his eyes, cowering back.

"Where?" said Albert, looking around. "He's mine!"

"He's running away. The fire helped!" said Lili. "Kill those bastards!"

That's when she heard Andrei's scream and growls coming from behind the house.

* * *

The fence fell with a loud crack. Andrei let out a terrified yell, only to attract the first growlers to his position. He randomly swung the axe, backing up toward the front of the house.

Lili and Albert soon joined him, and just in time, as Andrei stood little chance against the coming wave. Soon, the three of them were fighting growlers on the right-hand side of the house. Albert, ferociously swinging his huge axe, was doing the heavy work, putting down or maiming any growler that entered his range. Still, they were being slowly pushed back, and step after step they were getting closer to the front of the house.

Andrei was a bit behind Lili and Albert, jumping around nervously. He was afraid to put too much energy into a swing, fearing he might offer the growlers a suitable spot for a counterattack.

"What the hell are you doing?" asked Lili, taking a quick glance at him. "Kill them!"

"I am killing them!" yelled Andrei, jumping around some more.

Taking another step back, they finally reached a position where they could see the front of the house.

"Mat, no!" yelled Lili, and Andrei turned to look at what she was seeing.

Two growlers were fast approaching Mat, who was curled up in front of the open door, crying.

# 14 QUARRELS

In the morning, Flo barely made it outside the house before she vomited.

"Are you okay?" asked Dan with concern, seeing her pale face as she came back inside.

"No, I'm not," she said, holding her stomach in pain. "I'm sick."

"I'm not feeling too good myself," said Dan, "but I'm not as sick as you. What do you think it was, the pâté or the wine?"

Hearing this, Flo ran out again.

* * *

It was midday, and Flo was still in bed. Dan sat next to her, massaging her hands.

"It's a trick my mother taught me. Feel the pressure I put here? Feel these nodes? You should feel better after this."

"I know about it. My family knew this trick as well. It's something about the lymph nodes. I'm sick. This sucks!" said Flo, flipping out.

"Interesting. They made me think it was a family secret, ever since I was a kid. Maybe it's one of those secret tricks the entire world knows about," said Dan, laughing. "Relax! It happens to all of us. I'm still not feeling a hundred percent myself. Something must have been bad, and I guess it was—"

"Don't say another word, please!"

"Yeah, sorry," he said, continuing to massage her hands.

\* \* \*

They had about one more hour of daylight left, and, finally, Flo was feeling better and could stand.

"I guess if we go now," she said in a faint voice, "we can make it back in time. And the walking should restart my digestion."

"Okay," said Dan. "I'll hold you up if need be, and we can take it slow."

And so they left Grandma's house at last.

"We're too late to pick up things from that store," said Dan, checking the position of the sun. "I don't think we'll get there in time."

"We could spend one more night here and go back home tomorrow at dawn," said Flo.

"No, no, it's better now. If you can walk, now's the best moment. The others must be worried sick," said Dan, and Flo nodded.

Howler was quietly following them.

"How are you, boy? Are you okay?" asked Dan, as Howler's tail swung a few times.

\* \* \*

They could finally see the store to their right.

"Ah, food," said Flo with a bitter smile. "At least Andrei will be happy."

Now it was Dan's turn to smile. "Unfortunately, we don't have enough time nor light to make a full inventory, but let's grab some things anyway. We'll definitely have to return."

They entered the store and started stuffing things into their backpacks, having brief chats here and there about whether to take more sugar or more flour.

Suddenly, Howler assumed an alert position and, as he'd been trained, came to Dan's side, touching his leg.

"What's up—" Dan stopped instantly, turning off his flashlight when he noticed Howler's posture.

"Look, finally, deodorant! This is becoming a rare commodity," said Flo, unaware of what was happening. "It's frozen, but—"

"Shush!" whispered Dan, and Flo understood, turning off her flashlight as well and squatting behind a counter.

A few moments later, they heard a shriek. It seemed to come from outside, yet somewhere close, upfront, in the general direction of the church. The same direction they were heading.

They froze. Flo's eyes started making repetitive, uncontrolled moves, as Howler attempted to yelp. Dan grabbed Flo's hand, looking into her eyes. She relaxed a bit, then Dan quietly shifted closer to the door, trying to peek outside.

Suddenly, he heard growls, just as Howler came to his side, in the same alert state. The sound intensified and soon a few growlers passed by the front of the store, running toward the church.

Dan took a few steps back into the darkness of the store and pulled out his walkie-talkie.

"Hey, Lili, Andrei, are you guys there?" Dan tried a few more times before finally surrendering.

"We're still not in range," he whispered to Flo. "We need to get closer."

"Are you sure about this? What if they see us?"

"If they see us, we'll have to fight. But don't worry. They won't. Hey, boy, enemy! Do you feel the enemy? Enemy!"

Howler moved around a bit, but he didn't go into alert mode again.

"It should be safe now. I can't hear them anymore. Still, let's be careful. And let's leave our backpacks here. They're too heavy, and the food is already frozen, so it cannot go bad. We'll come back for them later."

They headed out, looking around with concern. Their eyes had adjusted to the darkness inside store, so they could see very well outside. On the plus side, there seemed to be no growlers around. However, they saw quite a lot of footprints, all leading toward the side of the village where their base and family were.

"Let's go," said Dan, and started advancing. "Keep your eyes peeled, Flo. If you notice any movement, let me know."

\* \* \*

They finally reached the church. Everything lay still. However, they discovered new tracks everywhere.

"See?" he asked, pointing out the area to Flo. "That wasn't like this yesterday."

"You're right," she whispered. "Our families are in danger."

"Yes, they are. Let's go."

"Try the walkie. It should work from here," said Flo, realizing the opportunity.

"Ah, you're right." Dan pulled out the walkie as they kept moving.

"Hey, Lili, are you there? Are you all right?"

\* \* \*

They were under siege and almost falling.

Lili saw the two growlers going straight for Mat. The kid looked so small, curled up on the doorstep, and the two growlers were only a few steps away. Their white faces blankly staring at Mat, and their mouths bloody and missing some teeth. A few more seconds and they would get him.

Lili yelled and charged toward the two, holding her spike forward. She made a lot of noise, and she managed to get the growlers' attention.

The two growlers used to be muscular people in their forties. It looked like they used to work the fields and do lots of manual labor. From afar, Lili was smaller and shorter than them, and it seemed like she didn't stand a chance.

Still, with a force she never believed she had in her, she put the spike all the way through one of them and made it stumble back on the ground. Screaming, she landed on top of it, right in front of the second growler. All this a few steps away from Mat, who luckily had his eyes shut and was still covering his ears.

The remaining growler's mouth had rotted and it was missing lots of teeth, probably from biting the fence. Nonetheless, it leaped at her, biting her back.

\* \* \*

"No!" yelled Andrei sprinting toward Lili. He grabbed the growler by its clothes. He started pulling, yelling, and fell off the porch, into the snow, landing on his back, with the growler on top of him.

The memory of the large growler that used to live in this house, the one that had suffocated him with its weight, came into his mind, as he realized a monster was, again, fully covering his face.

This time it was a growler's back. The creature was struggling, trying to turn to bite and scratch the living person beneath it. Luckily, this growler was a skinny one, and Andrei, who was still holding its clothes with both hands, easily pulled it down, toward his waist.

Unfortunately, the growler managed to turn its face toward Andrei. The putrid breath that came with every growl it made, engulfed Andrei, just as the monster's teeth bit his lower lip.

Screaming in pain, Andrei pushed it farther down, as Lili grabbed the growler from behind, pulling it off him.

The growler again turned its attention to Lili, trying to grab her, biting the air, scratching with dirty fingernails.

"Step aside," yelled Andrei, and Lili quickly reacted, releasing the monster and taking several swift steps back.

A moment later, Andrei stuck his axe into the middle of the growler's back.

\* \* \*

As she was catching her breath, Lili picked up a voice in her walkie-talkie.

"Hey, Lili, are you there? Are you all right?"

"Dad? Dad! So good to hear your voice! We're overwhelmed! Where are you, can you come help?" she yelled, trying to get up.

"We're still by the church. What happened? Overwhelmed by growlers?"

"Growlers, yes! Come quick! The back fence is down, and the fence in the front doesn't look too good either. Pay attention, Dad. There are growlers on the main street."

"My God, I had its tooth in my mouth!" yelled Andrei, spitting a black tooth into the snow. "How is it? Is there blood?" He pulled down his lower lip, showing it to Lili.

For all this time, Albert had been fending off the remaining growlers at the back of the house—eight or nine of them. Meanwhile, the front fence was losing beams and wavering dangerously.

Lili grabbed her spike and pulled it out of the growler next to Matei.

"There's no time for this. Hurry and take him inside!" she yelled, pointing at Matei, before rushing back to help Albert.

* * *

Dan and Flo were running through the snow as fast as they could, Howler a few steps in front of them.

"Look," said Dan, pointing. "It's a fire!"

Behind the trees and the houses, they could see the sky flickering red.

"Something is burning. Let's go!" said Dan, speeding up.

"Shit, I hope it's not the house," said Flo, also picking up the pace.

As they advanced, they finally came in sight of the house. But Howler suddenly stopped, looking at a fixed point in front of him.

"What is it, boy?" asked Dan closing in, and he immediately noticed a person standing with his back to them.

The moon was behind them, so as they approached, they could make more details. The figure was fully dressed in white, with only a little black patterning. No wonder they hadn't seen it immediately. With all the white snow and black buildings in the background, it had been well camouflaged.

The person seemed restless, moving left and right, sometimes putting his hand in front of his face, covering his eyes, especially when he glanced toward the fire.

He moved differently from a growler. There was no drunken swaying, and he had full control over his hands. He moved as a normal person would. But there was something strange about him, and Dan's heart missed a beat.

Straight ahead, in the distance, the growlers were attacking the front fence of their house. A lot of them lay on the ground, squirming or fully dead. Still, more than a dozen remained and were pushing forward, trying to break in. There were fires in the yard, but the house was not burning.

Dan let out a relieved sigh and continued his approach, carefully keeping an eye on that person.

They got to about fifty yards behind him, and additional details were now visible.

"He's fully naked!" said Flo, suddenly.

The sound of her voice, although way fainter than the noise of the fight, made the person turn.

"Oh my God, Dan!" yelled Flo. "It's like your disease! The skin you had!"

Dan saw it. Black vines traversed the man's entire body, just like the ones he used to have on his back.

"It's the Strigoi!" said Flo, stopping, looking around as if trying to find a way out.

Dan squeezed Tiny in his left hand and charged. The Strigoi stood his ground, then leaned forward, throwing his hands to sides and loosing a ferocious shriek.

Dan could see the black eyes and tongue moving as he released his demonic shout.

"You'll die now!" yelled Dan, charging and raising his axe.

Suddenly, the Strigoi veered to Dan's right and, with extreme agility, jumped over a six-foot fence without even touching it.

"Shit!" said Dan, looking around. "Go, boy, follow him! Enemy! Go!"

Howler started running down the main street, along the fences, going back toward the church. He was looking to his left, toward the side of the village where the Strigoi had disappeared. Dan followed close behind.

\* \* \*

Flo remained in the middle of the road. She saw the creature jump and after that Howler and Dan setting off in pursuit. In the distance, near the sieged house, she saw the growlers turning, leaving the fence and running toward her and Dan.

"They're coming back, Dan!" she yelled. "The shriek called them! They're coming here! Where do we go?"

* * *

Dan stopped and turned, seeing the incoming horde.

"Shit!" he yelled. "Come, follow me!"

Flo listened, and soon they were all running toward the church. Howler was far ahead, still following the Strigoi, looking left, to where he sensed the creature, which, by the looks of it, was heading for the church.

The growlers were gaining on them, and the noise grew louder.

"Howler, back!" Dan commanded, and Howler ended his pursuit, returning to his side. "Here!" said Dan again, pointing to a green-painted house to the left. "Come here. Flo, Howler, come on!"

They entered the house's yard, the one where he and Howler had trained for so many days. Dan closed the yard gate as they entered, pushing the latch into place.

"Hold this door," he said, and Flo pushed with her hands while he put his back against it, jamming his feet into the ground. "And be quiet."

The growlers came, pounding their bodies on the gate.

One after one, they hit it, crowding together until, finally, they went dormant.

Dan glanced at Flo and touched his finger to his lips. They moved away, quietly, until they reached the back of the house. There, they started whispering.

"We're safe, for now," said Dan. "Relax, Flo. We're good. Hey, look at me, relax. We're good."

Flo was looking around, panting. She slowly relaxed, only to collapse into Dan's arms.

"I'm afraid. What happened to the others? Are they okay?"

"It's okay to be afraid. I don't know about the others. I'll ask."

He realized his earpiece had slipped out. When he put it back in, he heard Lili's desperate voice. "Dad, please answer! Where are you?"

\* \* \*

"Ah, Dad, finally," said Lili, and she started crying, nervously. "I thought we'd lost you! How are you?"

"We're okay." She could hear his whisper in her earpiece. "We hid at the house we've used for training. How are you?"

"We're safe. A growler bit me, but don't worry, it didn't go through my coat. It hurts and I've got a bruise, but I think I'll be fine. Andrei wasn't so lucky. A growler bit his lip. There is some blood, but he's in one piece. After that we heard a new shriek, and all the growlers turned and left."

"On his lip? Jesus. And yes, the shriek. I think that was our doing. We saw the Strigoi. We attacked him, and apparently we scared him off."

"Really? Oh my God! Is it the same Strigoi or another one?"

"I have no idea. We'll come s—"

A new shriek made both Dan and Lili stop using the walkie-talkie. This time it was coming from the middle of the village, where the church was.

\* \* \*

All the growlers at the gate woke, got up, and then, growling, started running back toward the center of the village.

"The coast is clear," said Dan, whispering into the walkie-talkie and to Flo at the same time. "We're coming back."

They slowly opened the latch, peeked outside and then stepped into the street. They saw the backs of the growlers as they returned to their leader. Flo, Dan, and Howler took a right toward their house. As they walked, they caught sight of another group of growlers coming their way, about half a dozen strong.

"What the hell?" said Flo. "More Morois? Should we go back to the house?"

"No way. They're too close. We can do this. Howler, stay. Flo, come with me."

Howler stopped, waiting, at the same moment Dan and Flo turned back, running again toward the center of the village.

Dan made enough noise to attract and hold the attention of the seven growlers. He talked loudly, although he made sure not to alert the first group that was already on its way toward the church.

All seven growlers were following him. They went past Howler, ignoring him, as Howler stayed put, alert yet silent. The fastest one got close to Dan, and Dan stopped, turned, and swung his left hand. Tiny cracked open the growler's skull.

As another one approached, Dan pushed it back with his axe and got ready to strike. Still, the other five were near, and they would soon overwhelm him.

"Howler, bark!" he ordered. Howler started barking, while Dan suddenly went silent.

The six growlers slowed and then turned, going for the noisy dog, just as Dan killed the closest one, hitting him from behind.

Five growlers left, now all running toward Howler.

"Howler, quiet! Quiet, boy!"

Howler stopped barking.

"Hey, ugly monsters! Right here!" said Dan, making noise, as he hit another growler from behind.

"Just four of you left, aren't you?" he continued to banter in a loud voice. "Not so strong now, eh?"

His plan worked. As the remaining four turned once more time, one of them was faster and closer to Dan. And once again Dan put him down with a fast strike.

The remaining three closed in.

"Howler, bark!"

\* \* \*

"Oh my God, Howler, you're incredible!" said Flo, petting the dog. "I've never seen anything like this before."

"You're a smart boy, aren't you?" said Dan, joining in the petting. "Now, let's go back," he continued, looking at Flo. "All this noise might have attracted the other pack that was moving toward the church, and I'm in no mood to find out."

# 15 STAKEOUT

I t was a little past midnight, and the three of them were in the front yard.

Matei was sleeping in his bedroom. Andrei had carried him there after the kid cried himself to sleep in front of the house's door, during the growler attack.

Albert was resting his massive body on his axe, wheezing. His chest moved up and down, and it looked like he was doubling in size whenever he inhaled.

"Oh my God, Andrei, you saved my life," said Lili, jumping to hug him.

"Yeah, and you saved Matei. It was incredible what you did," he said, looking like he was trying to control his emotions.

"And your idea with the fire, I think it saved us all," continued Lili. "I saw him coming, the Strigoi. He was coming to kill us," she continued, crying some more. "But the fire pushed him back. I saw him cover his face. And you, Albert. If it weren't for you facing down a dozen growlers, alone, we would have been—"

"Ouch," said Andrei, touching his lip.

"Oh, how's your lip?" She instantly switched her tone to one of concern, trying to get a good look at his mouth.

"It hurts. It bled a lot, and I kept on sucking the blood out of it, then spitting it out. I'll go add some mashed onions and garlic. If Dan got some sort of bacterial infection when bitten, that should be enough to stop it from spreading."

"At least it didn't bite the lip off," Lili said, slowly petting his sweaty hair and looking at him with love. "You would still be ugly, but that war scar would have made you look sexy for a change."

"So you're into fat *and* ugly people?" said Andrei, mimicking surprise.

"Hey, open up!" They suddenly heard Dan's voice from behind the gate.

"What took you so long?" said Lili, as Flo, Dan, and Howler entered the yard. "You've been away for two days. What happened?" asked Lili, even as she gave Dan a long hug.

Dan told them about the store and how they'd postponed their return since they'd wanted to grab everything by daylight, and then about the further delays when they got food poisoning from the old cans. Or was it the cheap wine?

"Still, good thing we're back in time," concluded Dan. "However, I have to go."

"What? Go where?" asked Lili with a frown, as everyone else turned, looking at him.

"I have an idea about that Strigoi. I think I know where he is, and I want to gather some intel. And who knows, if I'm lucky I could end this."

"Is it really a Strigoi?" asked Andrei, looking around the yard without blinking. "Are you sure?"

Lili rolled her eyes, huffing.

"Ah, we forgot to mention," said Dan. "We saw the Strigoi, real close. I almost got him. Got to within eight yards of him, maybe less. I attacked him, but he ran away."

"I'll come with you and we'll kill him," said Albert, suddenly.

"No, no," said Dan, shaking his head. "You need to defend this place. I don't even know if my hunch is correct. Plus, he has an army of growlers with him. Now's not the moment to fight out in the open. Let me see what I can find out. It will be like a stakeout, back in the day."

"What do you mean 'end it'? Dad, you must be careful," said Lili, barging into the discussion.

"I will be careful, honey, I will. I'll act only if I get an excellent opportunity, one in which I'm positive I'd make it out alive. Just like a stakeout," he said, smiling.

"You should have seen Howler," interrupted Flo, grabbing everyone's attention. "He can sense where the Strigoi is. He followed him, even though we couldn't see him. He and Dan made a great team. They managed to kill seven Morois, just by ping-ponging them between them."

"How did you do that?" asked Lili.

"They split up, so as to be several dozen yards apart. Dan would make some noise, then Howler would make noise. Then Dan again, and so on. And the stupid Morois were just running between the two. And Dan was either behind the slowest one, killing it, or in front of the faster one, also killing it."

"Ah, you were kiting them?" said Andrei, with an impressed tone.

"What?" asked Dan.

"Never mind. It's something used in computer games," said Andrei, waving his right hand.

Lili rolled her eyes and continued. "But you told me you were safe. When did you meet seven new growlers?"

"I don't know why," said Dan, "but there was a second batch of growlers, after the first one."

"Hmm. Maybe it was the group that attacked at the back of the house? They probably needed more time to go around. Then they must have fallen dormant sooner, since they weren't chasing you," theorized Andrei.

"Perhaps," said Dan. "Now, I have to go."

"Please be safe out there!" whispered Lili, hugging her dad.

"Yes, I will, don't worry. I'll take Howler with me. Until then, clean up the yard. And do something about the back fence."

* * *

"Okay, we have to get rid of the dead growlers," said Lili, looking around the house. There were a few of them inside the perimeter and a lot more out front.

"Albert, Andrei, can you take them across the street, to the house under construction? We stored a few there in the past."

"Okay, Lili," said Albert, and he went to grab the first growler's leg. It immediately started squirming.

"Oh," added Lili, "and silence them."

"Not a problem," said Albert, with a flicker in his eyes.

* * *

"Come on, boy," said Dan, speeding up. "We need to get there fast. He mustn't have time to prepare or run away."

Howler let out a short, happy yelp, following Dan along the snowy road. The tracks were fresh and visible, and clearly a large number of growlers had moved up and down that night.

Soon, they reached the place where they'd killed the seven growlers. Dan stopped, put down Tiny, and, with his left hand, pulled out the knife.

He got close to the first growler and pushed the blade into its heart. It let out a dying hiss, waking the others. But that didn't bother Dan, who finished off the other six one by one.

He then went back, picked up his axe, and continued his journey.

* * *

They finally saw the good-old green-painted house, entered the yard, and moved on around back. As he examined the surroundings, Dan noticed that a house closer to the village center, a few hundred yards away, had a tall barn with an attic space.

"See that, boy?" he asked, squatting near Howler. "That's where we need to go. I bet we can see right into the churchyard from up there. But how do we get there?"

He looked around. The fences between the properties were tall. He could jump them, surely, but there was no way for Howler to do it.

"We could go back to the main street and check the house's gate. What do you think, boy?"

Still, Dan wasn't satisfied.

"I just don't want to go on the main road. What if the Strigoi comes back? No," he said, looking around, "we need to stay off the road, so we can hide quickly, in case of need."

As he moved around the yard, he saw the gate leading to the

back of the property. Like most others in the village, this house also had a split. The primary living area, containing the house and annex buildings was upfront, and behind the house lay the field, where people had their vegetable gardens, orchards, or various crops. This was a short, flimsy fence, with a simple door leading out back. They quickly passed into the field and looked around.

Luckily, the fences between the properties were smaller here than in the back gardens, only about three feet, and most were made from soft metal mesh. Moreover, unlike in the front yards, back here there were almost no trees or buildings, so the view was unobstructed.

"Shit, boy," whispered Dan as they approached the fence separating the green-painted house's field from the one next to it. "There are a lot of tracks in the snow here. Come, boy, let's be careful."

They slowly got closer to the fence.

"Oh, boy," said Dan, suddenly squatting and holding Howler. "Someone stepped this fence down. Tracks are going everywhere. So this is how that Strigoi put together his assault, without us even knowing it. See? He took the back roads. He went behind the houses and spied on us from back here."

Dan stood and glanced about, trying to get as much information as possible from the tracks. Luckily, the moon was up, so he could see into the distance. And as far as the eye could see, the tracks went from one property to another, fences broken between them.

"Hmm. These tracks have distinctive shapes and sizes, boy," he said, squatting again near the path. "This means he moved growlers through here more than once. That's interesting. We need to decide; do we take this route or the road?" said Dan, considering the two options carefully. He looked around a bit longer, petted Howler, then spoke to him again. "We're here already, so come on, let's go," he said, and started walking toward the church.

\* \* \*

They reached the field behind the house with the tall barn. Upon reaching the backyard, Dan gingerly opened the door to the front of the property. Inside, they were greeted by silence. Next to the gate they noticed a dog kennel, and inside it they could see the tiny snout of a frozen, skinny dog.

"Poor thing," whispered Dan, while petting Howler. "He probably starved to death. Come on, let's go, boy."

They quietly approached the barn.

It was unlocked. Dan opened the door cautiously, peeking inside. Because of the pitch-black darkness, he couldn't see anything.

"Boy," he whispered. "Enemy, boy!"

Howler got alert and started sniffing. Still, after a few dozen seconds, he relaxed.

"Okay, so I guess it's clear, huh? I sure hope you're not mistaken."

Dan took a few steps inside and stood there, waiting for his eyes to adjust. He could soon see the interior of the barn. It was about forty by sixty feet, and it looked more like an old garage than a normal barn. He discovered a few old cars, taken apart or just left to rust.

"What do you know, boy, an illegal chop shop? I bet the local policeman knew about this but turned a blind eye. What do you think, boy?"

Howler moved around a bit, enthusiastic.

The barn's ceiling was high, fifteen or maybe even twenty feet, and Dan noticed the attic could not be reached from the inside. He went out and walked the perimeter. He finally saw a wooden staircase behind the barn. It was built against the barn itself on the length of half a wall, at an angle close to forty-five degrees, going from the ground up to the large roof. You could actually go up and down without needing to use your hands.

He started up, and Howler followed, taking shaky steps and whimpering. When he reached the top, Dan saw there was no trapdoor at the entrance, so he went straight into the attic.

"Relax, boy," said Dan, turning back. "Come on, you can do it. A few more steps."

Finally, Howler reached the flat surface of the attic and frolicked around a bit, until Dan helped him relax.

Inside, it felt like a train wagon. The attic had a roof with two sides, at an angle which made the space feel narrow and long. On the two opposing sides stood two wooden walls, each with a large opening in the middle. One faced the churchyard, and through the other Dan could vaguely get a glimpse of the yard of their own house, far in the distance. This sort of place was usually built for storing hay over the winter, but luckily this particular one was empty.

"See, boy? We'll hide behind this wall and carefully gaze through these openings at the world outside. Make sure you stay behind me, right boy?" he said, looking at the dog.

He moved some wooden boxes around, trying to create improvised stools, making as little noise as possible.

"See, boy? Now we can sit on either side of the openings, and just slowly inch our heads out. You stay here, okay?" He petted the dog once more. "Let's see what the others are doing."

"Hey, Lili," he whispered, using his walkie-talkie. "Are you there, honey?"

"Yes, Dad, I'm here," she answered after a few moments. "What's up? You okay?"

"Yes, yes, I'm fine. I found a suitable place to spy on the church. I'll let you know what I find out."

"So you think he's in the church?"

"I guess so, yeah. It makes sense, given the info I have."

"Okay, Dad. Take care!"

"Yeah, I will. See you tomorrow. Go to bed if you can, but lock the door. Pay attention and be safe, okay honey? Oh, and keep the walkie nearby."

"Yes, yes, Dad. We will. We still have a few bodies to move. I'll leave this turned on. If you need anything, just say so, okay?"

"Yes, honey, okay."

* * *

Dan had a wide view of the church property, about fifty yards from his location. He could see the entrance to the church itself, the roof of the house in which he'd almost died, the gazebo covering the cellar at the back, and, most importantly, nearly all of the yard.

It was quiet, and he and Howler sat there, watching.

Minutes passed, and then hours. Dan had dozed off, when

suddenly Howler's head came under his right arm, waking him.

"What—" he said, and quickly controlled himself.

In front of the church, on its porch, stood the Strigoi. He was looking around, left to right.

Suddenly, he started walking, heading toward the main road, where he took a right, continuing in the direction of their base.

"Hey, Lili. Lili, answer!"

"Ugh, Dad, what's up?" said Lili in a sleepy voice. "Are you all right?"

"The Strigoi is coming your way."

"Shit!"

"Yeah, I know. I can't see him from up here anymore, so I'm not sure where he's heading. He might stop somewhere else, but he went your direction down the road. He seems to be alone, but stay alert."

"Fine. We'll make sure we have strong fires in the fireplaces, just in case he plans to enter the house."

"Right. That's clever."

"Exactly. But as a precaution, I'll wake Albert, you know, for his smashing skills."

"Right."

"So, his lair is at the church? Over," Andrei suddenly asked over the earpiece.

"Yes, he's here," said Dan, who now moved toward the other opening. "I saw him on the porch."

"It makes sense," said Andrei. "They probably live in the basement, where they don't freeze. Over."

"They?" asked Lili, before Dan could use his walkie. "I hope you mean the growlers."

"Yes, the growlers, not other Strigois. At least, I hope not. Over."

\* \* \*

For minutes and minutes, Dan kept looking left to right, sliding between the two openings, trying to get a glimpse of the Strigoi and his movements.

Finally, about twenty minutes into it, Howler let out a brief whine, and Dan joined him, just in time to see the Strigoi reaching the church's entrance, running.

"Man, he's fast," he muttered, picking up the walkie. "Hey, Lili. False alarm. He's back. Everything okay on your side?"

"Yeah, we're fine," said Lili. "That damn thing. We'll never sleep again until we get rid of him."

"I have a straight line of sight to him," said Dan, after a few moments. "I could try my gun. But it's far, and I still can't trust my right hand," he said, looking at the improvised cast keeping his finger in place. "I could try a left-handed shot. But I'm not confident at all."

"No, don't try it, unless it's a sure hit. If you miss, you'll be in danger."

"Ah, too late now anyway. He just entered the church. The bad news: he can open doors."

"Great," said Lili, audibly irritated.

"Yeah," he agreed. "Oh, he's out again. Let's see what he's up to. Over and out," he said, putting the walkie back on his belt.

The Strigoi stood on the porch, and, just like last time, spent a few minutes looking left and right.

Suddenly, he let out a shriek. This time it sounded fainter than usual. After that, he started walking toward the road once again. A few seconds later, Dan could hear growls.

"Hey, Lili," he said with an alert voice. "This is not good. Do you hear me?"

"Yeah, Dad, what's going on?"

"He's going toward you again, but this time he has about a dozen growlers with him."

"Are you sure?"

"Yeah. I see them."

"Shit… shit, shit!" he could hear, then a few moments of silence.

"Hey, honey. Stay put. Twelve growlers are a lot, but they can't enter the house if Albert holds the door. If you see them closing in, let me know and I'll come back and help."

"I've already woken Albert," said Lili. "He's ready. He wants to go out and kill them all. I've convinced him to stay put. But, Dad, we need to do something about that thing. We cannot go on like this."

179

"Yeah, I agree. Let's keep the channel open. Keep me posted," said Dan.

"I'll take care of everyone, don't you worry, Dan." Dan heard Andrei's voice, loud in his earpiece.

"Andrei, channel open means not talking," answered Lili.

"Yeah, I know."

"Then don't talk."

"You don't talk."

"Jesus," muttered Dan, putting down his walkie.

* * *

Minutes slowly passed. Lili gave regular status reports, saying "All okay so far" into Dan's earpiece. Dan acknowledged with a short "Roger", and then the waiting began once more.

Suddenly, Howler became alert.

"What is it, boy?" whispered Dan, trying to figure out what Howler sensed.

Shortly after, Dan realized he could hear a humming.

"What is that?" whispered Dan, moving between the two openings.

When he saw the procession, he suddenly understood.

The Strigoi was leading the way, walking confidently. He wasn't tall, he was actually shorter than all the growlers behind him, but the way he walked, almost pompously, made him look taller.

The dozen or so growlers were following him. Seven of them were pulling the seven dead growlers Dan had left in the street.

"Lili! Are you there?" whispered Dan.

"Yes, Dad. We're okay. No sign of the Strigoi or any growlers."

"Yeah, I know. I'm looking at them now. I think I know what he's doing. He went back to collect his dead. He's grabbed the seven growlers Howler and I killed earlier. Unless he picked up yours, but I suppose you had more than seven."

"No, we put our kills near the house under construction," said Lili. "We heard nothing, so probably they're yours."

"He can use the back roads. But in this case, he took the main street. Anyway, this is bad. He's resurrecting them, I'm sure!"

"This is bad, I agree. This is terrible. What's he doing now?"

"I'll stop talking. I don't know why, but I'm afraid he might hear me. I suspect he has incredible sight, so what if he has enhanced hearing too? I'll let you know what I see in a little while. Over and out."

The Strigoi let out a shriek, and the live growlers dropped the dead ones in front of the church. Moments later, they started falling, dormant.

The Strigoi moved around, looking at the growlers scattered in front of him. He seemed to make a decision, and he approached one of the dead growlers on the ground, a smaller one, and started eating its hands.

Dan stood there, watching from behind the wooden wall in the attic, as the Strigoi consumed first the dead growler's left hand and then the right one. He took his time, eating and chewing slowly, and about twenty minutes later, only the bones remained.

"Dad, are you still there?" he heard through the walkie.

"Yeah," whispered Dan, shifting back behind the wooden wall. Still, out of the corner of his eye, he glimpsed the Strigoi turning toward his attic opening.

*Shit*, thought Dan, as he pulled back his head. He stood there, quiet, his heart the size of a flea.

"Okay," he heard. "Glad you're good. I'll leave you to it. Over and out."

Dan finally built up the courage to look again, inching his head out. With his right eye, he could see the Strigoi was still on the porch. Now he wasn't looking all around. It seemed like he was focused on the barn.

Dan pulled back slowly. Could this be it? Had he been made? Another few minutes passed before he leaned his head forward again, trying to catch a glimpse.

The Strigoi was in the same position, hands behind his back.

*What if that's his way of going dormant?* As he relaxed a bit, Dan suddenly realized something was happening with the Strigoi. The moon and stars were reflecting their light onto the Strigoi's body, and Dan could see his belly moving. It was like something was inside it, pushing outwards from within.

This continued for several minutes, and Dan kept watching.

Suddenly, the Strigoi moved. He turned to his left and went to the first dead growler lying in the snow. It was the one whose head Dan had cracked open with the axe, then later pierced with a knife.

The Strigoi squatted over the dead body.

"Oh my God," whispered Dan, as he saw the Strigoi vomiting. Something like a gooey paste fell on the dead growler's head and oozed farther down its chest.

From the distance, it seemed much like toothpaste, but it was pitch black.

He repeated the move on the other six growlers, including the one with the eaten hands, and then he turned, suddenly, looking toward the attic where Dan and Howler hid.

Dan quickly pulled back, taken by surprise. "Shit, he saw us," he whispered to Howler.

A few seconds later, he peeped again. The Strigoi was gone, but the growlers were still there. On their chests and faces the vomit grew, a bit like a dough. It spread, fully covering their faces and the better part of their chests, and now it moved up and down fast, like accelerated breathing.

"Lili, I think I know how he resurrects them! You were right. The ones with strange faces and chests had been resurrected!"

Howler came to him, pushing against his hand.

Dan suddenly stopped, understanding what he meant. "Shit!" he exclaimed, putting down the walkie.

Howler was looking toward the access ladder. Dan ran over there, only to see the Strigoi just outside the barn, running toward the stairs.

"This time you're mine!" said Dan, dropping Tiny and picking up the gun with his left hand.

The Strigoi took a few steps up the stairs, before jumping the rest of the way. He looked up at Dan. He was grinning, and bits of putrid meat were visible, stuck between his teeth.

Dan aimed the gun and fired.

\* \* \*

"Dad?" said Lili, using the walkie-talkie, hands shaking. "This is horrible. But are you okay? What happening over there?"

Pause.

"Hey, Dan, answer!" She heard Andrei talking into his walkie-talkie.

"Give him time to answer, you idiot!"

"He had time to answer. Why are you yelling at me?"

"Be quiet!"

They waited for a few more seconds.

"Dad! Dad, are you there? Please answer."

\* \* \*

The gun went off. But the Strigoi wasn't there anymore.

Dan looked through the opening, but he didn't see him. Howler was looking out the attic opening facing the church. Dan joined him and he soon saw the Strigoi running toward the church, jumping over any fences in his path.

Dan fired two more shots, trying to get him, but he missed. Just then the first golden rays of sunshine burst from behind a hill.

"Goddamn it!" he said, picking up his walkie. "Yeah, I'm here," said Dan with a bitter voice.

"Oh, thank God! Are you okay?"

"Yes, Lili, I'm fine. I had a clear shot, but I missed."

"What do you mean?"

"He was coming up a ladder in the barn attic I'm in. I pulled out the gun and fired. I guess he understood something bad was going to happen, so he pushed on the barn's wall and jumped to the side. I heard a noise right after. I think he hit something, but he didn't seem hurt."

"Don't worry. We'll get him eventually."

"Yeah. We're coming home, over and out," said Dan.

# 16 HEARTS ARE BURNING

It was a beautiful morning. The sun was shining, and Dan and Howler were just entering the yard of their house.

Albert was there, opening the secured gate for them.

"Hey Albert. How are you, buddy?"

"I heard you found that son of a bitch," he said, spitting on the ground. "Let's go get him."

"Yeah, we will. Wait a bit. We need to discuss."

"What is there to discuss, Dan? I want to kill him."

"And we will. But let's talk for a moment. Hey, Albert. Look at me. We'll get this guy, this thing, whatever it is, okay? Trust me on this."

"Okay, Dan," said Albert in a calmer tone.

"How's the back fence?"

"I put it upright after the Morois, um, growlers left. But it's in awful shape. A lot of the beams are broken. I'll need more time to do a proper job."

"This is bad. It was a sturdy fence," said Dan, looking at it from afar. "Let's talk and we'll see what we can do."

"Where's the kid?" asked Dan, once they got inside.

"He's sleeping, Dad. Let's not waste time, as he might wake at any moment. And we need to sleep afterwards," said Lili, yawning.

"Okay. So I've seen with my own eyes how he resurrects the dead growlers. He eats some growler meat, after that something happens inside of him, and about half an hour later he vomits on the wounds. That disgusting goo was pitch black and looked thick. I guess it fixes the growler, which, as a result, then has that strange face and chest like we saw at Albert's house."

"That's it then," said Andrei. "It was nice knowing all of you."

"Stop it," said Lili. "I said let's not waste time. Dad, in that case, how can we kill the growlers?"

"I know my mother had some details about how to kill a Moroi, but I never really listened properly, so I might be wrong," he said, looking down, trying to remember. "She said something about burning their hearts."

"My mother told us a lot of things on this subject," said Albert, while Flo nodded.

"What did she say?" asked Lili.

"It's basically some gruesome thing, as Dan mentioned," intervened Flo. "You need to cut the heart out and burn it."

"Probably the burning is just superstition," said Andrei, frowning. "Sounds more plausible that the removal of the heart does it. To me, it's clearer than ever that's where their core is." As he finished his sentence, Andrei's expression remained blank, looking through the people, like he was ruminating.

"Sounds about right," said Dan. "Yet what I've seen gives me the shivers. I wonder if we just remove it, maybe he can put back the infected heart then 'glue' everything in place with his vomit."

"Jesus, that's gruesome," said Flo.

"Back where?" asked Andrei, returning from his thoughts.

"Back inside the growler, dufus," said Lili, rolling her eyes. "Pay attention!"

"Ah, you're probably right, Dan," said Andrei in a hyped tone. "Possibly that's why Grandma mentioned the burning of the heart. There might be some religious stuff involved, but the fundamental reason was to make sure the heart was gone. That way, the Strigoi can't bring a Moroi back to life, no matter what. It's like a computer. If you remove the processor, the CPU, it doesn't work anymore. And if you further destroy the CPU, no one can put it back in."

Everyone sat there, thinking.

"Okay, then, I will say it," said Flo. "We have to remove the hearts from all the Morois we killed."

Everyone took a deep breath, while Flo quickly added, "I propose the men do it!" at the same moment Andrei opened his mouth to suggest something else.

"Damn," added Andrei, grieving the lost opportunity. "We can't. Dan has his right hand in a cast. And I'm also suffering from—"

"I'll remove the cast," said Dan, interrupting his plea. "I think I'm fine. If I feel any pain, I'll put it back on."

"Are you sure?" asked Andrei. "For your own health, you should—"

"Yeah, right, you're thinking about his health," interrupted Lili. "Now, go do the job."

"Why don't you do it?" asked Andrei. "Why is this a man's job?"

"It's not," said Lili, "but Flo already called you should do it," she continued, grinning.

"That doesn't count."

"Yes, it does."

"No, it doesn't."

"Stop it, both of you," snapped Dan. "We'll do it. Yes, *we*, the men," he added, just as Andrei wanted to say something.

\* \* \*

Dan was sitting at the table, slowly removing the bandage and then the splints. He looked at his thumb. It was white, with long traces where the splints used to be.

"It doesn't look swollen anymore," he said, turning it around.

He gingerly squeezed his hand into a fist.

"This hurts a bit. And it feels odd. But I think it's way better."

"Is it?" asked Flo, who was sitting beside him.

"Yeah. Thank you."

"No problem," she said, smiling happily.

Lili entered the room at that point and glanced quickly between the two of them.

\* \* \*

A short while later, Dan, Andrei, and Albert were in the yard of the house under construction. That's where they'd stashed the twenty or so growlers from the previous night. The cold had frozen them, and the ice seemed to have glued them together.

Below this pile were the growlers they had already dispatched a few weeks ago when they cleaned up the house they were now using as a base: the huge man who had almost killed Andrei, the woman, and the two children. Since several weeks had passed, it was clear these were fully frozen. Way in the back was the cradle with the toddler in it. Still, no one wanted to go and check on that.

"This will be a tough one," said Dan, looking around.

"I'll get all their hearts out, no problem," said Albert with a crazy look in his eyes.

Dan and Andrei exchanged a glance.

"What if we set all of them on fire as they are?" asked Andrei.

"We'd need too much wood," said Dan. "And I'm not sure I want to build a huge funeral pyre just to kill two dozen growlers."

"I see what you mean," said Andrei. "Well, I guess it's up to you, Albert." Andrei tried a smile, but no one else joined him.

"Let's do it," said Albert, squeezing his huge axe in his left hand. He got close and grabbed one growler with his right hand. Luckily, the growlers on top of the pile were not yet completely frozen, so they could be easily moved.

He pulled it a few steps away, onto the ground, then swung his axe and split the growler's chest in half, clothes and everything.

Dan stepped closer, sizing up the situation. The cut was large, but it wasn't enough room to put his hand inside. "Those bones look sharp," he said. "I'll need some worker gloves, and I don't want to ruin mine."

"There are some in the house, left behind by the construction crew," said Albert, pointing toward the house. "I used some myself when I did the insulation."

The heavy-duty gloves were duly found, and with them on, Dan was able to pull apart the sliced chest and expose the heart. He could do that without using his thumbs. Still, there was a slight shake in his right hand when he tensed his muscles.

"Oh my God," said Andrei, almost vomiting. "Why is it so black?"

"I guess this proves your CPO, SPO, or whatever theory you

had," said Dan.

"CPU."

"That's where the new brains are. And here's that black thing all over again."

"If we impale this," said Albert, pointing at the black heart, "the growler dies. Then the Strigoi comes, vomits black shit all over it, and the growler lives again?"

"Succinctly put," said Dan.

"Okay, then remove it," said Andrei.

"Okay, fine. But you need to keep the chest open," said Dan, looking up at Andrei.

"What? No. I can't."

"Why not?"

"Ahh… I don't have gloves?" tried Andrei.

"There are a few extra in the house," said Dan. "Go get some."

Andrei went to retrieve the gloves, mumbling.

"Kids these days," said Albert. "I had to force mine to learn to kill a chicken for soup. Chopping its head off was too much for them. They were so opposed. 'They are living creatures', 'they have feelings', 'I can't do this to another being'," he said, with a sigh. "They learned, eventually, but they wouldn't even hear about killing pigs. They help, they hold it and all that, but I'm still the one putting that knife in the pig's throat every Christmas."

"Yeah. Still, this is different, Albert," said Dan, looking up.

"Why is it different? These are not human beings anymore. Even worse, they're monsters."

Dan said nothing, studying Albert's face as he looked at the opened-up growler with hate in his eyes.

"Come on, already," yelled Dan, just as Andrei showed up.

"Yes, yes, hold your horses," said Andrei, pulling on his worker gloves with little enthusiasm.

"Okay, good. Now, hold this open while I take out the CPO."

"CPU!"

"Right, that."

Andrei put his hands into the growler's chest, looking the other way.

"Okay, now separate the two parts. Yup, like that. Pull. Stronger, come on. Yeah, great," said Dan, while he grabbed at the exposed heart with his left hand. "It's larger than a normal heart, I think."

"How can you tell?" said Andrei, looking anywhere but at what Dan was doing.

"I learned in school it should be the size of your fist. This is double that. Oh, and it's linked to other organs."

"What do you mean 'linked'?"

"It has tubes going everywhere."

"Yeah, that's normal," said Andrei sarcastically. "The heart links with veins and arteries. You know, for blood to flow."

"Yes, but there are more than usual. Way more. A few dozen of them. These aren't all veins and arteries, right?" asked Dan. "I need a knife," he said, trying to grab his with his right hand. The knife sheath was on the left-hand side, so he had some issues getting it.

"Now, if I just cut these links," he said, and started cutting. "Oh, it's bleeding," he said, more alert.

"Bleeding? No way," said Andrei, looking the other way.

"No, not bleeding, but some black stuff is leaking out. Ah, not too much. I jumped the horse on that one. Sorry," said Dan, his voice spiking in tandem with his moving right hand as he cut the heart free. "Puah, it stinks. It's that moldy odor again."

"If anyone had told me a few months back I'd be doing this," said Andrei, "I would have said he was crazy. Yeah, that smell is awful," he continued, retching.

"Tell me about it. I'm the one doing the actual cutting. There, it's out!" said Dan, holding up the heart. "But my right thumb hurts a bit. I think you'll need to do the next one."

"What?" said Andrei, who finally glanced at the heart Dan was holding. That's when he started vomiting.

"Oh, man," said Albert, puffing. "Kids."

* * *

A few hours later they had two buckets filled with black hearts.

"Now, let's burn these," said Dan. "Andrei, can you start a fire?"

Andrei was pale as a sheet of paper. He had vomited three more times during the process, but he got good at cutting out the growlers' black hearts.

"Yeah," he answered faintly.

\* \* \*

The fire was burning hot, and Dan put in the first heart. He kept on adding the others, slowly, until all lay in the pyre.

Lili approached. "Oh, so this is the cause of the smell," she said.

The odor was foul. It smelled like burned meat, but there was something else alongside that.

"It's the same thing I smelled in that basement," she said, "when I was looking for you, Dad. It's this moldy odor. It's so powerful it's suffocating."

"It's probably the black tar stuff," said Dan, nodding. "We noticed it since we started cutting the hearts out."

"Oh God, this is horrible," said Andrei, retching.

"Move away," said Lili, looking at him with concern. "How is he?"

"He vomited four times!" said Albert, filled with laughter that shook his enormous belly.

"Yeah, he's not that well. But I wanted him to go through this. It might help him in the long run," said Dan, with a concerned voice. "He'll be fine."

"Yeah, I hope so," said Lili.

\* \* \*

At lunch, Andrei didn't want to touch any of the meat. And when he saw the contents of the black beans can, he ran out of the room.

"Ugh," said Lili.

"What's wrong with Dad, Mommy?" asked Matei, looking puzzled.

"He's sick, honey. Don't worry about anything, just eat."

"Why is he sick, Mom? Is it because of his lip?"

"Oh, that? No, that's fine. He ate something bad. He'll be okay, don't you worry."

"Give him some pills, Mom."

"There's nothing we can do. Eat!"

"But I'm not hungry anymore. I'm done," he said.

"Okay then. Go out and take Howler with you."

"But, Mom, I want to stay here with you."

"People who stay here clear the table and then do the dishes. So, yeah, that's a splendid idea. Stay."

"I'll go out!" he said, and ran to the door.

"How long do you think you can pull that off?" asked Flo, smiling.

"I don't know," answered Lili, smiling back, "but I'll use this trick for as long as it works."

* * *

"We have properly killed those Morois out there," spat out Albert. "Now, it's time to go kill the Strigoi."

The others around the table threw glances at each other. They were well fed, and they'd just finished clearing the table.

"What? You promised! We have to do this!" said Albert, the pitch of his voice rising.

"Yes, no one is challenging that," said Dan. "But we need to be certain of success."

"What's that supposed to mean? We go to the church and lay waste to that son of a bitch!"

"We still don't know what's inside that church," said Dan. "We do know he has at least nineteen growlers with him. The twelve that were following him and the other seven they resurrected."

"I can take on nineteen growlers!" said Albert.

"No, you can't," said Dan, "and you know it. We need to be smart. Plus, he might have rounded up more than that. I only saw nineteen, but there might be more."

"Okay. Fine. So what do you propose?"

"Let's gather some more information," said Dan, looking around the table. "I'll go back again tonight, to see what he's up to. If we learn his movements, his habits, we might find a weakness."

"But Dad," said Lili, "he already made you once. Now he'll know where to look."

"I have another plan, don't worry. I want to see if he comes to pick up the dead we killed for good. I want to see how many growlers he brings with him on this run. I want to check if he's even still at the church."

"Why don't we build a trap at the house under construction?" asked Andrei.

People nodded, agreeing.

"That's not a bad idea," said Dan. "What kind of trap?"

Everyone contemplated the question.

"No idea," said Lili after a while.

"We could stand inside the house, hidden. And when the Strigoi arrives you can shoot him," said Andrei.

"And what if I miss? And what if the nineteen, or more, growlers attack us? It doesn't sound safe."

"You've got to crack a few eggs to make an omelet," said Albert.

"But when the eggs are people, you need to be careful," said Lili.

"You guys don't understand," yelled Albert. "You didn't lose two children, a daughter-in-law, and your mother to these monsters!" He rose from his chair. "We must kill that thing!" His face was red, and he was squeezing his enormous fists.

"Albert, we'll do it. But we need to find the best way to go about it," said Lili calmly. "We want to live to tell the story afterward."

Albert took several deep breaths. Then he slowly unclenched his fists and sat back down.

"Now," said Dan, "we need a plan, a way to do it safely. Other ideas?"

Silence immersed the table again.

"We could storm the church," said Albert. "But, I know, too many Morois. If only there was a way to trim his numbers!"

"Indeed. If he had half of his nineteen, I think we could get him," said Andrei.

"Let's not forget the Strigoi himself. We've never fought him directly. What if he's got some sort of superpower?" asked Dan.

They all nodded.

"Okay, enough of this. We're wasting valuable time," said Dan. "I'll go spy on him some more. You reinforce the fence behind the house. You've already put it back up, now make it stronger. Basically, prepare for a possible second siege."

"Yeah, we'll reset the fires, everything," said Lili. "If he comes with only nineteen growlers, he'll never get in."

\* \* \*

A few hours before sundown, Dan and Howler were on the move. They advanced down the main road, heading toward the church. Dan held Tiny in his left hand and a plank tucked beneath his right armpit.

When they had almost reached the church, they stopped at the house with the barn and attic. The front gate was locked, and Dan had to jump over to force it open from the inside. As he did so, he realized the house's front door was smashed open.

Dan approached quietly. He struck the doorframe with the side of his axe, waiting for an answer. Since nothing came out, he returned to the gate. It had a padlock that was holding it close. He used Tiny as a lever and broke it.

It was rather noisy, but still they heard no growling. The house looked clear, even with the smashed door, but Dan was not interested in it. He went to the back, toward the barn, Howler following him.

They climbed up, and Dan looked out through the opening, trying to check the churchyard. It was still sunny and he could see it very well. There were no more growlers in the yard.

"He must have called them back in, eh, boy?" said Dan, squatting next to Howler. "Fine. Let's go," he said, and started down the stairs.

Behind him, where the trapdoor should have been, Dan laid down the plank. He put it in such a way that it was barely visible from below, yet it would be impossible not to touch it if someone climbed the stairs.

\* \* \*

They reached the green-painted house as the sun set, and Dan opened the front door. He had cleared that house of growlers in the past, so he advanced quickly to the first floor. Up there, he found a window facing toward the field out back.

"This is where we'll stay, boy," said Dan. "I'll open the window, so you can sense him. But you have to be quiet."

It was an attic floor, so they could see and even touch the roof of the house when he opened the window wide. The action disturbed some snow, which tumbled in.

"Such a shame about letting in all this cold. This is a well-insulated house, and the warmer air coming from the tiny basement below kept it from freezing. Oh well, not to worry, boy," said Dan, as he stuck his head out and looked at the roof. "We're safe."

* * *

A few hours passed when, suddenly, Howler became alert.

Dan noticed the change and focused his gaze out the window. Soon, he heard a humming, which was slowly replaced by overlapping growls.

He could finally see the group, advancing through the backyards' improvised trails. In front was the Strigoi, with a bunch of growlers following him. Dan counted seventeen, but he might have missed some.

"See, boy?" said Dan, trying to make the dog relax. "Just as I expected. He's using the back road, going to pick up his dead, to raise his army."

He took out the walkie-talkie. "Hey, Lili. I see him. He's coming your way, just as expected. Stay alert."

* * *

Ten minutes passed, then twenty. Suddenly, a loud shriek cut through the silent night. It was different from before. This time the sound was full of hate and frustration. And a bit of rage.

"I guess that's 1–0 to us, isn't it, boy?" said Dan, smiling.

# 17 TRAPS

In the morning, Dan and Howler returned to their base.

"Welcome back," said everyone, greeting him happily.

"What did you learn?" asked Lili.

"It was as I expected. He's stayed in the same place, so he feels confident. It doesn't look like he wants to move. On the contrary, he went to check the barn. I'd left a marker, and it was moved. He was definitely there, looking for me."

"He also went to the house under construction," added Albert. "I went over there just now. He's moved the bodies, and some of them are missing, so he must have taken them."

"Yeah, probably to eat," said Andrei, scoffing.

"Well, what do you know, you're both foodies. You could probably be friends," said Lili.

"No, we couldn't," said Andrei, his expression grim.

"I mean, you already kissed a growler. You seem to have many things in common." Lili grinned.

"No, we do not."

"I'm joking. Jesus. What's wrong with you?"

"Look, we need to talk," said Dan, stopping their exchange. "I've been thinking."

"We have a few options, really," continued Dan from the comfort of the living room. Everyone was around him again, while Mat was still sleeping.

195

"We can go into strategic attack mode. Go by the church, see if we can thin his numbers, yet make sure we don't have an all-out confrontation. We can put traps here and there, where we expect him to be. Some guerilla warfare, if you will. We can play that game. However, he will always have the upper hand."

"Why is that?" asked Lili.

"Because he can see during the night, dufus," answered Andrei.

"No, it's because his army is way bigger than ours," said Dan, stopping them once more. "And if he breaks into every house in the village, he can produce ten times the army he has now. Where do you think he got his current growlers? By opening houses around the church, that's my guess. I saw one house with the door smashed open, yet no sign of growlers. Imagine what would happen if he decided to expand."

"If I were him, that's what I'd do," said Andrei, nodding. "If he tried to get his dead back and then he went to look for you, it means he's on high alert, stressed out by your presence. However, he will want to reinforce his team by enlisting new growlers, if we give him the space to do that."

"Then we must leave," said Flo, suddenly. "That must be our best option. To get the hell out of here."

"That's the third option, yes," said Dan, nodding.

"And the best one!" said Flo.

"What's the second?" asked Lili.

"The second option is to go all-in. He's in the church, we know that. We march in there, we play to win, we kill everything that moves, and if all goes well, we kill the Strigoi."

There was a brief silence while everyone reflected.

"I say we flee!" said Flo.

"And go where?" asked Lili. "Remember what happened in town. We're no safer there than here. For all we know, the town is now filled with Strigois."

"What if," interrupted Andrei, "this is not the only Strigoi out there? What if this is a different one from the Strigoi back at Albert's house?"

"I think it's highly probable it's the same one, Andrei," said Lili condescending.

"And why is that, my incredibly wise wife?"

"Because, my incredibly witless husband, from all the information we have on him, he looks the same. And the fact that he dropped my backpack off here certainly reinforces that."

"Ah, yes. The backpack part does sound legit. The other, not so much. What if all Strigois are small and skinny?"

"Anyway," interrupted Flo, "to answer Lili's question, I say we go south, to onion county."

"Ahh, I see," said Andrei, smiling. "To have a ton of onions at our disposal. Smart!"

"No, dufus," said Lili. "To meet more people. Living, normal people."

"Exactly!" said Flo with enthusiasm.

"Why should there be more—"

"Oh, come on, Andrei! Jesus!" exploded Lili. "I guess in, gee, 'onion county'," said Lili, air quoting the title, "the people eat lots of onions. Which makes me believe there might be more people like us out there, who survived because of the onion overdose."

"True, true," said Andrei, nodding. "They could have larger communities, that's right."

"I vote we go. Plan three over here!" said Flo, raising her hand, happy.

"I vote we attack now," said Albert. "Plan two. Afterwards, we can go wherever you want."

"I would also be inclined to leave, and I love your proposal to go south. However, we can't travel in this weather. I mean, we can," said Dan, "but we will be putting ourselves at great risk if we go on foot. It's at least 150 miles, and walking such a long distance it's no easy feat. The roads must all be covered with snow. No, I think we have to stay."

Everybody was quiet, until Andrei raised four fingers.

"How about plan four?"

Everybody looked at him, waiting.

"Well, what is it? Spit it out! What, we have to beg for it?"

"Hold your horses, my cute little wife," he said, with a grin. "How about we play the attrition game?"

"The what?"

"We go around the village, door to door, properly killing all the growlers we can find. Not just kill, but take-out-their-hearts-and-burn-them kill. The complete deal. Eventually, the Strigoi will have little army left to attack with. Now I think of it, we could call this," said Andrei raising both his hands over his head and forming an invisible banner, while using a deeper voice, "'The Culling of…'." He abruptly stopped, hands mid-air, looking at the others. "By the way, what is this village's name?"

"That doesn't sound half bad," interrupted Flo, "but are you ready to remove a few hundred hearts from dead growlers?"

"And there's always the risk of getting hit, bitten, scratched, or, even worse, killed by one of those growlers during this culling of yours," said Dan. "Not to mention what such a deed would do to your very soul and wellbeing."

They sat in total silence once more, until Lili took over.

"Then I vote for plan one. The guerilla fight."

"If we can't leave, the same vote for me," said Flo.

"Yeah, me too," added Andrei. "We need to keep the Strigoi busy, not give him time to move around and get new growlers from nearby houses."

"I would go for plan two if Albert and I were the last people on Earth. But if we think about you guys and the kid," said Dan, looking at the people around the table, "I think I'll also vote for plan one."

They all agreed, except for Albert, who, with a grunt, got up and left.

* * *

"Hey, buddy, we need you. We'll get to the proper fighting, but until then, let's improve our odds." Dan was following Albert as he restlessly paced the yard.

"You keep on saying that, Dan," said Albert, coming to a halt and turning to look at Dan. "And you'll keep saying it until that damn Strigoi gets an army large enough for us to never be able to defeat him. And then we'll all die. And mind you, I don't care about dying. But I want to take that devil down with me, even if it's the last thing I do!"

"I hear you, buddy, loud and clear. And trust me, I want to kill that thing as much as you do. But let's try to improve our odds. If we see we can't, I promise I'll go with you myself."

Albert nodded, with a grumpy look.

"Until then, fix these walls, make sure we're safe. If we're safe here, there's nothing he can do to us. Oh, and if you have any ideas about traps we can use, please build some."

\* \* \*

Lili, Dan, and Howler were closing in on the church. It was midday and the sun was shining.

"Remember, if anything happens," whispered Dan, "we run."

Lili nodded.

They entered the yard cautiously, looking left to right. As they approached the church, Howler became alert. Dan petted him and they continued to move.

Lili touched her nose, then pointed at the church. Dan nodded. That moldy smell was here and it was probably coming from the church itself.

Dan signaled Lili, who stopped moving. He closed in about ten yards, then he placed a walkie-talkie on the snow.

He removed its earpiece, then returned to Lili.

They moved out of the yard and stopped at the open gate. Behind them, dropped onto the snow by Dan a few minutes before, stood the shield that Albert had put together, with its handles removed.

"Where should we put this?" whispered Lili.

Dan took it and put it on the ground, in the middle of the gateway, spikes up.

"Cover it with some snow, to make sure it's not visible, Dad."

Dan threw a glance at her, shaking his head. Still, with care, he started covering it with snow. Soon, it wasn't visible anymore, yet a careful eye would have been able to tell something was off with that pile of snow on a beaten path.

"Ready?" whispered Dan, and Lili nodded.

They moved back a bit, walking along the main road, quickly reaching the corner of the church's land, right where the next property's fence started. The church's fence was only around three foot, about half the size of the next property's. Squatting there and looking over the short fence, Dan pulled out his walkie-talkie and started talking.

"Hey, e-o, what's up! Are there any growlers in the house?" His voice came out loud through the walkie-talkie in front of the church.

Lili looked at him, squinting, while Dan shrugged and offered an embarrassed smile. "What," he whispered. "I'm not good at this."

"I guess you're good enough," said Lili, pointing, as a group of growlers came out of the church. They had emerged, but they soon seemed lost.

"Hey, over here!" yelled Dan, this time from behind the fence.

The growlers turned and started running toward them. Unfortunately, since the church's fence was short and the monsters had a direct line of sight, they went straight toward the yard's corner and not to the access gate, where Dan and Lili had hidden the spikes.

"Shit," said Dan.

Suddenly, they heard a shriek, and all the growlers turned and headed back to the church.

"Hey, come back!" yelled Dan, jumping up and down. "You idiots, come back here!"

Immediately, the last two growlers turned again and came after Dan, while the other three entered the church. As they reached Dan, he promptly put them down with two good hits to the head.

"Why are you still using your left hand?" asked Lili.

"I don't trust my right hand yet," he answered, looking at it. "I'll need some time to adapt."

"What do we do with these?" asked Lili, nodding at the two squirming growlers.

"We should silence them and remove their hearts."

"Puah," said Lili with disgust.

Dan jumped the short fence, pulled out his knife, and stabbed the two growlers in the chest. As they released their dying growl, they heard a new shriek coming from within the church. And this time, it seemed all the growlers came pouring out.

One after another, they swarmed through the church doors, going after Dan and Lili.

"Run!" said Dan, and they jumped the fence and charged toward their base.

Behind them, they heard another shriek, and when they turned their heads, they saw the growlers going back inside the church. Only this time, they were carrying their two dead.

* * *

"That's disappointing," muttered Lili, as they walked back to base.

"Yeah, it is," confirmed Dan in a similar tone. "We killed two, but I bet he'll resurrect them in no time."

"We left the spikes at the gate."

"That will not kill nineteen growlers. It will probably take out one and slow the others a bit. But that's all. We've got nothing."

"What if we organize better?" asked Lili.

"How do you mean?"

"I mean, if we kill more growlers. We do a similar thing, then we kill the ones that come pouring out, one by one."

"We can't do that; they'll overwhelm us. That's basically plan two you're talking about. And we just tested it. If we make too much trouble, they come out in full force. And if they do that, they'll wipe us out."

"You're right. if only there was a way to get them out in small groups."

* * *

Back at the house, everyone was worried after hearing about Dan's and Lili's adventures.

"We need to go," said Flo. "There's no other way. These traps don't work. We're probably lucky he didn't let those growlers follow you."

"He didn't let them follow us because he knew we could kill them one by one," said Dan. "But, yes, who knows, we might be lucky."

"I say we strike now," added Albert.

"I feel I've witnessed this discussion in the past," said Andrei. "Now it's your turn, Dan or Lili, to propose something in between."

"Andrei is right," said Dan.

"In what way?" asked Lili, turning her surprised face toward her dad.

"I'll propose something in between."

Both Albert and Flo puffed.

"But not what you expect. We need a more effective trap, so I propose I try to assassinate the Strigoi. I'll go to the barn and try to lure him in. If he comes, I'll be ready, and this time I'll take a better shot. If he doesn't take the bait, I'll just gather some more intel."

"Are you sure? That sounds risky," said Andrei. "He'll know about the gun. He'll not make the same mistake twice."

"But what if he does?"

"Dad, this is dangerous. You'll be all alone. Don't do that," said Lili, as Flo was nodding, approving.

"Should be less risky than last time. Now I know the place. It has a thin access point, through the stairs. There is only one direction he can come from. And this time, I'll have a secret weapon with me."

Dan turned toward Albert. "Buddy, please, have some more patience. Please stay behind tonight and guard the others."

\* \* \*

When evening came, Dan and Howler hid in the attic of the tall barn. However, he made sure he was more visible than last time. Not too obvious, but not the stealthiest he could be.

As the hours passed, he wondered if the Strigoi was still inside the church.

"Hey, Lili, do you hear me?" he said, using the walkie-talkie. As instructed, they'd all switched channels on the walkies, to make sure the one left in front of the church stayed silent.

"Hey, Dad. Loud and clear. How are things?"

"We're fine, I guess. No movement from this bastard."

"Maybe you should come back?"

"I don't know. I have a feeling it's safer here than out there. He might be watching and waiting for me to move first. We'll see. I have my secret weapon, so I should be safe up here. Over and out."

\* \* \*

When there were only a few hours left before dawn, the Strigoi finally left the church.

Just as before, he let out a shriek and a few growlers followed him. He went to the back trails, behind the houses, and walked toward their base.

"Hey, Lili!" said Dan, using his walkie-talkie. "He's coming your way, using the back road. He's taking the same trail, so I guess he feels safe. I counted four growlers with him. He might try to bring back some more of the growlers, but please be careful."

"Okay, roger. We'll keep our eyes open."

\* \* \*

One hour into it, Howler became alert. Dan followed, squeezing his axe.

He looked out and saw the Strigoi pass by his barn, jumping some fences, and finally reaching the church property. He walked toward the church, but, as he took his steps, he slowly turned his head, looking straight at Dan.

"Bastard," mumbled Dan, just as the Strigoi looked back toward the church and shrieked.

More than a dozen growlers came out and surrounded him. The Strigoi then turned, fully facing Dan's hideout, and pointed his hand toward him.

The growlers took a few steps, directly toward Dan's barn, until they hit the first fence.

The Strigoi gave another shriek, and suddenly the growlers became highly aggressive. They started pushing at the fence and soon after, they put it down. They continued to advance, running, the Strigoi still pointing at Dan.

"Boy, this is bad," said Dan to Howler. "We have to run for it!"

They got down the stairs just as the Strigoi and his minions reached the last fence. Dan and Howler dashed through the yard gate, got out into the main street, and sprinted toward their base.

As they ran, the dozen or so growlers followed, with the Strigoi between them. The Strigoi was very agile, and it looked like he was not even trying too hard.

"He's toying with us, boy," said Dan to Howler, as they struggled to keep the growlers at a distance. "He's waiting for us to get tired. But keep running. Don't you stop, okay, boy?"

Suddenly, the Strigoi took a left and jumped the fence into one of the yards. The same side as their base.

"Shit," said Dan, panting into the walkie-talkie. "He might come for you."

"Who, the Strigoi?"

"Yes."

"Dad, why are you panting? What's going on?"

"We're running. They're after us. This was a very bad plan!"

"Do you need help?"

"I might need you and Albert to wait for us near the gate. We may have that fight after all."

"Roger, Dad. We'll come rescue you."

"No! Stay inside. Wait for me."

As he finished these words, the Strigoi leaped from their left into the middle of the street, cutting off their retreat. In front, some thirty yards away, was the Strigoi, and behind them, about twenty-five yards back, over a dozen growlers.

Dan looked around, squeezing Tiny, and suddenly recognized the green-painted house.

"Here, boy!" he yelled, opening the gate and closing it behind them. He rushed to enter the house, locking the door just as the growlers busted into the yard.

Dan turned and saw a heavy armchair a few steps away. He grabbed it, pulling it as fast as possible, trying to push it up against the door.

Growls started everywhere.

And they were coming from inside the house, from upstairs and from the tiny basement.

* * *

"Shit," said Lili.

"What?" asked Andrei in a sleepy voice. "What time is it?"

"It's time to save Dad."

"What? What happened?"

"He's in danger. Go wake Albert. I need him."

\* \* \*

The front door was being pushed from outside, and Dan could hear the usual banging and scratching. Inside, coming down the stairs, were two growlers. Closer, a few steps away, were two more, coming up from the tiny basement. No way to retreat in that direction. Howler was standing beside him, alert yet quiet, looking at all of them.

Dan kept his back against the door, pushing it closed. He'd locked it, but he knew without his support it would soon break.

He then opened his winter jacket, exposing his secret weapon: two large strings of onions and garlic wrapped around his neck.

The first growler climbed the last step and came near, and Dan recognized it as the one with the eaten hands. It seemed to be impervious to the onion and garlic, as it continued its attack.

"What the…" said Dan, while pushing at the growler with the tip of his axe. The growler took two steps back, but the second one was coming fast. They bumped into each other, and both growlers came heavily toward Dan.

Dan pulled out his knife with his right hand and held it forward while adjusting his body just enough for the second growler to come chest-first right into the blade.

The first one, the one with the eaten hands, smashed into the door on Dan's left, biting it and breaking some of its teeth with a screeching noise. The creature seemed slightly bothered by the onions, but that didn't prevent it reaching toward Dan's neck.

Dan couldn't hold on to the knife as the stabbed body fell to the ground. He raised his left elbow and struck the biting growler in the head. It wasn't enough to stop it, but it gained him a few seconds. The creature jumped again, reaching. Luckily, Dan now had enough time to use his right hand to grab the growler's forehead and keep its mouth away from the left-hand side of his neck.

The two other growlers were fast approaching, so Dan gave Howler the signal to bark, which immediately attracted them. He continued to bark while the two went after him, inside the living room.

"Run, Howler," yelled Dan holding the front door closed while also keeping the growler's head from his neck. "Run, boy!"

Howler moved quickly between the growler's feet, making them bump into each other; then he sprinted up the stairs to the first floor, barking for attention.

The growlers turned and followed, all while Dan fought the growler with eaten hands.

Dan's left hand was between him and the growler, and it held Tiny. The growler was pushing and trying to bite his neck. Dan started turning Tiny, let the axe slide down until his hand reached the metal head. Now, holding the axe right near the blade, he raised his hand and pressed the sharp side between him and the growler's neck.

The growler continued to push, even as Tiny cut into its neck. It didn't seem to care as it struggling aggressively, pushing until the axe reached its spine.

The good part was that the growler could not properly control his head anymore. The head fell to the side, no longer held together by any muscles or tendons.

Dan could now release his grip on the forehead, grab Tiny in his right hand, and give a firm push, putting some distance between him and the growler, before cracking open its skull.

Meanwhile, the banging on the door continued as a dozen growlers tried to enter.

To make it worse, Howler appeared at top of the stairs, and sprinted down, barking.

The two growlers were following.

Dan waited, still and silent, yet making sure his back remained against the rattling door.

The first growler—a fat old man—passed by, followed by a skinny old woman.

Dan swung Tiny and put the woman down.

"Good boy!" whispered Dan. "Now run! Go up!"

Howler didn't need to hear Dan's command. He already knew what he had to do, as he sprinted again up the stairs, barking.

The fat man turned, only to get an axe to its head.

"Great, boy! You were awesome!" Dan yelled.

He then heard a shriek, and the pushing on the door intensified.

\* \* \*

"We should be close," said Lili to Albert. "Get ready."

"I am ready."

"I hear them!" said Lili. "Look, there, at the green-painted house! Let's go."

They sped up, just in time to hear a loud shriek which woke the entire village.

\* \* \*

"Boy, where are you?"

Howler appeared at the top of the staircase.

"Good boy! Stay there!" yelled Dan, panting. The armchair was close. In one swift move, he grabbed it and finished the job, pushing it against the door.

"Go, boy, go!" he yelled, and started running up the stairs.

The door was moving violently. He reached the top floor the moment before it broke with a loud creak. He continued running toward the open window, the one facing the field behind the house.

"Come here, quick!" said Dan, and he grabbed Howler. He lifted him out of the window, directly onto the roof.

He quickly followed, just as the first growlers reached their floor. Dan and Howler turned and climbed upwards, toward the top of the roof, stepping on the untouched snow. Then they waited.

The house below them creaked from the heavy steps of the growlers. And every now and then the Strigoi shrieked, further startling them and making them move even more aggressively.

They waited there for a few minutes. The sky was already showing lighter shades of blue, signs that the sun was about to rise.

Suddenly, the Strigoi joined them on the roof, coming out through the same window.

He looked at them, showing his teeth and a black tongue, and let out an aggressive shriek. The sky was clear, so they could see him well, and his black vines seemed even thicker than last time.

Dan started shaking his onion and garlic strings, looking at the Strigoi. The Strigoi glanced at them only briefly, not seeming to care.

He moved fast, like he was in a hurry, advancing toward Dan and Howler. His movements were a little strange, however. It looked like the light was already bothering him, as he used his left hand to cover his eyes.

Dan quickly pulled out his gun, but before he could fire, the Strigoi leapt to the right, tumbling down the side of the house.

"Damn!" growled Dan.

The Strigoi shrieked, the sound loud and full of frustration, and the house creaked and groaned once more.

\* \* \*

"They're getting away!" said Lili, as they reached the gate.

The growling sound was fainter, instead of becoming louder.

"Hey, over here!" said Dan, and they both looked up.

"What are you doing up there, Dad?" asked Lili.

"Surviving," said Dan, smiling. "Grim news. The garlic and onion strings don't work. I think Grandma Gina exaggerated or misunderstood that bit. Ah, so good to have you here, Albert. We have four hearts to take out."

# 18 THE CULLING

Albert started talking once they'd all sat down at the table. "We have to—"

"Yes, I know," said Dan. "We have to do it now."

"Do what now?" asked Andrei.

"Sometimes I think you're really thick," came Lili's answer. "What has Albert been pushing for these past weeks?"

"Killing the Strigoi."

"Yeah, so what's up with the question?"

"I wasn't paying attention. You're cute when you're annoyed."

"Yeah, and you're annoying when you're annoying."

"Coming back to it, we have to do it. Now's the best time. He's down four more growlers," said Dan.

"But why don't we repeat this for a few more nights?" asked Lili.

"He won't make the same mistake again. Last night he set a trap. A very smart trap. He knew I'd been to that house, and he knew I'd think it was safe. I'm impressed how smart he is."

"I hate that we keep on calling him 'he'," said Albert.

"Doesn't matter either way. He or it is smart. And if it wasn't for Howler, I would be dead."

"I believe we've been very lucky," said Lili.

"Yes. And unfortunately, the garlic and onion strings don't seem to work. At least not when the growlers are in highly aggressive mode, controlled by the Strigoi. Yeah, they seemed to notice it, but it wouldn't stop a group of charging growlers. And the Strigoi didn't seem to care about them either. Maybe freshly cut, or made into a paste, for the smell to be extreme, would have a different result. But the plants, as they are, put on a string, don't work."

"Then what's up with Grandma Gina's story? Why was she protected by the strings of onion and garlic around her neck?" asked Lili.

"She probably wasn't, and it was only a projection of her beliefs. What if the Strigoi let her live just to make sure the returning people wouldn't leave? You know, since we would have to stay there to take care of her. That way, he could make sure he got everyone," suggested Andrei. "Injuring a member of the pack, you damage the whole pack. Unless the pack leaves the injured one behind, which, of course, we don't. Now I think of it, the Strigoi probably counted on that."

"That sounds plausible," confirmed Dan.

"Shit! This is bad! If that's true, that Strigoi is really smart."

"Language, honey," said Andrei with a superior smile.

"He's sleeping, you irritating oaf."

"He is, but what if you get used to using that kind of language?"

"The Strigoi is down to fifteen growlers now. It's still a lot. But better than nineteen," continued Dan in a louder voice. "And please stop with this nonsense, you two; it's getting tiring. I want options. What can we do?"

They went over the options they'd already covered in the past.

"To conclude," said Dan, "we risk fighting fifteen growlers and a Strigoi. And there's five of us. That's three growlers each."

"That's too much!" said Flo.

"It is. I think we can kill them if we're smart and organized. But we might be unlucky. Still, the main issue is, I don't know much about the Strigoi's strength. He's fast, agile, and he has enhanced hearing and vision. And, probably more importantly, he's smart."

"Yes, you probably won't be able to kite them again, like you did with those seven," said Andrei, nodding. "He'll likely coordinate them properly."

Everybody nodded, agreeing.

"When you were sick, Dan," said Andrei, suddenly, "with that bite in your neck, did you feel like you had something extra?"

"No, I just felt weakened, sleepy, and sick. I had a high fever."

"So no extra abilities, no night vision, nothing?"

"Where are you going with this?" interrupted Lili.

"I'm trying to figure out if maybe we have a secret weapon we could use. What if that black thing, in small doses, gives us extra strengths? The speed, agility, and strength of the Strigoi himself. Staying smart and alive."

"You're still dreaming you could be like that Watcher dude?"

"It's Witcher, honey," said Andrei, scoffing.

"Whatever. Just to answer your question, I don't think anyone would willingly put that black thing into their body. And if someone did, he would probably die. Yes," said Lili, interrupting Andrei, who was about to say something, "I assume the Strigoi is dead."

The group fell silent.

"What if we never fight them?" asked Andrei.

"Yes! I love this idea," said Flo, pointing at Andrei. "Let's leave."

"No, that's not what I meant. I mean, what if we kill them, but we don't have to fight them?"

"You can call an airstrike on half of the village and we're not aware of it?" asked Flo, raising her eyebrow.

"Nope," said Andrei, starting to grin.

"You're enjoying this, aren't you?" asked Lili, shaking her head.

"No, honey," said Andrei, with fake modesty. "I just strive to enlighten you all." He then switched to a serious note. "We know they're inside the church. And the church is made of wood. What if we lock them in, then set the entire thing on fire?"

Everybody fell silent.

"You want to burn down the church?" asked Lili, disbelief in her voice.

Andrei shrugged. "It's for a good cause."

"I love it!" said Flo.

"I don't know," said Albert, shaking his head. "I'm not sure God would be happy about this. I want to kill that son of a bitch, but not like that."

"Let's put it this way," continued Andrei. "The church, a holy place, is overrun by demons. I'm not getting into the 'how could this happen' discussion. However, I guess it would please God if we cleansed the land and banished the evil from that place."

"And you also get to burn down a church and flip it as a good thing," said Lili.

"Yeah, a dream come true," said Andrei with sarcasm.

"Come on, I know your theories," said Lili. "Don't hide it."

"Yes, I do believe there are too many of them around here. I think it's a miracle there's only one in this village. And whenever you build a church in Eastern Europe, you can never take it down. A million years from now and we'll probably have all the land covered with churches. Still, my proposal has nothing to do with that. If we do this right, we can get rid of that Strigoi, once and for all."

"I don't enjoy burning churches," said Lili, looking at her father.

"Me neither," said Dan, after a few moments of silence. "Still, if we do it for a good cause, if it feels right, it should be a good thing, I think. Too bad we don't have a priest with us."

"Yeah, that's exactly what we're missing," said Andrei, scoffing.

"Anyway," continued Dan, "we have a tactical advantage. They are probably all inside, including the Strigoi, and their numbers are thin. Plus, that Strigoi really hates daylight. He could barely look at me on top of the green-painted house and the sun wasn't even up yet."

"God have mercy on our souls," said Albert, getting up. "Let's get ready."

"Wait for a bit," said Dan. "We still need to discuss logistics."

"Okay," said Albert, sitting back down.

"Who goes and who stays?" asked Dan, looking around the table.

"I'll go," Albert instantly raised his hand.

"Me, too, although I'd rather not," said Flo. "I'd still rather go far away from this place. But if we can do this without a fight, I'm game."

"I can go as well," said Lili. "But someone needs to take care of Matei."

"You're right, honey," said Andrei quickly. "I can take care of him, since you've already offered to go. I mean, I would, but I'm still not feeling a hundred percent like myself after all that vomiting. And my lip, I'm not sure it's fully healed. See? It's still swollen. But worry not, I'll stay here and hold the fort."

"But this was your plan. I thought you'd want to participate."

"Ah, I would," said Andrei, trying to hold a straight face. "But someone needs to defend the base, right?"

Lili rolled her eyes, while Dan shook his head.

"Okay, fine," said Dan. "Let's get ready."

"I have some ideas that you can use," said Andrei, getting up. "You know, to make sure the fire picks up quickly."

\* \* \*

When the group departed, only Andrei and Mat remained.

"Why aren't we going with them, Daddy?" asked Mat as Andrei closed the front gate.

"They have some work to do and we'd be in their way."

"What work, Daddy?"

"Hmm," said Andrei, trying to find an answer. "Why don't you help me barricade this gate?"

"Okay, Daddy. But what work are they doing?"

"Shush, Mat, let's do this."

"Okay," said Matei, coming closer. "What can I do?"

"Well, we need to put this beam up here, and then these two other beams at an angle, see, in these spots, so no one can break in."

"But I can't raise beams, Daddy. They're too heavy."

"Yes, they are. You can sit and watch me."

"But that's not helping."

"Yes, it is. You'll be a big help. See, now we put this up... right here. Perfect. Now we take the other two. See? You're helping."

"But I'm not doing anything. Daddy, tell me what work they're doing?"

"They want to take the snow away from the main street. You know, to make it easier to walk."

"Really?"

"Yup. Remember how difficult it was to walk. Well, they want to fix that."

"But why were they carrying so much firewood with them?"

"They might need to melt some snow, so they'll build an enormous fire."

"Daddy, are you joking?" asked Matei after a while.

213

"No. What makes you say that?"

"I think they would need two times more firewood if they wanted to clean the whole road."

"Ah, they might find some more in the village," said Andrei, trying to hide his smile.

Matei paused, thinking. "Daddy? Are they going to kill the Strigoi?"

Andrei turned. "What makes you say that?"

"They seemed scared. And they only took one small shovel with them."

Andrei stopped, looking at his son, his eyes getting a bit wet. "You are smart, aren't you, little one? Yes, that's what they want to do," he said, hugging his son.

"I'm not little!"

* * *

It was midday, and the group was on the main road, next to the church's fence, at the corner.

Albert, as instructed by Andrei, had put together a few planks and built some three by five solid pieces, like a sled. On it, he'd stacked a lot of firewood, covering everything with a tarp, which he then encircled with a thick rope, to keep everything together. He pulled that thing through the snow up to the church.

Dan was pulling a similar contraption. It seemed to have three times the same volume, but it was all hay.

Lili and Flo were carrying all the weapons. Except for Albert's axe, which was too heavy for them, so they'd strapped it onto Albert's improvised sleigh.

Between them was Howler, who seemed to be enjoying the walk.

"Ah, look," whispered Dan, pointing at the church's opened gate. "That's where we hid that stupid trap. Looks like no growler has stepped on it, so let's make sure we don't."

"Where do you want these?" asked Albert, pointing at his cargo.

"Leave it here, but we should all get a little closer. The church is about thirty yards from the gate, so I guess we could move ten yards deeper."

"Right," said Albert, grabbing the sleigh's rope and starting to pull.

"Wait," whispered Dan. "Lili, get that trap out of the way so we can enter."

Lili carefully removed the trap, pushing it to the side of the road.

"Right," continued Dan. "Now, let's go as slowly and quietly as possible. Albert, I'll go first and I'll stop when I think it's a suitable spot. Lili will come with me, bringing my axe. Then I'll signal to you, and you two come."

"Why aren't we all going together?" asked Albert.

"The sleighs make noise. The snow squeaks when we walk on it. This way we'll be less likely to wake the growlers. Ready, Lili? Boy, stay!"

Lili nodded, and they started moving.

They took tiny steps, and a few minutes later, they stopped about twenty yards from the church, in the alleyway. Closest to them was the front right corner of the church, and they had a direct view of the main doors.

Dan turned around. He looked at Howler while gently tapping his thigh, and Howler came. He then signaled the others, and Albert and Flo followed.

* * *

"Now," whispered Dan, "let's open these up. Remember, be silent!" He waved Albert closer, so he could whisper. "Make sure you have your axe ready."

Albert nodded, and then he went back to his sleigh. He started untying the rope, and he was soon holding his trusty axe.

Dan did a similar thing. He removed the rope on his sleigh, then unloaded the nine sheaves of hay and set them to the side. He had spent a few hours, together with Flo, putting together these large sheaves.

He moved his empty sleigh a few steps away, then he put one sheaf down in the alley, choosing an area with less snow. On top he added firewood, brought by Albert and the women. At first, he placed about seven pieces in a circle. He went on to stack others on top, in the middle of the improvised star.

He took out a lighter and, shielding it from the wind, lit it. He held the flame to the haystack in various places, and soon the fire caught.

\* \* \*

Minutes into it, as the fire took off, the four of them started moving around the church.

They could see the church was built on top of a visible basement, and the wooden part was one and a half feet above the snow. But they were ready. They went back to Albert's sleigh, where the men picked up a few heavy items.

After that, they made their way to the back of the church, taking a wide, circular path, always keeping at least fifteen yards between them and the church building. Flo and Albert stopped at the closest corner, while Dan and Lili moved to the farthest one, on the opposite side from where Dan had lit the first fire.

The men let down a large wood stump each, next to the back corners of the church. This way, what was coming on top was level with the wooden part of the church. On top of the stumps, Lili and Flo placed the sheaves of hay they were carrying.

They all returned to Albert's sleigh, taking the same long route. There, they started packing pieces of firewood. The men were holding out their arms while the women stacked the wood.

They moved to the back of the church with this new payload. The men stood next to the stumps while the women took the firewood and stacked them, a piece at a time, on top of the hay, two by two, like Lego, building a tall, rectangular pyre that leaned against the church's walls. They even had some newspaper, made into balls, which the women set here and there amidst the wood.

They did a similar thing out front, where they were even more careful when moving, because of their proximity to the front doors. Only this time the church had a porch, so there was no need for the stumps.

At last, they were done.

\* \* \*

"Ready?" whispered Dan.

The fire in the middle of the churchyard was burning hot. Everybody nodded.

"Hey, guys, how's it going?" they all heard in their earpieces.

"Andrei, this is not a good moment," Lili whispered, covering her mouth with one hand and turning her back to the church. "We're just starting the fires!"

"Glad you're okay! Good luck! Over and out."

"Okay," whispered Dan. "Let's go."

Everyone grabbed one of the seven concentric pieces of wood. The end they grabbed was not burning, but the other end, the one in the middle of the fire, was ablaze.

The four of them started moving at the same time, in a coordinated action—Lili and Flo out back, Dan and Albert up front.

They set fire to the pyres and then slowly returned.

\* \* \*

"Pfft," said Andrei, pacing the front yard.

"What, Daddy?"

"Nothing."

"What?"

"It's nothing!"

"What is it?"

"They're doing something now. I hope they'll be okay."

"Are they killing the Strigoi now?"

Andrei stopped for a moment, looking in admiration at his kid. "I guess so."

Suddenly, they heard a loud roar coming from dozens of voices. It was far away, but it sounded like it was coming from hell itself.

"Shit," mumbled Andrei, looking toward the church.

Thick smoke was visible in the distance.

\* \* \*

The church was burning. There were now enormous fires at its four corners, and the flames were coming together high up. They would soon engulf the roof.

"They're awake!" yelled Dan, as the growlers started making

217

noise. "Let's go!"

He and Albert charged toward the main door. Then they heard a shriek.

Albert had his heavy axe in his right hand, but he also held his improvised sleigh as a shield. Andrei was the one who'd come up with the idea of building sleighs to carry the wood and hay, and he'd also suggested this double usage. That's why, back home, when he built the sleigh, Albert had added two handgrips, and now he had the sleigh slung across his forearm, like a short but very wide shield. The flames were making his face glow, and Andrei would have said he looked just like an angry Viking.

The door opened and three burning growlers burst out. They slammed into Albert's shield, and he pushed them back with a roar, while Dan started hitting them with his axe.

He smashed one head. He missed the second, yet he cut open a shoulder. The growler hit in the head fell to the ground, squirming and on fire, while an unstoppable Albert pushed back the other two.

A few seconds into it, four more growlers appeared and found Albert's improvised shield, slowly pushing him back. The heat from the nearby fire was too much for Albert, anyway, and the air had become too hot to breathe.

As Albert took a few steps back, Dan continued to strike, and more growlers fell with their heads cracked open. They all used to be older people, as the village's population was aging, and a few had those tumors on their faces.

"It's working," yelled Lili, when they heard another shriek.

All the advancing growlers pulled back, and another came out through the burning door of the church. It used to be an old woman, and it was missing its entrails. Still, on its chest was the same tumor the Strigoi used to bring growlers back to life.

Parts of its face were missing, bitten and eaten, but Lili and Dan would have recognized her with their eyes closed.

"Mom?" yelled Lili, dropping her weapon.

Dan stood there, stunned, just as Howler started barking.

"Dad!" yelled Lili, coming back to her senses. "It's not Mom! She's not Mom anymore!"

But Dan couldn't move, as the growler that used to be Maria slowly advanced to get him. She was rotting and they could see maggots crawling. She was a slow growler, and her approach seemed to take ages. As the seconds passed, Dan's hands felt like they weighed a ton and his will left him.

At the same time, Howler charged toward the left-hand side of the church, barking.

Albert put his shield between Dan and Maria right when she was about to scratch and bite. Her partially eaten face had white, empty, and fixed eyes. Albert pushed her back, into the burning church, and, with one swift move, cut her in half with his massive axe. Her two pieces fell, left and right, and the fire took them.

"It's not your wife, Dan. Dan, look at me!"

"Where's Howler going?" asked Dan, coming back to life, when he suddenly realized the dog was on the move. "It's the Strigoi! He sent Maria here as a decoy. Look, Howler is after him!"

Albert didn't need to be told a second time. He dropped his shield and started running after Howler, axe in hand.

The Strigoi had a burning left hand, and he was using his right hand to cover his eyes. Still, he was moving fast. Luckily, he hit the back fence, the one he usually jumped so easily, and he turned to his left, dazed, running blindly toward the priest's house.

"He can't see!" yelled Flo. "Get him, Howler!"

Howler, who was in pursuit, jumped high, going straight for the Strigoi's face, biting. The hit was powerful, and they both fell. The Strigoi was on his back, with his white face scratched and pieces of hardened skin pierced by Howler's teeth, while Howler flew a few feet to the side, twisting in the air.

Albert was coming, axe up, roaring.

Suddenly, the Strigoi threw his hands to the side and let out the loudest and most terrifying shriek they'd ever heard, looking right at Albert. His black tongue was moving and his charcoal eyes were piercing Albert, filled with rage. The village came alive and hundreds of growls started everywhere, much the same as when the pack of dogs used to wake all the growlers when they'd first arrived here.

"Do it, Albert!" yelled Flo and Lili simultaneously, and Albert's axe split the Strigoi's body, from his head to the middle of his chest, then got stuck in the frozen ground beneath.

The Strigoi was twisting, trying to get up, but the axe held him in place.

Albert was spitting on the creature, kicking it with his large boots, cursing and cussing.

Dan arrived and thrust his knife into the Strigoi's heart. The Strigoi gave a final twitch, then stopped moving. Dan removed the knife and looked up at the others. They were all nodding and smiling, and tears had appeared on Lili's and Flo's faces. Dan got up and took a few steps toward them. But then a noise rose behind him.

He turned again, only to see the Strigoi twisting and moving.

He slammed the knife into the Strigoi's heart again. The Strigoi stopped. He removed the knife, and the Strigoi came back to life a few seconds later. Dan stabbed the heart again and again. When he finished, he stood up, panting. He'd cut the Strigoi's chest to ribbons, yet it was still moving, albeit the shrieks were weaker and different, more metallic.

"Leave the knife in," said Lili, and Dan did just that.

The Strigoi did his twitch and then remained there, immobile.

"That explains the legends of burying Strigois with stakes through their hearts," said Lili.

"We must remove the heart and burn it, at least according to Grandma Gina's stories," said Flo. "I can't believe her stories were true."

They turned around, looking at each other, all of them in tears.

The church was burning high and fierce, and no growler ever came out of it again.

\* \* \*

"Hey, Andrei, we did it," said Lili. Her voice was coming through the walkie-talkie. "Your idea was great. It worked!"

"Oh, wow, well done, honey! What, are you crying?"

"We killed him! He's dead! The bastard is dead."

"Why are you crying?"

"You're an idiot!" she said, sobbing.

"I love you, honey. You guys did an amazing job!" said Andrei, putting down the walkie-talkie.

"What's up, Daddy?"

"Nothing, boy. We're safe."

"They killed the Strigoi?"

"Yeah, little one," said Andrei, grabbing Mat and tickling him. "They did. Tell me who the master is!"

"You… are… Daddy…" said Mat, laughing.

\* \* \*

"Good boy, Howler!" said Dan, petting the dog. "So good you saw the Strigoi and followed him."

"So, he ended up using the side basement exit?" asked Flo.

"Looks like it," said Lili.

"But when we discussed what to do, we agreed that was impossible."

"We agreed it wasn't worth the risk of making too much noise and alerting the Strigoi by barricading that exit. We thought he would use the one inside since the sun is too strong for him." She turned, pointing to the handrail visible near where they'd killed the Strigoi. "See, the door is down there, but you need to take a few turns before climbing out. He probably sent… Mom to the front door as a diversion, hoping he would then have enough time to run out blindly and quietly and hide somewhere in the village. Lucky we had Howlie, who sensed him and tracked him down. Good boy. Who's a good boy?" she said, petting the cheerful dog.

"Guys, let's check this out," said Dan, pointing at the Strigoi. "What we suspected is true. It's really the same skin I had, right?"

"Yes," said Flo, "only the vines are thicker, and the skin is turning black around them as well. I wonder if this keeps on growing and spreading until the Strigoi eventually becomes fully black. Anyway, it looks the same."

"I don't remember my mother ever talking about the Strigois' colors," said Dan, while they all shifted closer to check the dead Strigoi. His black eyes were open, yet immobile, and the mighty axe had split his black tongue in half, together with the head, neck, and part of the chest.

"Me neither," said Albert. "Yet my Mom kept talking about their black soul."

"Check his palms," said Dan, coming close and turning the Strigoi's left hand. "See? It's so rubbery and wrinkly, like it spent a few hours under water."

"Ah, look," said Flo, glancing over Dan's shoulder at the Strigoi's left hand, near its wrist. "Here, see? It's the same bulge, the same growth that Dan had on his neck. See this, Dan? That's how it looked."

"And you had the guts to cut this with a knife?" he asked, looking with admiration at Flo.

"Yes," she answered, with some pride in her smile. And something else on top of that.

Lili threw a quick glance between the two, then looked back at the bulge. "I see the vines radiate the same way from this growth. I think you dodged a bullet, Dad. And so did we."

"I think so too," said Dan, barely controlling a shiver. "But you realize what this means? It means there could be more of these things."

"That may be so," said Albert, "but I have a heart to rip out and toss in the fire behind us. Stand aside," he said, and squatted near the dead Strigoi's left hand.

"Do you need help?" asked Dan.

"Oh, no. I have this," he said, removing Dan's knife from the Strigoi's heart and throwing it into the snow.

The Strigoi started twitching once more. Albert held his left hand on the axe, which was fixed in the frozen ground, and with the right hand, he grabbed the left side of the Strigoi's body. He pulled, and, with a horrible noise, accompanied by a horrifying yet faint metallic shriek, that part broke, exposing the insides, including the heart.

"It's so black," said Lili, shivering. "Everything is black," she added, as she and Flo held each other. "And that moldy stench is nauseating."

"Yeah, it's coming from the ones burning in the church, but also from this one," said Flo with disgust.

Albert let go of the axe and grabbed the heart with his left hand. He started pulling, and the Strigoi convulsed. His gurgling was horrible. They were not shrieks anymore, and the volume was lower as the entire neck, mouth, and head had been split by the axe.

"Do you need a knife, buddy?" said Dan, pointing at his own knife in the snow, where Albert had thrown it.

"Na, I have this," said Albert, ripping at the heart with a violent move, accompanied by his own yell. "This piece of shit deserves nothing else," he added, spitting on the Strigoi's face. Pieces of meat tore as Albert snapped out the heart, and the Strigoi stopped moving.

"I say we also burn his body," said Flo, and everyone nodded.

Albert took a few steps toward the burning church and threw the heart into the fire, then he came back in time to see Dan pulling the dead Strigoi by his legs toward the church.

"Oh, Dan, you don't have to tire yourself doing this. No, we never have to get tired due to this son of a bitch again," said Albert, putting a hand on Dan's shoulders. "Wait a bit."

Albert went back, pulled his axe from the frozen ground, then returned. "Stand aside, Dan," he said, and he started chopping the body into pieces.

"Even the meat is fully black," said Flo, getting closer, pointing toward a clean-cut limb. "This is horrible."

"See? Now it's easy to throw into the fire," said Albert, grabbing a few pieces that used to be the Strigoi's legs and heading toward the burning church.

* * *

The fire was burning high and very hot, and the church's roof was on the brink of collapse.

"It had a nice interior," said Dan, who was hugging Lili. "It's a shame."

"I know," said Lili, with teary eyes. "It was a nice little church. Yet this is for the best."

Dan said nothing and continued to watch. A few dozen feet away, watching the fire from the other side, were Flo and Albert. They, too, were holding each other and seemed to be crying.

"The poor souls," said Lili, looking at them. "They've lost so much."

"Yeah. Wife a while back, mother, two children… Albert is a hero for taking all this on."

"He's crying. I fear his thirst for revenge kept him going. Now, he might wither. You know those folks who grow old together?

When one of them loses the other, he or she soon follows."

"We'll let him be for a while," said Dan, after a few moments of thinking. "He needs to mourn. Then we must show him he still has a reason to live. I know he really loves Flo, and she needs him. He's her only family now. She, too, has lost so much."

"Yes," said Lili. "What happened back there? That bastard resurrected Mom? This world is upside down."

"Maria?" said Dan, looking at her. "At first, I froze. That Strigoi played us. But now, now I realize, that was not Maria. I feel relief, *knowing* that Maria died weeks ago, in that cabin. What we've seen since is her body, but it's not Maria. The real Maria is up there, in heaven. And I'm sure she's looking down on us, loving us and taking care of us."

Large tears rolled down Lili's cheeks, and soon Dan joined her. Still, both of them were smiling, contemplating Dan's words.

"We have to keep going for her sake," said Lili, just as the church's roof collapsed, throwing a spray of sparks all around. "We have to be happy and help others be happy. We need to build a future for Mat. And, on top," said Lili, turning her eyes toward Dan's, "I think she would like *you* to be happy, Dad."

"What do you mean?"

"Oh, you know what I mean," said Lili, turning her gaze toward Albert and Flo.

# 19 WHAT NOW?

"There are more," said Andrei. "Definitely."

"How can you know?" asked Lili. The two of them were walking alone in the backyard.

"If something can happen, it will happen. And statistically, it's probable."

"Why?"

"Until recently, we knew two ways to die and two outcomes. Not eating onions makes you die because of the disease. If that happens, you wake up to be a fast, non-rotting growler. Die from other causes, like being eaten alive by dogs, getting hit by a car, having any kind of accident—"

"Yes!" interrupted Lili. "I'm familiar with all this."

"—you wake up to be a slow, rotting growler. Ah, and let's not forget what happened to your mother. She was a growler, a fast one, until we force-fed her onions. She then became a slow one, as the onions pushed out the disease, making room for the body to rot for a few days until coming back in full force."

"I know. Jesus!" said Lili, shaking her head.

"Sorry, honey. Well, now we have yet a third way to die," said Andrei, nodding. "One just needs to die because of the black bulge and vines resulting from a growler's bite, and puff! You've got yourself a fresh new Strigoi."

"So you're saying this could happen often?"

"Just imagine a gigantic city. A person is running from a growler, barely closing the door behind her. The person's hand gets bitten. One week later, a Strigoi is born. It's science!"

"Oh, now it's science?"

"Well, you saw Dan," he said, concerned. "He almost became one of those creatures."

"How can this be science? Plus, I remember a time when you said zombies didn't exist, because of scientifical proofs."

"Yeah, well, I don't remember that. And even if I ever said that, I was surely joking."

"Yeah, I bet."

"Ah, now that I think of it, I remember a time when you said Strigois don't exist, that they were just folklore. How's that now?"

"I'm strong enough to admit when I'm wrong."

"And?"

"And I'll let you know."

"Pfft," said Andrei, and they both laughed.

They walked for a few more minutes, smiling.

"No, but really, Grandma Gina was right. She was right all along. The Strigoi are real. I bet there's a scientific explanation as to why they exist, why they act as they do, and why they have those weaknesses, like being ultra sensitive to light," said Andrei, and their radiant smiles changed into sad ones. "I just hope we'll learn more about all these things, so we can survive in this new world."

Lili nodded.

"What do we do now?" asked Andrei a few moments later, looking around. "We could continue to stay here. It's not a terrible place. And if we can solve the generator problem, I'm sure we could replace that horrible outhouse with a decent toilet."

"We'll be able to stay here in the village for a while, while there's enough food up for grabs, no matter what toilet we have," said Lili, shaking her head. "Maybe even for half a year, who knows. But the food won't last forever. Eventually, we'll be forced to go to town."

"But we can grow crops. Become farmers, rear chickens, eat eggs. Eggs are good," said Andrei, rubbing his tummy.

"Do you know anything about growing crops? We don't even have seeds. Plus, I haven't seen a live chicken or cow anywhere. They all died, I guess. At some point, we'll have to go into town, find a supermarket, and eat canned food and such. Which is not so great."

"And what's wrong with that?"

"When I said you were an idiot, I wasn't joking."

"Ah, and what if there are Strigois in town?" asked Andrei, a shadow of fear clouding his face.

"That too, but I had another point. It's probably not that healthy to keep eating canned food," said Lili, thinking. "We need fresh, healthy food as well."

"Yeah, I can't believe I'm saying this, but I wouldn't say no to a large salad," said Andrei, nodding.

"Yes. We might have to do what Flo proposed."

"What, she finally proposed we repopulate the earth?" Andrei's grin returned.

"Hmm, never heard that one before. Marvelous thing you're original. Anyway, if she ever wanted that, you're not the one she'd pick."

"What do you mean?"

"Nothing," said Lili, waving her hand. "You're oblivious to everything."

"I don't understand."

"No surprise there."

"Pfft. Fine. Don't tell me. So, we go south. Is that really better?"

"Yeah, it is. It really is. We need to find more people. We need to build or join a community. We need to defend ourselves. And, if we're lucky, we'll find some people who know how to plant and grow crops and vegetables. Especially onions. Who knows, maybe they'll also have some livestock. Here," she said, indicating their surroundings, "we survived by luck. Pure luck. That Strigoi almost killed us a few times. You, me, Matei, Dad, Lili, Albert. All of us were, at one point or another, in danger. What if a second Strigoi comes here? Or, even worse, what if he's here already?"

"Ah, so now you trust my judgment, that there are definitely more out there."

"Yes, dufus, of course I trust your judgment. You're the smart one. You have excellent ideas, and I think you understand best how these monsters function."

"And you're the cute one," said Andrei, blushing a bit.

"I know," she said, and got closer to Andrei.

"I've also seen you're getting very courageous," he said, holding her. "Of course, you take after me in that regard." They both laughed.

"Right," said Lili, taking a deep breath. "I don't enjoy doing it, but I guess there are things that need to be done."

"And come spring," said Andrei, after a while, "we can find a huge car, stuff everyone in it, and drive for a few hours to onion county. If we don't find anyone there we can just come back."

"Yes. I really hope there are more people out there. Not just for us, but for Mat. And that's the fundamental reason why we should go."

Andrei looked at her, with a questioning expression, so she continued.

"Imagine we survive here. Imagine us growing old, then dying. What happens to Matei? He'll never have a wife. He'll never have kids, and he'll eventually be all alone."

"Kids are a pain in the ass," said Andrei, but his tone said otherwise.

"I know," said Lili, in a similar voice.

"Mommy! Daddy!" said Matei, running and jumping toward them like a frog.

All three of them hugged.

"See?" said Lili. "We have to do it for him."

* THE END *

# ABOUT THE AUTHOR

John Black has spent most of his adult life working in the entertainment industry and helping create virtual worlds.

He is a gamer, husband, father, pancakes enthusiast and more recently he followed his life dream of becoming a fiction author, writing in the horror thriller genre. His approach to writing is to go all in, keeping it fast paced and immersive.

John likes to think a lot of 'what would happen if' scenarios, and he will continue to explore the genre.

\* \* \*

If you would like to get in touch with John, or be notified about the release of future books, drop a line at *john.black.author@gmail.com*.

\* \* \*

Readers trust other readers.
If you enjoyed this book please leave an honest review on Amazon. Thank you!

Printed in Great Britain
by Amazon